DUCHESS IN DIAMONDS

SATIN AND SILK HISTORICAL ROMANCE
BOOK ONE

JENNIFER ASHLEY

JA / AG PUBLISHING

CHAPTER 1

*M*ake ready." Eleven-year-old Eamon Stone's whisper held tension.

The two boys with him, who until this morning had been his enemies, nodded.

One of them had dark hair, flinty gray eyes, and an arrogance he'd been born with. Lord Dominic Wolfe, whose father was a lofty marquis, held himself apart from the students at Hallbridge School for Young Gentlemen in Buckinghamshire. This had earned him mockery and a few beatings, until his attackers had gotten a taste of Wolfe's fists. Nothing weak about Wolfe.

The second youth's flame-red hair was like a beacon, his freckled face and blue eyes holding an incessant cheer that could be as irritating as Wolfe's brooding. Eamon had made McCormick put on his knit cap so his bright head didn't give away their position, but it had been a futile attempt. Their enemies were closing in.

Eamon and his companions would have to fight hard to get

past Pebbly Pollard and his compatriots, the vilest bullies in the school. These included the Viking, a boy who was six feet tall at twelve years old, with white-blond hair and blue eyes that held both ingenuousness and petty cruelty.

This morning, Eamon had persuaded the Viking to pinch cakes from the hamper Pebbly's indulgent nanny had sent to him and bring them to Eamon. When Pebbly discovered the deception, he'd rallied an army to go after Eamon. The Viking had turned coat, joining Pebbly's troops and putting the full blame on Eamon.

Pebbly and his crew had cornered Eamon in an empty lecture room, but he'd found unexpected allies in Wolfe and Hayden McCormick, who'd been caught in the chase. Wolfe had temporarily baffled the mob with disdainful words, while McCormick helped Eamon wrench open a window so all three of them could flee.

They now hid together below the ridge over which passed the only road to the school. Eamon had discovered this hollow soon after he'd been dumped at Hallbridge, his late father's man of business having no idea what else to do with him. Evidence of Eamon's refuge here—cigar ends, dog-eared books, a well-used notebook, and a flask of brandy—littered the yellowed grass.

Eamon had expected Wolfe and McCormick to turn on him once they reached his hiding place and blame him for their current predicament. Instead, McCormick sat cross-legged on the ground, calmly leafing through Eamon's notebook of drawings, while Wolfe kept a sharp eye on the enemy below.

When Eamon apologized for catching them up in his war, Wolfe spat on the grass. "Pollard needs to be crushed."

McCormick looked up from the notebook in amazement. "You expect *us* to do the crushing, do you, Wolfe?" he asked in his accent of the Shetland Isles.

Wolfe lifted his well-clad shoulders. "Why not? The three of us have more brains than Pollard's dozen toadies, and we each have our strengths. I've been drilled in tactics since I could crawl. McCormick, you're brilliant at maths. Stone, you—" Wolfe broke off, as though at a loss.

Eamon's eyes narrowed. "I what? Can draw pretty pictures?"

"Good ones too," McCormick said in admiration. "This is beautiful." His tattered glove rested on a portrait of a young woman whose silken ringlets framed a comely face, the gleam in her eyes matching her coy smile. "Who *is* she? I'd be obliged if you could introduce us."

"I have no idea," Eamon answered. "That's a copy of an Albrecht Dürer. You've fallen for a woman three hundred years gone."

"Oh." McCormick's syllable held vast disappointment.

"Your gift is your golden tongue, Stone," Wolfe concluded. "I've listened to you nattering since you arrived this term. Even Wilson is putty in your hands."

Wilson was the Classics master, who used martial tactics to drill Greek and Latin into small boys who'd rather be anywhere but a stuffy lecture hall. Eamon had managed to sidestep the worst of Wilson's assignments and had yet to be called upon to recite.

"Wilson just wants a bit of flattering," Eamon said reasonably. The man pretended to be tough but was in truth sentimentally in love with heroic poetry.

"But it's a trick to know exactly *how* to flatter," Wolfe said. "Somehow you convinced the Viking to steal from Pollard, when the Viking would die for him."

Eamon shrugged. "Neither of them is what I'd call quick-witted."

"Whereas you ..." Wolfe shook his head. "Never mind. I'd rather have you on *my* side, where I can keep an eye on you." He gazed down the hill where Pebbly and the Viking were conferring. "McCormick and I are going to think of a way out of this mess. Stone, you will execute the plan, and we'll back you up."

Eamon stared at him. "You'll throw me out to take the first blow, you mean?"

"It's you and your tongue that got us into this situation," Wolfe pointed out. "That same tongue is going to take us to safety."

Mirth trickled through Eamon's uneasiness. "My tongue, eh? I'm not *that* fond of Pollard."

"Don't be disgusting." Wolfe wrinkled his aristocratic nose. "I mean *you're* going to talk, while McCormick and I focus on strategy."

"Not sure I can help you there." McCormick moved on to landscape drawings Eamon had copied from seventeenth-century Dutch painters, and paused at an original Eamon had done of the school grounds from this very hill.

"Maths are very helpful in military planning," Wolfe informed him.

"I don't think we have time for all that," McCormack said, reluctantly dragging his attention from the notebook. "Look."

One of Pebbly's search parties had returned to him, and several lads pointed up the hill toward Eamon's hiding place. Eamon knew he and his new friends were well concealed, but if they stayed too long, they'd be trapped.

"We'll have to rush them," Wolfe said tightly. "Both of you, get in as many blows as you can to thin the ranks and then make a dash for the senior common room. All the masters will be there."

"They'll thrash us," McCormick protested. "*And* throw us into the brig." The brig was a cold, grimy room in the cellar where the worst miscreants were shoved for a day to think about their transgressions.

"That is where Stone's gift of the gab will come in handy. He'll talk them out of punishing us." Wolfe stuck out a fist, his pristine kid glove fitting him like a second skin. "We're in this together. Right?"

McCormick touched his fist to Wolfe's, his freckled hand peeping from holes in his woolen glove. "If you two take me out of here alive, I'll be glad to call you my brothers."

"As will I," Wolfe said. "We will be there for one another, no matter what."

They eyed Eamon, waiting for him to join the pledge. Eamon balled his hand—his bare fingers dry, cracked, and stained with blue paint—and bumped it against the others.

"Be careful about this vow," Eamon said. "It means that wherever we are, whatever trouble we face, we each must answer."

His respect for Wolfe rose when the man didn't demur. McCormick nodded. "Done."

"Very well then," Eamon said.

Their three fists touched, sealing the pact.

A shiver ran through Eamon, as though something had begun on this hill, something whose ending he could not see. He always liked to know outcomes three moves in advance, but since the day his father had died, his life had become more uncertain than ever, an empty and sometimes terrifying sensation.

Forming a bond with these two boys who'd followed him without question felt strange, but it was a welcome change to the bleakness.

On Wolfe's signal, they charged down the hill, yelling like Highlanders at Culloden Moor, and took on their enemy.

They ended up fairly badly beaten, but Eamon's charm, as Wolfe predicted, landed Pollard, the Viking, and their followers in the worst trouble, including a stint in the brig. The three newfound friends, let off with only a lecture, met on the hill again that evening, wounded but triumphant, to share a celebratory cigar and brandy.

This was definitely the beginning of something, Eamon reflected as the three bruised boys passed around the flask. It would be interesting to see what.

June 1815

"MAKE READY." EAMON'S WHISPER COULD BARELY BE HEARD ABOVE the noise of battle, but his friends caught it.

The two men at his side were poised to run, though Wolfe could barely walk with the wound he'd sustained to his leg. They had no choice. It was flee or die.

"When I give the signal," Eamon said.

McCormick acknowledged this with a nod of his filth-streaked red head.

Wolfe remained flinty-eyed. "What signal?" he croaked, hoarse with pain.

Eamon grinned so hard he felt the dirt cracking on his cheeks. "You'll know."

"God help us then," Wolfe muttered.

The three had been sent to report on Bonaparte's right flank, which stretched southward toward a thick wood. They were to discover weaknesses and do any damage along the way that they could.

They'd slunk through the grass and brush in the long June twilight, taking cover on a low rise above a stream, backed by woods. Bonaparte did indeed have a hole in his defenses nearby, where several columns had been moved away to confront the new danger from the Prussians. Eamon used his drawing skills to sketch a quick map of the enemy's positions for their commander.

Unfortunately for the three scouts, someone in Bonaparte's forces had also seen the hole, and a line marched up to plug it.

As the three men had fled, Wolfe had taken a bullet in the leg, and they'd been cut off from their escape route.

The three at last managed to find cover, but here they were, trapped between enemy lines and a long way from their own camp.

While they waited for darkness, Eamon had slipped out on his own to complete the second part of their orders—inflict whatever damage they could. Eamon had found the powder horn in his bag useful, as well as a few musket balls and a slow match.

Both Wolfe and McCormick relaxed in relief when Eamon returned unscathed, then pretended not to, as though they hadn't worried about him. Their expressions of nonchalance amused Eamon at the same time their concern touched him.

Their commander, a congenial colonel who'd be more at home with books and a brandy, had sent Eamon with Wolfe and McCormick because he'd learned they'd been comrades since boyhood. They'd aid and protect each other, he'd reasoned.

What the colonel hadn't realized was that Eamon and McCormick hadn't seen each other since they'd dispersed from Hallbridge, though they'd kept up an irregular correspondence.

McCormick's red hair had darkened somewhat, and his rawboned body had filled out to the rugged sturdiness of his warrior ancestors, though his freckled face and wide smile hadn't changed. He'd returned to his native Shetland, after a few cursory years at Cambridge, to study maths with a brilliant tutor. He'd spent part of the Peninsular War on Wellington's staff, making perfect maps and plotting trajectories for the artillery.

Lord Dominic Wolfe had shared a regiment with Eamon in Spain, but Wolfe had grown into a hard man Eamon barely recognized. He quickly realized that Wolfe's coldness came from grief at his father's death coupled with Wolfe's older brother's enmity for him.

Wolfe had done what many second sons had—bought a commission, then moved rapidly through the ranks in field promotions until he reached the rank of Lieutenant Colonel. Eamon suspected he'd gained his epaulets by terrifying the enemy with his gray-eyed gaze, very like a wolf's.

Now, in Belgium, the three had been thrown together as veterans to answer the new threat from Bonaparte. But Eamon had no idea if they were still friends.

"If we go separately, we'll have a better chance of making it through," Wolfe said. He lay supine on the dried summer grass, his leg stiff, blood dark on his uniform trousers.

"No, we won't," Eamon argued. "At least, *you* won't. You'll need our help to get you out of here."

"Aye, that's so," McCormick put in.

Wolfe let out a growl. "If you expect me to say you should leave me here and save yourselves, I won't," he snapped. "I want to live too. So, very well, you'll take me out."

"Agreed," McCormick said. "Which way is best? Skirt the hill just below the ridge?"

"I wouldn't," Eamon said quickly.

"Why not?" Wolfe mouth tightened. "What the devil did you do, Stone?"

"Trust me." Eamon stuck out his fist. "Remember our vow?"

"The one that got me into more difficulties than anything else in my life?" Wolfe demanded.

"And me," McCormick put in. "Usually because of you, Wolfe. Don't blame it all on Stony."

Wolfe's dark brows rose, but he didn't argue.

Three fists came together, their hands so covered with mud it was impossible to see skin. Wolfe had more or less retained his gloves, but his valet—he'd brought the man to Belgium with him—would be unhappy.

Eamon pulled out a pocket watch, one he'd blackened so it wouldn't gleam. "Soon," he said.

Below them, flashes of blue showed Bonaparte's men marching into position. They moved with precision, looking neither left nor right, luckily for the three men barely hidden in scrub a few feet above them.

"I'll be glad to finish this," Wolfe whispered when the French line had passed. "Old Nosey was wise to pin him here. No chasing Bonaparte all over the Continent again."

"What will you do after?" McCormick asked. "Regiment's been my life for a while. Might stay with it. Or become a maths tutor, which sounds less exciting."

Wolfe didn't answer, but his eyes flickered, as though he hadn't wanted to think much further than this night.

"Me, I'll marry and settle down," Eamon said. "I need some rest."

The other two stared at him in amazement.

"Marry?" McCormick asked with a muffled version of his good-hearted laugh. "Wolfe could, yes. He's titled, but the pair of us are nobodies."

"My *brother* is titled," Wolfe corrected him. "Once his dear icicle of a wife gives him a son, I will inherit nothing."

"I intend to marry for love," Eamon informed them. "I'm a romantic, me."

"There is no such thing as marrying for love," Wolfe stated. "It is a business arrangement. Only on the stage does it happen, and you'll notice that the lovers always turn out to have wealthy relations or be disguised princes and other such rubbish."

"Interesting that you know so much about these plays," Eamon said in a mild tone.

"Dragged to the damned theatre by my grandmother. Give up, Stone. You have nothing to offer a lady but your clever conversation. Which grows wearying, trust me."

"Good thing I don't want to marry *you* then. Believe me, I will search until I find a lady who loves me for who I am." Eamon shrugged. "If she has a fine dowry, so much the better."

"Her family will forbid it," Wolfe predicted. "Wisely."

"He must have someone in mind," McCormick said. "Who is the lady, Stone? Anyone we know?"

"No one specific, more's the pity." Eamon gave a heartfelt sigh. "These are musings to while away an idle hour."

McCormick flashed his grin. "Care to make a wager?"

Of course, the man who could skim through complicated odds in his head would say that.

Wolfe scoffed, but Eamon let anticipation bubble inside him. They might die this day, unable to escape the troops that surrounded them. At McCormick's words, though, something within Eamon believed they would live. Perhaps this very wager would compel them to survive against all odds.

"What terms?" Eamon asked.

"You find a lady willing to marry you," McCormick said. "Legally, I mean, in the parish register, with the blessing of her family and all."

Eamon leaned in. "Let's make it more interesting, shall we? We each attempt to find wives—the loser is the last bachelor standing."

McCormick's blue eyes twinkled. "The stakes?"

Wolfe broke in. "Dear God, the pair of you. What can any of us wager?"

"A bottle of the finest brandy smuggled from France?" McCormick suggested. "Or, let's say, the final bachelor has to host a spectacular soiree for the lucky couples."

Eamon shook his head. "I have another idea. We pool what we have—money, any property we acquire, whatever we have that is worth anything. The dividends go to the sons and daughters from these marriages so they won't have to scratch for a living like we did. That way, we all win. Once we produce offspring, that is. We'll think of some amusing forfeit for the losing bachelor."

Wolfe contemplated Eamon a moment, thoughts hidden

behind his flinty gaze, then he relented. "It's never likely to happen, so why not?"

He held out his tattered-gloved fist once more. McCormick and Eamon met it with theirs so rapidly that they both laughed.

Wind scraped branches above them. Eamon went quiet and again checked his watch.

As the long hand clicked to the top of the hour, a blast sounded down the ridge to the right.

"There we are," Eamon said in an everyday tone, but McCormick had already hauled Wolfe to his feet and was staggering with him away from the explosion.

The ridge suddenly cleared of Frenchmen who raced toward the noise. Eamon caught up to the other two, lending his arm to steady Wolfe. The three gained the top of the hill, deeper twilight and smoke giving them cover. Wolfe paused, Eamon beside him, to catch his breath.

"Don't stop, my friends," McCormick said in alarm. "We need to get clear."

"We are clear." Eamon readjusted his hold on Wolfe, who grunted with pain.

McCormick shook his head. "You should have told me you'd lit a slow match, Stone."

Wolfe's eyes filled with apprehension. "Why is that?"

"Because I wouldn't have lit mine."

A second explosion roared into the night.

The three men jerked forward along the path toward Wellington's army, moving as fast as they could with Wolfe stumbling between them. The boom of powder and the shouts of panicked French soldiers barely muffled Wolfe's continuing curses and Eamon's echoing laughter.

CHAPTER 2

May 1816

Caroline, the Duchess of Aylesmore—Caro to her family and closest friends—took the pale card that Singleton, the household's butler, presented to her. On it an engraving of a picture frame enclosed the words:

Eamon Stone, Esq.
Assessor, art collections.
Paintings, sculpture, objets d'art.
Valuations, estate sales, art placement.

Very small letters at the bottom declared: *No fee for consultation.*

The very reason Caro had hired Cheswell's gallery was because they would send someone to value the paintings at no charge. Mr. Cheswell had assured her in his last letter that they would take their fee from the proceeds of any sale.

"Who is it?" the dowager duchess demanded imperiously from her favorite corner of the sitting room. Her voice retained the aristocratic French lilt from her girlhood. "The picture man at last?"

"It seems so," Caro answered. "They've sent someone called Mr. Eamon Stone. Do you know him, *Maman?*"

"Stone." The dowager lifted her keen blue gaze from the novel she perused. Her face was thin and pointed, her figure as elegant as the day she'd married the Fifth Duke. "There were the Bedfordshire Stones, but no, they fled to the Continent years ago, to escape their creditors. Living in Lucerne now, I believe, near the lake. Beautiful land. I traveled there when I was a girl."

If Cheswell's gallery didn't purchase a few paintings from the ancient Aylesford collection, Caro and the dowager, along with Caro's son, Leo, might find themselves fleeing to Lucerne as well. They'd learn to eat goat's cheese and climb about the mountains behind their tiny chalet.

Caro had only a dim idea where Lucerne was in Switzerland, but mountains were bound to be nearby, as well as chalets. And goats.

"This Mr. Stone is here in London," Caro answered.

"Then I do not know." The dowager lightly touched her lip. "I find that odd. Ask him who he is when you speak to him." She returned to her book, unbothered.

"Where have you put him, Singleton?" Caro asked.

The Grosvenor Square house of the dukes of Aylesmore was vast, with a complex hierarchy of rooms into which visitors should go. The first-floor drawing room was for dukes and duchesses and the occasional royal visit, while the second-floor drawing room housed lesser nobility. Various nooks and crannies existed for everybody else, based on lineage and rank. Singleton knew every place for every person.

"Ground floor reception room, Your Grace," Singleton answered in his lugubrious tones. He wasn't an ancient specimen, his hair still black, his gait sprightly, but he'd cultivated an antiquated air. "The blue one."

Caro felt sudden pity for Mr. Stone. "Oh, dear. That bad, is he?"

Singleton looked down his long nose. "He has no precedent, Your Grace."

Which meant Singleton hadn't known how to classify him. A man who assessed paintings for a gallery likely was not much more than a tradesman, but Singleton's hesitation indicated that Mr. Stone might exist in the space between tradesman and impoverished gentleman struggling to earn a living. The end of the long war with France had returned many such men to England.

"Well, it's a pleasant enough room." Caro kept hold of the card as she moved to the mirror and forced a stray lock of dark hair back into its severe knot.

The dowager's head popped up again. "The blue reception room? It isn't pleasant at all. It's dreadfully cold, and the chairs are hard. Apologize for it, my dear. We don't want the picture man to rush off."

Caro turned from the mirror. "Are you certain you still wish to sell? These are paintings from your husband's collection, after all."

Caro had never met the Fifth Duke of Aylesmore, who'd been gone before she'd married his son. By all accounts, he'd been quite a man.

"He liked looking at the damned things more then he enjoyed talking to people, including me," the dowager answered decidedly. "If he could have married *them*, he'd have been very happy. Sell them, my dear. We need the blunt."

As always, Caro's mother-in-law spoke to the point.

"Very well." Caro tucked the card into the pocket of her everyday gown and left the room, followed deferentially by Singleton. "Send him to the second-floor drawing room," Caro instructed the butler.

By Singleton's intake of breath, Caro knew this was a breach of protocol. Only barons and above went to the second-floor drawing room. But a worse breach would be for her to descend to the blue reception room to greet Mr. Stone herself. Singleton would faint in horror if she did that.

Caro and the dowager—the former Eugenie Duval, daughter of a French marquis with a very long title and surname—had been reposing in the private sitting room on the fourth floor, a level Caro rarely went below these days. Her bedchamber was directly above this floor, with the nursery above that.

This cozy sitting room held a large shelf of books, and the dining room was next to it, so Caro had all she needed. She'd resurrected the out-of-use dumbwaiter a previous duke had installed so Singleton didn't wear himself out climbing multiple staircases to serve meals or bring the dowager her cup of chocolate.

Caro skimmed down two long flights of the wide stairs to the second floor. The staircase filled the middle of the house, which had been the largest on the square when built. Other townhouses had squeezed against it in the intervening years of the last century, but this abode remained grandiose and immense.

The May day was warm, and the second-floor drawing room, which Caro hadn't entered in ages, proved to be stuffy. Caro went to the window once Singleton left her, ready to admit some fresh air.

The window latch resisted her tugs. Caro struggled with it, at last forcing the brass catch out of its slot.

When she'd first married Aylesmore, ten years previously, the house had swarmed with maids and footmen who'd have opened the window for her. Now there was only Singleton, the cook who never left her demesne below stairs, and Jeanne, the dowager's lady's maid, who'd made it clear she did not perform manual tasks.

The window sash proved even more stubborn than the latch.

Caro wasn't feeble, being rather tall for a woman and what she'd heard others call *sturdy*. Plus, she'd been chasing Leo about this big house, the park outside, and Mayfield Hall—the Aylesmore estate—for nine years, which had given her stamina. Even so, as much as she wrenched at the window, it wouldn't budge.

"Open, you blasted thing."

A pair of strong hands in well-fitting leather gloves landed on the sash on either side of hers.

"Allow, me, madam."

Caro jumped, and crashed into a man's body that was as solid as his hands.

She looked back and up into a hard face that held a crooked nose and summer blue eyes filled with warmth. The man had dark hair as unruly as Caro's and a clean-shaven face framed by a high collar and a simply tied cravat.

His arms hemmed her in, his body enclosing hers. The scents of cashmere, smoke, and warmth clung to him, hinting of dark nights, firelight, and intimacy.

Caro flooded with unaccustomed heat. She had no idea where these images came from, why she had any business mixing the word *intimacy* with this man, who'd sprung from nowhere.

He regarded Caro with amusement as well as curiosity. She sensed a watchfulness behind both those emotions, like an animal who was never certain it would be accepted or kicked aside. If he was accepted, his eyes promised, he would provide her an experience like no other.

Caro had no idea where *that* thought came from, either.

She made herself come out of her frozen stance and duck from beneath his arms.

The gentleman politely stepped aside for her, then attempted to sweep the window upward with a magnanimous gesture. The sash resisted. He gave it two mighty heaves before the window finally screeched open a few inches, then stuck fast.

Caro laughed. She couldn't help herself.

The man's answering smile stole her breath. His gaze fixed on Caro, as though she were the only being in the world, the only person he ever smiled for.

But of course, that couldn't possibly be true. He must bestow his smile on any he thought it would affect.

This, Caro whispered to herself, *is a dangerous man.*

From the doorway came Singleton's aggrieved tones. "Mr. Stone, Your Grace."

Mr. Stone started when Singleton said *Your Grace,* and stared at Caro in shock.

Any tradesman who'd accidentally been in a near embrace with the lady of the house—a duchess, no less—would have backed away hastily, apologizing in consternation. Duchesses came attached to dukes who could make a tradesman's life hell if they chose. Though Caro could assure this man that the current duke was nine years old and a sunny-natured boy.

Mr. Stone only studied Caro all the more closely, then made a courteous bow.

"Your Grace."

His voice was deep like a rich wine.

Caro gave him a nod she hoped was regal. "Mr. Stone."

Singleton hovered in the doorway, a terrier ready to leap to Caro's defense. Singleton hadn't much approved of Caro when the Sixth Duke had first married her, but he'd soon converted from long-suffering enemy to staunch ally. He'd been a rock when Leopold had died suddenly, leaving his wife, mother, and little boy with a vast estate to maintain and a staggering amount of debt.

"Thank you for coming, Mr. Stone," Caro said. "Singleton, would you bring coffee while I show Mr. Stone the paintings?"

Singleton obviously did not want Caro to lead Mr. Stone down to the gallery herself, but who else could do it? The curator of the duke's collection had been one of the first to desert them, when he'd realized his salary wouldn't be paid. More retainers had rapidly followed.

"Yes, Your Grace," Singleton said stiffly.

Mr. Stone watched the exchange with a quirk of his lips, though Caro wasn't certain what he found so entertaining.

"Please follow me, Mr. Stone," she said with a cool dignity she'd learned from the dowager.

Keeping her head high, she stalked across the large room past Singleton and out onto the landing.

Chill air poured up the stairwell, but Caro resisted shivering. She'd discovered long ago that never reacting to weather, bizarre circumstances, or taunts drew more respect than falling into hysterics at the least provocation.

Mr. Stone's tread echoed as she led him down one flight of stairs to the gallery. While he stayed a few paces behind her, she felt his presence like a flame at her back.

The Third Duke, Caro's husband's great-grandfather, had turned almost the entirety of the first floor into a gallery for his budding art collection. The next three dukes had added to the artworks—the dowager's husband contributing the most of all —and the collection was now famous throughout Britain.

Four windows marched along the gallery's front wall, letting in what feeble light trickled through London's clouds and smoke. The walls had been papered in a pale green, faded now, chosen to allow the deep colors of the artworks to catch the eye.

The dukes had mostly collected paintings, though small marble sculptures on plinths dotted the room. Caro's husband had always shielded her from the nude Daphne and Apollo with his coat, which had made her laugh.

Poor Leopold. He'd been cowed all his life by his hard father and had vowed never to put his own son through what he'd suffered. Probably the bravest thing Leopold had ever done was to make sure small Leo knew he was loved for himself.

Caro swallowed regret and swept her arm in faded lavender silk to indicate the paintings filling the walls.

"Some of these are in dreadful need of cleaning," she said in apology. "And many are from artists who never became famous —my husband's forebears simply liked them. But *these* should be of interest."

She led him toward the two Rembrandts, which reposed in quiet splendor on easels Singleton had set up for them.

One depicted a young woman draped in sumptuous silk and brocade, with a crown of flowers on her head. The second was a portrait of the artist himself, his wrinkled face and bulbous nose solemn under a beret.

"I hope to find a buyer who will treasure them," Caro said with admiration. One of the solaces in a life grown desperate was to wander the gallery and view beautiful things. "It is a wrench to part with them, but—"

She broke off when she realized that Mr. Stone wasn't listening. He'd stepped to the paintings, his attention caught.

Her heartbeat quickened as she watched him.

Mr. Stone possessed a restlessness Caro had never encountered in the gentlemen carefully chosen to speak to her as a debutante. Nor had she seen it in her husband's circle, made up of older men who held the power of the nation in their hands. Mr. Stone was perfectly still, but she sensed he could dash away at any moment and be gone.

Which would be a pity. Something had awakened inside Caro when she'd been in his near-embrace at the window, as though a lamp long doused had suddenly been ignited.

Mr. Stone was well-muscled under his thick wool coat and simple trousers tucked into boots, as though he rode a lot. Or perhaps he wrestled bears—who knew what art assessors got up to in their own time?

His jaw held a shadow, as though his whiskers grew back as

rapidly as he shaved them. They fascinated her, those whiskers, though Caro could not say why.

The shadow could not hide the long scar that began on his cheek and ran down under his collar. She could not say why that fascinated her either.

Raw men had never been allowed into Caro's world, kept far from her curated, fenced-off girlhood as possible. Caro would have grown up innocently gullible if it hadn't been for her much more worldly friends. She'd never dared breathe a word to Mama what she, Louise, and Jo had laughed about together in private.

Caro's gaze strayed to Mr. Stone's firm hip cupped by fawn wool, and then he cleared his throat.

He was staring straight at her. As Caro dragged in a swift breath, a knowing smile danced on his lips.

Heat boiled through her. She was a matron, for goodness' sake, the mother of a duke, and not the sort of widow who pursued torrid affairs. Mr. Stone was here to purchase the Rembrandts, nothing more.

Mortification and an unfamiliar longing twined inside her in a confusing mix.

"Your conclusion, Mr. Stone?" Caro asked, rather breathlessly.

The hint of a smile became a broad one. It was teasing, though, nothing lustful or lewd, as had been the case with a few other creditors before Singleton had escorted them out. Perhaps Mr. Stone was flattered that such an aging crone had so lustfully gazed at his well-honed body.

Mr. Stone focused on the paintings once more. "They are quite good," he said in all seriousness.

Caro's hopes rose. Rembrandts were valuable, and perhaps their sale would clear the worst of the debts so Leo could grow up unencumbered by them.

"Excellent," she said, striving for dignity. "I do not wish to be gauche, but how much exactly do you think they will fetch?"

"Mm." Mr. Stone stepped to the self-portrait and very gently touched a corner. "As you say, they will have to be cleaned. But even then ..."

"Yes?" Caro asked with some impatience.

Mr. Stone faced her again, his smiles gone. "Duchess—er, Your Grace—however I am to address you. These pictures *are* very, very good."

"I am pleased to hear it." Caro's worry returned. "Has the grime ruined them? Surely, they are worth something even with that."

"They would be." Mr. Stone's voice gentled, and his expression was, if anything, sad. "If they were true Rembrandts. What I am trying to say to you, Duchess, is that they are very, very good forgeries."

CHAPTER 3

*E*amon hated saying the words, but the duchess deserved the truth. The dismay that rushed over her face was heartbreaking, as was the sweet sparkle dying from her eyes.

Eamon fought the need to pull her into his arms, soothe her, whisper to her that everything would be all right. He'd fix it all for her.

But she was a duchess, and Eamon was nobody, the son of a gentleman swindler. Not allowed to touch a lovely duchess in distress. He could only stand in helpless anger and watch her despair.

At an ungodly hour this morning, Cheswell had commanded Eamon to hie himself to Grosvenor Square and value a few paintings for a widowed duchess. Eamon had obeyed with reluctance, expecting to find a withered specimen in black stumping about with a tall cane and a sour countenance. She'd harumph at Eamon's assessment, no matter what he told her, declaring he was no better than a cheat.

Or else she'd be a frail thing who'd crumple to the floor if he valued her paintings too low. She'd have a steadfast companion at her side to wave a vinaigrette under her nose and glare daggers at Eamon.

He'd entered the drawing room in this vast house to discover who he'd thought was a pretty lady's maid struggling to open the window. The visit, Eamon had decided, was looking up. Whatever else he had to endure, he could enjoy the aesthetics of gazing at a comely young woman.

The comely young woman now stared at him as though her entire world had crumbled around her.

Her eyes were the lightest brown touched with green and flecked in places with gray. Eamon was too much of an artist to simply say *hazel*. Her dark hair held waves that struggled against bonds that tried to tether it, unsuccessfully, to a fashionable style.

This woman should throw fashion to the wind and wander about with her hair flowing, her garments loose and gauzy, her feet bare. Eamon would paint her like that, without the strictures the labels of *widow* and *duchess* placed on her.

He'd briefly considered, when he'd seen the Rembrandts, that the duchess or her family was trying to trick Cheswell's into paying for fakes. Her expression now told him she genuinely hadn't known.

"How can they be?" she asked, her voice ringing with disbelief. "The Fifth Duke—my husband's father—acquired them from a reputable dealer. There are papers ..."

"As I say, they are very good." Eamon had to admire the forger, even as he wished to beat to a pulp whoever had introduced these paintings into the house. "Dealers—and dukes—might be fooled."

"The Fifth Duke was a canny man. Not easily duped." The duchess stated this flatly, as though daring him to argue with her. "Mr. Stone, I have been warned that dealers will sometimes name a price too low, so that they may turn about and sell the paintings for their true value, reaping a profit. Please tell me you are not such a man. I shouldn't like to think so."

True that unscrupulous assessors and outright confidence tricksters apologized as they sadly claimed they could pay only a few pounds for a priceless masterpiece. Rubbed their hands in glee when they toted away the Raphael or Claude from under the ignorant owners' noses.

"I understand your skepticism. But look."

Eamon beckoned the duchess closer to the supposed self-portrait. She came to him without hesitation, her indignation overriding her earlier embarrassment when he'd caught her blatantly staring at his body. He'd been sorry to break short her scrutiny, regretful he'd had to interrupt what might have become a very interesting encounter.

"Rembrandt painted much of his work from the 1630s to the 1660s," Eamon explained. "He rarely used bright green, yet both paintings have more than a few tints of it." He indicated the artist's sleeve that dipped toward the frame, where splashes of green glowed among the black and dark rust. A person might miss it, because the duchess was correct—these paintings were filthy.

"Perhaps he made an exception," the duchess said tightly.

"Not when he painted this." The self-portrait portrayed Rembrandt as an older man, his aging countenance shown without vanity. "He'd taken to only very dark colors and stark whites by then. And this." Eamon moved to the painting of the lady in the sumptuous robes. "The model is Hendrickje Stoffels, but it should not be."

The duchess regarded him in irritation. "Why not? Was she ill that day?"

"Hendrickje is one of his later models," Eamon said. "He painted his wife, Saskia, as the goddess Flora, not Hendrickje. The original of this was done in 1634. Notice the brighter colors, the smoother textures, the shine on the fabric. The forger got much of it right—it is an exact copy, except for the model. I wonder why he—or she—did that? To avoid being called a forger? If caught, she could have claimed she copied it to practice her technique."

"Why do you suppose a woman did this?" The duchess sounded indignant.

Eamon quickly shook his head. "I don't—I am only speculating. In any case, whoever did paint these, man or woman, might be long deceased. Some of these pigments are no longer obtainable, or not easily so. And it has taken a while for so much grime to build up. But it might have been a woman who painted it. Talent is the same whether one is male or female, in my experience. Look at Madame Vigée Le Brun."

The duchesses' stare told him she wasn't interested in discussing art history.

"What you mean is, these paintings are worthless," she stated.

Eamon tried to soften the blow. "To the right collector, they are not. They will never fetch the price of genuine Rembrandts, but someone interested in forgers might pay a few guineas for them."

"A few guineas."

The duchess abruptly turned and strode away from him down the gallery, her slippers whispering on the bare wooden floor. Eamon wondered if she'd shout for her butler to show Eamon the door, but she turned at the far end of the gallery and headed back.

Her pace slowed as she neared the paintings, her fingers splayed across her mouth.

Eamon watched the duchess try to calm herself, to make herself not care that someone had cheated her family out of tens of thousands of pounds.

"If not these, then perhaps other paintings might be valuable," she said. "The previous dukes amassed quite a collection."

And why, Eamon wondered, was she so desperate to sell? Though a noble title did not preclude a peer from being insolvent, dukes seemed less susceptible to the whims of economic change. Dukes were lofty beings, raised high above the other titled nobles, often with blood ties or very close friendships with the monarch—not that monarchs were very good at keeping accounts themselves.

Eamon had noted no fire in the reception room, though he'd assumed that was to encourage unwanted guests to leave. There hadn't been one in the drawing room he'd been taken to, and its closeness indicated it hadn't been used in a long while.

Instead of a dozen footmen scurrying about to light the mistress' way up and down the stairs, there was only the spindly butler who might blow over in the next strong gust.

Cheswell had said, *Go charm the Duchess of Aylesworth out of a few paintings we can turn a profit on*, without giving him much information on the Aylesworth family itself.

The duchess's lavender gown was several years out of date and covered her from neck to ankles. She'd come out of full mourning, but Eamon was acquainted with ladies who spent their mourning year planning their future wardrobe down to the last button, donning it the moment the requisite time of grief was officially finished.

Either this woman had respected and loved her husband too deeply to leave off dull half-mourning for frivolous gowns, or she had no other choice of garments.

All signs indicated that the once-wealthy Aylesworth dukes were now skint.

Eamon's wisest course would be to apologize to the duchess and claim he couldn't help her. Cheswell's gallery did not have time or resources to waste scouring a collection of forgeries to try to assist a bankrupt. He'd put it in more polite terms, of course.

Eamon opened his mouth and found himself saying something quite different.

"You are likely right, Duchess. This gallery might hold many treasures, and the rest of the house as well. I can go through it all for you, catalog and value it. Who knows what we will discover?"

Eamon liked the way her eyes lit with hope, though the hope quickly vanished.

"That is kind," the duchess said. "But I am afraid I will not be able to engage your services."

She couldn't afford the fee, she meant. Her attempt to hide this fact behind a chilly, aristocratic dismissal increased Eamon's admiration for her.

"Duchess, do you still have my card?"

She blinked then reached into a slit in her gown and pulled out a rectangle that had been curled in her warm pocket. Eamon tried not to envy the card.

"Will you read what it says to me?" Eamon asked as she held it up.

"*Eamon Stone, Esq. Assessor, art collections. Paintings, sculpture, objets d'art,*" the duchess said in a clear voice. "And so forth. I did glance at it when Singleton announced you," she finished with impatience.

"The last line, if you please. There." Eamon stepped closer and touched the bottom edge of the card.

The duchess drew a breath, her fetching bosom rising. "*No fee for consultation.*"

"Precisely." Eamon made himself increase the space between them, though it was cold anywhere not close to her. "I am happy to rummage through your home and see what I can turn up. I only take a commission on the sale."

The card curled further as hope glimmered in her eyes once more. "My husband employed a curator," she said, as though persuading herself to argue. "I'm certain he left a detailed record."

"His records will help," Eamon acknowledged. "But he did miss these rather obvious forgeries."

Or perhaps he hadn't. Could the curator himself have long ago disposed of the real Rembrandts and hired a forger to replace them?

"That is so," the duchess agreed. Eamon heard the worry behind her words. What if the rest of the so-called priceless collection was worthless?

"I promise you, I'll find *something*," Eamon heard himself say. "Something hidden in the attic, maybe, well-guarded from thieves and forgers."

"I will have to consult with the dowager," the duchess said quickly. "Her husband purchased many of these things."

"By all means." Eamon made her a bow. "You consult and then write to me at Cheswell's. I shall eagerly await your missive."

The duchess relaxed into a sudden smile. It beamed from her, revealing her sincerity all the way down. It warmed the chilly room, that smile.

A dozen ways went through Eamon's head for coaxing out the smile again, including her drowsing beneath him in a tumbled bed. She'd gaze up at him with her green-brown eyes, and the smile would turn sultry. *Eamon,* she'd whisper, and his name would be music.

Eamon shut off the thoughts lest they show on his face—or lower down his body.

"I will write," the duchess said, her politeness less brittle. "Thank you for your honesty, Mr. Stone. You will hear from me soon."

Her tone said the interview was over. As much as Eamon wanted to linger, he knew when it was time to leave.

He bowed again, resisting the urge to seize her hand and

press a kiss to it, and headed for the stairs. The butler appeared like a ghost on the landing, waiting to show the barely tolerated guest out.

Eamon couldn't resist a backward glance at the duchess as he descended. She stood where he'd left her, in front of the false paintings. She was like a pillar of flame in that cold room, a light in Eamon's darkness.

He'd be back. No matter what he had to do, Eamon would return, would spar with his duchess again.

When Eamon set his mind on something, it fell into his hands, even a pretty duchess troubled about funds. He'd solve those worries and lay her troubles to rest. On this, he was determined.

"Thank you, Singleton," he sang at the butler as he passed. "I know the way."

Eamon skimmed down the rest of the stairs and out the massive front door, breaking into a whistled song as he sailed into the street.

———

"Ah, I have it," the dowager said, gazing into mid-air.

Her attention had wandered when Caro, dry-mouthed, had explained that the Rembrandts were forgeries. The dowager had listened without change of expression then returned to the puzzle of Mr. Stone.

"I recall now," the dowager continued. "His father was Sir Benedict Stone. Knight of some order I can't remember, deceased. Came from Dorset, or so he claimed. Sir Benedict was quite a one with the ladies. A rogue of the deepest kind." The dowager turned to Caro. "Tell me, daughter-in-law. Is his son as handsome?"

CHAPTER 4

as he handsome?

Yes. In a way that was a bit frightening.

Was it Mr. Stone who was frightening, Caro wondered, or the feelings he brought to life?

She recalled too forcefully his arms around her at the drawing-room window, and the heat that burned from the inside out when he caught her studying him in a most unladylike manner.

"He certainly is charming," Caro managed.

"His father could coax the birds out of the sky," the dowager said in reminiscence. "Sir Benedict was a bit of a swindler, in fact, as I recall. Are you certain this young man told you truthfully about the paintings?"

"I am not," Caro had to admit. "But if he was trying to cheat us, wouldn't he have simply taken the pictures away with him? Perhaps leaving us with a token amount? He would do so if they were genuine, and then sell them on, would he not?"

The dowager nodded, the tapes of her lace cap fluttering. "I suppose that is true."

Mr. Clive, the former curator, had said nothing about the paintings being forgeries. Caro had to wonder why not. Was

Mr. Stone the liar? Or Mr. Clive? Or had Mr. Clive simply not known?

Mr. Stone had been winsome and delightfully informal, chatting with Caro as though she were a person, not an untouchable duchess. Most gentlemen since her marriage had regarded her either in abject terror or as though she were a challenge—the forbidden young wife they wished to conquer.

Mr. Stone had spoken to Caro as herself, that debutante of ten years ago with giddy dreams and no idea what life would bring.

When she'd accepted Leopold's proposal, Caro had imagined traveling to intriguing places full of glamor and excitement, but she'd quickly learned that the pace of one's existence depended upon one's husband. If the duke enjoyed staying at home gazing at paintings and dusty books, then the duchess remained home with him.

Caro's own family had never had the funds nor the inclination to travel, so Caro had quietly put her dreams to rest. Now that she was a widow with no money and a child to raise, the possibility of viewing the world retreated even further.

For some reason, the sparkle in Mr. Stone's blue eyes had dredged up the yearnings Caro had long ago learned to ignore. They were dangerous, those yearnings.

It would be best if Caro never saw Mr. Stone again.

His card, which she seemed to still be holding, creased her palm. He would return to assess the collection and discover if anything was worth selling.

Regardless, Caro didn't need to speak to him. Singleton could admit him to the gallery and watch to make sure he didn't steal anything. Caro would remain on the fourth floor, where she belonged, and never set eyes on Mr. Stone.

Never let him stir the odd feelings that had bubbled to the surface when she'd looked over his fascinating body. Never let him step close to her, the strong warmth of his arms enclosing her, promising both comfort and delight.

Caro straightened her spine and thrust his card back into her pocket. No, she'd write Cheswell's to accept Mr. Stone's offer to assess the collection, but she'd stay far from him when he returned.

It would be for the best.

———

EAMON PUSHED A GOBLET OF BRANDY ACROSS THE CLUB'S DARK walnut table to Wolfe and pegged him with his best commanding stare. "Tell me everything you know about the late Duke of Aylesmore," he said.

"Aylesmore," Wolfe repeated. He frowned and moved the walking stick he sported these days from one side of his chair to the other. "You mean the Sixth Duke of that title, I suppose, deceased a year ago."

The two men sat in a relatively empty room in the club for veterans of their infantry regiment, a modest building compared with the sumptuousness of White's or Brooks's. Wolfe was a member of both those lofty establishments, but he often met Eamon and McCormick here, at the Twenty-Fifths Club, where they could stretch out their legs and rub elbows with fellow survivors of Waterloo.

Eamon had always found White's stuffy. He went only as Wolfe's guest, as he was not a member himself, though Eamon's father had been one. Dear Father had gained membership into almost every club in London, where he'd sat in cushioned chairs and tricked aristocrats out of money, brandy, land, horses, or whatever he decided to turn his hand to.

Surprisingly, none of those aristocrats had caught on. They still greeted Eamon warmly whenever they saw him, nostalgic for the beguiling conversation of his father.

Yes, Sir Benedict had been quite the raconteur. Pity he hadn't held on to the things he'd obtained. *One last game,* had been his favorite phrase. *Then we'll retire in style, my boy.*

Sir Benedict had dropped dead quite suddenly one evening, before his last game could be played. He'd left the boy Eamon with no cash, no home, and no relations that would admit to him. Sir Benedict's equally slippery man of business had obtained a place at the Hallbridge School for Eamon and deposited him there. Hence Eamon's friendship with the man reposing across from him.

"Nothing very interesting about Aylesmore," Wolfe continued. "Sat in the Lords and never spoke. Never did much of anything, from what I understand. Married the daughter of a country gentleman—Arnott, I believe the name was. She was Aylesmore's second wife. A scandal, because she was a nobody and half his age, but everyone quickly forgot about them. Aylesmore was forgettable." Wolfe pinned Eamon with a sharp gaze of his own. "Why?"

"I met the widowed duchess today." Eamon turned his glass on the table but didn't drink. "In her house in Grosvenor Square. She is very out of place there. Thought she was a maid, at first."

Wolfe's brows rose. "She couldn't have been a maid, my short-sighted friend. No more maids, no more footmen in that household. Aylesmore and his father—and grandfather, for that matter—couldn't hold on to a farthing for more than a minute. When this Aylesmore died, most of the staff evaporated, knowing they'd never be paid." Wolfe kept his stern gaze on Eamon. "What the devil were you doing in his house?"

"Looking at paintings for Cheswell." Eamon tapped his fingertips on the table. "Surely the dukes of Aylesmore have estates with peasants farming away, bringing in crops and paying rents."

"In the past, certainly." Wolfe nodded. "But while the wars

with France made some rich, for others, it was a disaster. Aylesmore invested heavily in ships that never made it past Boney's Continental System. His father married a Frenchwoman whose father had vast estates with yes, many peasants, which provided her an enormous dowry. That was before the Terror."

"Didn't meet this Frenchwoman," Eamon said. "If she's even still alive."

"She is but can't help in the area of funds. When her father's estates were confiscated by the new French government, the dowry, which was tucked into banks in Paris as well as tied up in the land itself, vanished. The marquis fled with what he could carry in a cart, ending up in England to die at the Aylesmore country house. Anything left, the Fifth and Sixth Dukes frittered away buying pieces of art and old books. The Sixth Duke's bride, Miss Arnott, didn't bring much of a dowry at all, which was part of the scandal. She did bear him a son and heir, which he hadn't managed in his first marriage."

A sad tale. Sadder still for the lovely widow, left with a child and no income.

"You know much about it," Eamon observed. He'd suspected Wolfe would have the information tucked away in his complicated brain, hence Eamon's invitation for the pair of them to take brandy at their club.

"My grandmother," Wolfe said. "She collects gossip as a hobby, and she never ceases speaking. I learn by absorption."

Eamon lifted his glass. "Here's to absorption."

Wolfe didn't join the toast. "You never finished explaining. You were viewing paintings and mistook the duchess for a maid. *Why* did you mistake her?"

Eamon shrugged. "I didn't expect a duchess to be rushing about in drab gowns or escorting visitors through the house."

"Or to be young and pretty?"

"To be honest, no."

The duchess wasn't comely in the conventional sense, which these days tended toward wisps of women with painfully fair skin and pencil-thin limbs. This duchess was relatively tall and had wonderful curves hidden by the ugly purple gown. Instead of perfectly tamed locks, dark wild waves had cupped her head, threatening to tumble loose at any provocation.

She had the body of a lover, but her blushes told of her inexperience. She'd shared a bed with her middle-aged husband and produced a child, but Eamon suspected that was the extent of her carnal understanding.

"You said she was a country gentleman's daughter," Eamon prodded. "Were there no daughters of the duke's noble cronies he could marry, if he was looking for an heir?"

"It was a love match, according to my grandmother. The duke's first wife was a sprig of the aristocracy with a long pedigree but weak constitution. She passed away within a year of their marrying, leaving the duke heartbroken."

"Poor man," Eamon said feelingly. "I will guess the rest. He realizes years later he's beginning to age and looks about for a companion. Stumbles across Miss Arnott and hears angels sing." He had definitely heard them humming in the background when she'd turned her startled gaze to him at the window.

"Caroline Arnott," Wolfe supplied. "If you are fishing for her Christian name. Not that you are in any position to use it."

"Certainly not." Eamon feigned shock. "I address her as Duchess."

"I'm surprised you weren't tossed out on your ear for that. You grovel and call her Your Grace, if you deign to speak to her at all."

"Because I am a lowly creature not fit to be trodden on, I know." Eamon grinned and lifted his glass. "To beautiful women met at the wrong place and time."

That, Wolfe conceded to drink to.

"I will be cataloging her art collection for her," Eamon said.

Wolfe coughed and quickly set down his goblet. "You'll be *what?*"

"Cataloging her art. No, I do not intend to put any paintings under my arm and walk out with them," he added in irritation at Wolfe's suspicious gaze. "She showed me two dodgy Rembrandts she thought were genuine. Someone deceived her —or the Aylesmores in general—and I have to wonder how sound the rest of the collection is. If I can find something that will bring her some much-needed cash, then I will."

"You sound like an honest man. Wanting nothing more than to help a long-suffering widow."

"Even a scoundrel can turn his hand to a good deed," Eamon said easily. "Speaking of good deeds, where the devil has McCormick got to these days?"

"Tutoring." Wolfe resumed his usual somber expression. "Maths. To youths who care nothing about it."

"Poor fellow. Well, we must all make a living."

Eamon waited for Wolfe to announce how he was keeping his own head above water, but the man drank and didn't answer.

"I intend to win the wager, you know," Eamon said quietly.

"Eh? What wager?"

"How soon he forgets. Have you erased your memory of that evening at Waterloo, when we were certain we wouldn't make it back to our regiment alive? We vowed to marry and pool whatever moneys we gain to raise our families."

"Ah, yes, that bit of foolishness." Wolfe's frown became a scowl. "You'll never win it chasing a penniless duchess, Stone. If she'll even speak to you again."

"One never knows," Eamon said. "One never knows."

Wolfe huffed and downed the rest of his brandy, but Eamon sipped in thoughtful silence.

———

HAYDEN MCCORMICK, AT THAT MOMENT, WAS EXITING A HOUSE in Upper Brook Street in extreme disgust. "Bloody Sassenach ingrates," he muttered under his breath.

He'd been asked to leave by the snobbish father of the household, whose two unruly boys refused to settle down and learn the numbers their father believed would put them at the top of their classes when they entered their prestigious school.

Those two would never be at the front of any class except to be ridiculed by the master, Hayden growled to himself. If they calmed down and paid attention, they'd perhaps keep themselves from the bottom of the heap, but as it was, they had no chance. The boys were dullards, like their father, with no intention of applying diligence to better their lot.

They'll be running the nation in fifteen years, Hayden thought with a shudder.

Their enraged papa had refused to pay Hayden's fee and advised him to return to Glasgow where he belonged.

Hayden decided it wasn't worth it to explain that Shetland was nowhere near Glasgow and that its inhabitants had descended from an entirely different stock, namely Vikings who'd torn apart soft Englishmen like him.

He'd stomped away into the growing darkness, making for his club.

"You just missed Wolfe," Stone told Hayden when Hayden reached the Twenty-Fifths and called for a large pint of their strongest ale.

"Damn him," Hayden growled, then nodded reassuringly at the waiter who'd brought him the pint. "Not you, lad. Thank ye." When the waiter left, he resumed. "I wanted to pull another recommendation from Wolfe. I've been sacked and need employment."

"I am sorry to hear it," Stone answered as Hayden took a long swallow of ale. "Did you know we are not to admit we work for a living? We are supposed to exist in genteel poverty, as though it is a virtue to go hungry."

"I wasn't raised to believe it shameful to earn an honest crust," Hayden said without offense. "Wolfe knows everyone in London and can persuade someone they need to hire a tutor."

Stone regarded him in quiet sympathy. "You should be at a university, explaining to the three men who can understand you about higher maths and the whirling of the planets and so forth. Not grubbing with little boys who'd rather be running through the mud."

Hayden took another fortifying gulp of ale. "Universities hire men they know, who were usually students in that college themselves, not outsiders with no connections. I don't mind teaching the lads, as long as they're willing to learn. Besides, fellows at the highest colleges are notoriously penniless."

Stone shrugged. "They give you a place to live. You can write papers for obscure journals and retain your dignity."

Hayden relaxed into his chair, his fit of pique assuaged by the decent ale and the chance to vent his spleen. "Dignity doesn't make one rich. I don't need much but wouldn't mind something to put by for my old age."

"You are always maddeningly cheerful," Stone said with a hint of a grin. "Leave it with me. I met a duchess today who has a small boy. He might need your skills. Although—" Stone pointed a stern finger at Hayden. "Confine your attentions to teaching. The duchess is not for you."

"Oh, aye?" Hayden raised his brows, his attention caught. "She's for *you*, is she? You intend to carry out the wager?"

Stone nodded and looked wise, but Hayden could pry no more information from him.

Interesting, Hayden mused to himself and succumbed to the comfortable chair to enjoy the rest of his ale.

———

It was ridiculous to fuss about one's garments when one was simply going to greet Mr. Stone and then leave him to wander the gallery alone to make his notes.

Caro had changed her mind about avoiding him altogether, convincing herself it would be rude not to at least say good morning. After all, Mr. Stone was doing them a great favor, charging nothing to root around in the house's vast and dusty gallery.

Caro surveyed the frocks she'd laid out on her bed. They were sadly few in number, every one of them out of fashion and many times mended. She hadn't minded before this, because she went out so seldom these days and paid little attention to her appearance beyond being tidy.

Handsome Mr. Stone with his charming smile was the sort of man who'd effortlessly attract women to him like butterflies to a flower. And like butterflies, those ladies would be elegantly beautiful in stunning gowns and dripping with jewels.

Their hair likely stayed in place as well, Caro thought impatiently as she pushed back yet another strand. Sleek topknots, perfect ringlets.

Ah, well. Unless one had a devoted hairdresser, one had to make do.

Caro was becoming thoroughly tired of making do.

Why hadn't she worried about the cut of her gown and state of her hair when Leopold had been alive?

Answer, because she'd been happy. There had been contentment in knowing that another person accepted her as she was.

Mr. Stone had already engendered completely different feelings inside her, and such emotions could not be good.

Caro sighed and lifted the best gown of the lot. It had long sleeves and a matronly cut, but it was a pretty shade of dark green with lighter green flowers embroidered on the hem. Several of the embroidery's colorful threads had worked loose, but a few snips with her small scissors took them off. She rubbed the rest of the threads to hide the gaps in the pattern.

The gown went over her shift and small stays. The ensemble wasn't *too* dowdy, Caro decided, as a chance beam of sunlight caught the sheen of the broadcloth.

She donned her worn leather shoes, tucked in strands of hair once more, and sailed forth.

Mr. Stone was punctual. Cheswell's gallery had replied to her letter accepting Mr. Stone's offer to look over the collection, telling her to expect him Monday morning at ten o'clock. At one minute to ten, Mr. Stone tapped the knocker on the front door.

Singleton admitted him, and this time showed him straight to the gallery, where Caro pretended not to have been lingering for the last half hour, waiting for him.

Mr. Stone's brilliant smile struck with force as Caro turned from studying a painting, as though she was surprised to see him.

"Good morning, Duchess." Mr. Stone made a gallant bow, while Singleton glided haughtily back down the stairs. "Oh, I beg your pardon. I was told by a man who knows much about such things that I should not address you thus. I should say Your Grace. But then, you might not like that either. Which designation do you prefer?"

For one wild moment, Caro almost told him to use her given name, but that would be highly inappropriate, especially for the nobody miss who'd beguiled a duke.

"Duchess will do, Mr. Stone," Caro said, striving to appear unruffled. "*Your Grace* is rather formal."

"Ah, she blesses me with informality," Mr. Stone said to the air around him. "I did not dare to hope. As we are barely acquainted, I must remain Mr. Stone, that dull stick. Though one day perhaps we will be such friends that I will be Eamon to you."

"Eamon," Caro repeated before she could stop herself. She liked the feel of the name on her tongue. "Is it Irish?"

Mr. Stone lifted broad shoulders. "My antecedents are rather obscure. I know of no other Eamons in the family, and my father was Benedict, which is very English, I believe. I've never been to Ireland."

His gaze had touched her lips as she'd spoken the name, and in the tingling heat that consumed her, she missed most of his explanation.

Flustered, she turned away. "Would you like to begin with the paintings?"

"That will do." He spoke calmly behind her, his footsteps measured as he followed.

"I dug out Mr. Clive's books," Caro babbled. "He was our curator. They were a bit puzzling." She'd felt at sea when going over Mr. Clive's crabbed handwriting. Caro did not consider herself ignorant, but his shorthand had left her bewildered.

"Catalogers often have their own codes." Mr. Stone spoke without worry. "I'll look them over and see what I can find."

"I've left them here." Caro diverged her course to a table against the wall, where a bust of a Roman emperor watched over a stack of leather-bound ledgers.

"Ah, Vespasian," Mr. Stone said as they halted. "One of the few fortunate emperors to die in his bed."

"My husband admired him for taking his duties so seriously." Caro lapsed into an affectionate smile. "He often spoke to him when we passed." She caught Mr. Stone's amused expression. "My husband was whimsical, not mad."

"I quite understand." Mr. Stone gave Vespasian's balding marble head a pat. "Art is marvelous for listening to our troubles." He regarded the books. "I believe I will look at the paintings first and peruse the ledgers afterward. To see if I agree with your curator's assessments."

Caro scarcely heard him. She realized they were standing quite close, and they were very much alone in the gallery.

Mr. Stone wore a frock coat similar to that of his first visit, though this one was a deep blue. It smelled faintly of warmth and rain, the outdoors, and something indefinable. His hair was damp from the mist outside, droplets glistening in the light of the few candles in the sconces above them. Caro had persuaded Singleton that Mr. Stone would need light to see the paintings, as the day was overcast, and not much sunlight penetrated the windows.

Mr. Stone fixed on her in a way that made Caro grip the table to keep her knees from buckling.

"Well." She drew a breath, trying to clear her head. "Shall I leave you to it?"

"No." The word was abrupt, almost sharp. As Caro stared, her heart thumping, he softened his tone. "No," he repeated. "Stay."

CHAPTER 5

She'd run. Eamon braced himself, waiting for her imperious duchessness to slap his face, declare him a menace to decent ladies, and stalk away.

Instead, she fixed him with a perplexed gaze, her eyes unwavering. Beautiful eyes, the gold flecks dancing in candlelight. Eamon wanted to gaze into them for as long as he could, to reach out and cup her face, to discover if the skin of her cheek was as silken as it looked.

"Why?" she asked him breathily.

So I can bathe my senses in you, so I can delight in you. I intend to marry you, after all.

Good Lord, where had that come from?

Maybe because of the stupid wager, which Eamon had brought up at the club to put off Wolfe's curiosity?

No, hang the wager. His declaration had come from a place deep inside him, far beyond the frivolous charm he used to keep the world at bay.

Eamon wanted his duchess—Caroline, Caro, or however she preferred he address her once they were lovers—to be his simply for the joy of it.

She'd obviously liked her ducal husband, her smile betraying such when she'd described him chatting with the bust of Vespasian. She'd had a comfortable marriage, Eamon decided.

But the duchess deserved devotion, desire, and blatant admiration, not mere companionship. He wanted to show her what depths passion could stir. Eamon would kiss her body, tumble her hair, and bring her joy every day, morning or evening, whichever she preferred. Both, he hoped.

What means they would live on, Eamon had no idea, but he never let practical considerations stand between him and something he wanted. He dove in and then ascertained what needed to be done, as he had that day at Hallbridge when he'd first become friends with Wolfe and McCormick.

The duchess—Caro, she would be to him—waited for his answer, never realizing what wild fantasies whirled through his head.

Eamon seized the first explanation that came to him. "Because you know the collection. Show me what the dukes considered important, in their eyes. Take me to what they treasured most."

Caro's dark brows rose, but she did not question him, thank heaven. She turned without hesitation and skimmed down the gallery, her dark green skirt flowing.

The gown she wore today had been fashionable when Eamon had been shooting at Frenchmen on the Peninsula, when skirts had been cut to cling to a lady's legs. Caro must have worn this years ago, when she'd been first married, or perhaps before that. Gentlemen must have fallen over in a heap whenever she passed.

"You have already seen the Rembrandts. Poor things," Caro was saying, jerking Eamon's attention from his dreams. She waved a hand dismissively at the two paintings still on their easels as she passed them.

Eamon barely gave them a glance. The false Rembrandts had

brought him here, so he was grateful, but he mostly he focused on Caro's upright back and the wavy dark tendril that had tumbled from her knot of hair.

Caro paused to remove a candle from one of the few sconces that had been lit and cupped her hand around the flame as she led him deeper into the shadows.

Light squares on the wallpaper at this end of the gallery indicated that paintings had been taken away in the past. Sold long ago? Had they been genuine, or forgeries as well?

Caro halted in front of a large square landscape painting. It had been hung so that the sky, clear blue with halos of golden light, seemed to stretch upward, as though the viewer stood in the foreground with the awed figures there.

"I like this one," she said softly.

The painting was beautiful. Towering trees framed its edges, while a cliff in the far background overlooked a tossing sea beyond. Ancient buildings in the Greek style lined the cliffs, far from the viewer, while a ship flowed toward the vanishing point on the horizon.

Eamon admired the technique, the seamless use of color. The scene was so real, he could feel the breeze in the trees, was certain he could reach out and touch the rocks. They'd be warm and rough under his hand, and cold spray would shower him.

"*Why* do you like it?" Eamon asked. He knew why he did, but he was thoroughly weary of his own opinions. Caro's would be more interesting.

"Because I want to go there." Caro breathed a laugh, her formality fading. "I know this isn't a real place—Claude Lorrain painted myths and historic legends, like the Queen of Sheba sailing off wherever she was heading. But it makes me want to find that clifftop, that sea, that *place*. When London becomes dreary and dark, I pretend I am there." She waved a hand at the painting. "The Dukes of Aylesmore have a house in Kent, but at this time of year, everything is gray and knee-deep in mud." Her laughter trailed off, her wistfulness sharp.

This was too difficult. Eamon couldn't stand next to her, watching her gaze with soft longing at the painting, without wanting to pull her into his arms and promise her the world. He'd take her anywhere she wanted to go, perhaps to the warm climates of Sicily or a Greek isle, where she could gaze upon old ruins by the seashore as long as she liked.

He hated to go on breaking her heart.

"This painting is in the style of Claude," Eamon said gently. "Possibly a copy done by someone in his studio or by someone trying to emulate him."

Caro swung to him in dismay. "You mean it isn't real, either?"

"If it was, it would be worth even more than the Rembrandts. Landscape wasn't as appreciated in Claude's time, but it is today."

The despair in her eyes cut him. "Are *any* paintings in this gallery genuine?"

Eamon wanted to reassure her, but he also couldn't lie. Someone had been stringing her and her family along, and Eamon refused to continue their deception.

"Possibly," he said. "We have a long way to go. But just because someone who worked for Claude or was his student painted this doesn't mean you must cease loving it. The light, the clever use of color, are masterful. He or she had talent, this painter, even if his name or hers wasn't Claude Lorrain."

Caro drew a shaking breath, as though trying to prevent herself from bursting into tears. "I wonder if the artist was given their due," she said without much conviction.

Eamon shrugged. "Many an artist aspires to be great, but sometimes they can only manage to borrow another's genius. Our own paintings are overlooked, so we console ourselves with being talented copyists. Many of Bonaparte's savants who went to Egypt to record what was there were blessed with such talent."

Caro switched her assessing gaze to him. "Are you a copyist?"

"I am, for my sins." Eamon gestured at the false Claude. "I'd be honored if you'd allow me to copy this piece. Not to sell," he added hastily. "I would pin it to the wall of my dreary lodgings to brighten up the place."

He'd already copied several paintings, courtesy of Caravaggio and Canaletto, that made his rooms a little more colorful.

"I suppose it would do no harm."

Caro did not sound at all in transports that she and Eamon could be gazing at the same painting at the same time, even when they were apart.

And when the devil had Eamon become so bloody sentimental?

When he'd gazed into Caro's green-flecked golden eyes, that was when.

"Continue loving the painting," Eamon said. "I'm certain the original artist would be thrilled, even if he's been dead and gone these several hundred years."

Caro returned her reluctant attention to it. "You are right— the picture is beautiful, no matter who painted it. It would be a shame to toss it away because it isn't worth the large amount it was supposed to be."

Eamon wondered who'd managed to sell the thing to what- ever Duke of Aylesmore had plunked down his money for it in the first place. The dukes seem to have been happy to pay for art without being very wise about it. They'd been the sort of purchasers who liked the look of the thing with no idea as to its true value.

"Did your husband treasure this?" Eamon asked.

Caro softened. "He actually wasn't one for paintings. He

liked some of them, but his true love was books." She plucked her candle from its holder and continued down the gallery to the far shadowy corners.

A bookcase covered the end walls of the gallery, framing a doorway and climbing to the high ceiling above them. Books lined the shelves, tomes of all sizes bound in leather, cloth, and paper, some with covers cracking, others with the spines falling away from neglect.

A ladder hooked to a runner reposed at the end of the shelf, so the collector could climb to the top and caress the books there.

Eamon gazed at the shelves in dismay. "Quite a lot of them."

"Leopold could never resist a book if it was dusty and faded," Caro confessed. "He said that one never knew what was inside if one didn't take a chance on it."

Eamon pulled a small volume from a lower shelf, its leather so worn he could not make out the title. The binding gave an alarming creak as he opened the book, and the first two pages curled away from the threads that had fastened them to the spine. "I see he did not resist many."

The book was nothing very ancient, a twenty-year-old reprint of Daniel Defoe's *Robinson Crusoe*. Eamon could have found this in a secondhand bookshop in Covent Garden.

"Leopold adored his books," Caro said. "I sometimes teased him that he ought to have married them instead of a wife who only had conversation to recommend her, and not much of that. He would smile and say, *Nonsense, my dear*, then return to his reading."

Her eyes filled with sudden tears, and she quickly turned away.

She'd loved the old fool, damn him. Eamon's heart burned.

This was not a lonely young widow eager to succumb to the wiles of the first rogue who came her way. She'd mourn her husband until the end of her days, leaning against his pile of worthless books for comfort.

She'd been no empty-headed girl, proud she'd landed herself a duke, Eamon assessed. She'd had a true marriage with a man she'd liked and held in high regard, and she'd borne him a son. The newest Duke of Aylesmore was a product of *this* marriage.

"I must admit to you, I don't know much about books," Eamon said to give Caro time to regain her composure. "A consequence of my misspent youth. I was more apt to draw in the margins than read the words."

When Caro turned back to him, her eyes were dry again but held sadness. "Mr. Clive examined them. He did not find much of value."

Eamon was beginning to consider Mr. Clive a perfect fool. If he'd missed that the Rembrandts and the Claude were fakes, would he know a Shakespeare First Folio if it hit him on the head?

"It does no harm to go through them again," Eamon said. "I am fortunately acquainted with those who have more expertise in books than me. My friend Wolfe, for instance, who grew up in homes with vast libraries, and my friend McCormick, who is a genius. By the bye, if the young duke has need of a tutor, I can recommend none better than Hayden McCormick."

"Oh." Caro regarded Eamon uneasily. "A tutor would be welcome, but to be honest, Mr. Stone, I could not pay the fee." She flushed, embarrassed.

Eamon wanted to kick himself. She must think he was an obsequious leech, worming his way into her household, eager to discover something valuable so he could receive his commission. Now, he was suggesting he bring in his friends to take advantage of her hospitality, more or less demanding noblesse oblige.

"As myself, they offer their services gratis," Eamon said, trying not to imagine explaining this to his annoyed friends.

"McCormick loves to shape young minds, and Wolfe is at home among obscure texts. Let them come and speak to you about the books, in any case."

"Well…"

Eamon held up a hand to spare her having to refuse. "My apologies, dear lady. I will not foist my friends upon you. It is no matter. I will say nothing of this to them."

Caro flushed, her eyes betraying distress. "Oh, dear, now I've offended you."

Eamon stared in astonishment. "You, offend *me*? My dear Duchess, you are incapable of offending me, even if you threw me to the ground and trampled on me."

With difficulty he staved off the delightful vision of himself on the floor with her pretty feet on his chest. He could cup her lovely ankles while her skirts swayed to let him enjoy his fill of the view.

When Eamon could breathe again, he saw that Caro had dropped her gaze, but he realized her downcast look wasn't from shyness.

She was studying him as she had yesterday, with interest. At the moment, her focus was on Eamon's throat, his skin revealed by his carelessly tied cravat. From there, she moved up his chin to his lips.

Don't kiss her, Eamon admonished himself. He clenched his jaw to maintain control. So easy it would be to lean to her, caress her cheek, draw her to him for a touch of lips…

He'd destroy everything. This trust she had to stand here alone with Eamon in a dark gallery would be gone in an instant. She'd summon the loyal Singleton to throw him out, or perhaps do it herself. She was robust enough to manage it.

Caro raised her gaze to meet his. They regarded each other in silence, the only sound the sputtering of the candle Caro held.

Wax splashed to Caro's fingers, and she drew a quick breath.

Eamon quickly snatched the candle from her, and it extinguished itself, the tip of the wick glowing red. He dropped the candle to the nearest table and grasped Caro's hand.

"Are you all right? Did it burn you?"

She let him examine the skin between thumb and forefinger, now pale with a thin coat of beeswax. Only the best candles for a duchess, even a penniless one.

Caro tried to shrug. "It's only wax."

"Very hot wax." Eamon gently rubbed the offending patch, which obligingly flaked away.

Eamon brushed his thumb over the area once more, then lifted Caro's hand to his lips and pressed a quick kiss where the wax had fallen.

He felt her start beneath his lips. He expected her to become outraged, snatch her hand away, and order him to go. *Knave. Peon. Remember your place.*

Instead, Caro smiled shyly. "My mother used to do that when I was hurt."

Now she was comparing Eamon to her mother. Ah, well, better that than having him flogged for his impertinence.

"I'd like to tell you *mine too*, but I don't remember her," Eamon said.

Instantly Caro radiated sympathy, as though he'd told her the most distressing thing she could imagine. "Oh, I am sorry."

Eamon did not relish pity from anyone, but it was different when coming from a beautiful woman whose hand he held.

"You are kind," he said. "Thank you."

He should release her now. Under Caro's compassionate gaze, Eamon never wanted to let go of her again.

He *did* want to sneeze, because these books probably held a century's worth of dust, not to mention mites and other things that ate paper. Eamon held it in, because he'd have to step away from Caro and make an exploding, inelegant noise.

The next few seconds would decide things. He'd either

sneeze or pull the woman of his dreams close and kiss her. Then the woman of his dreams would either allow the kiss or show him the door.

A dry cough sounded behind them.

The moment shattered and scattered its pieces at Eamon's feet.

"His Grace, the Duke of Aylesmore," Singleton intoned.

CHAPTER 6

aro's face lit, and she abandoned Eamon in a heartbeat.

For a brief instant, the words *the Duke of Aylesmore* conjured in Eamon's mind the middle-aged duke with a love of books and an indulgent smile for his duchess. He'd charge to Eamon and demand to know what he was doing holding his wife's hand, perhaps call him out for his audacity.

Then Eamon remembered that, of course, the duke these days was a child. Caro's son.

Caro ran on light feet to a lad with unruly dark hair in a too-formal suit, with a somewhat rebellious expression on his small face.

"Darling, what are you doing out of the schoolroom?" Caro reached her son and leaned to kiss his forehead. "It's history today. You like history."

But a healthy boy could only sit and stare at musty books for so long, Eamon well knew.

"Art is history," Eamon said as he moved to them. "And there must be history in all these tomes." He waved a hand at the bookcase looming behind him. "I well remember Waterloo and the Peninsular campaign. That's history for you."

The boy's mutinous look evaporated as he riveted his gaze on Eamon. "You were in the war, sir?" he asked with youthful eagerness.

"I was indeed. A captain, for my sins." Eamon gave the lad a military bow. "At your service, Your Grace."

His Grace grinned, showing charming dimples. "My name's Leo. How do you do, Captain Stone?"

"Plain Mister now. I sold my commission."

"I shall call you Captain anyway," Leo announced. "It's more exciting. Were you really at Waterloo?"

Caro, instead of admonishing her son for speaking familiarly with a stranger, gazed at him with so much love it was heart-wrenching.

"I was indeed," Eamon told the lad. "Had a grand adventure in the middle of that battle, stranded on a ridge with the French army all around me and my friends. But we escaped, mostly unscathed, as you see." He spread his arms.

Leo listened in round-eyed fascination. "What happened?"

Eamon glanced at Caro, who gave him a minute nod to proceed. Eamon launched into the tale of the harrowing few hours on that ridge, brushing aside his, Wolfe's, and McCormick's real conviction that they'd not make it back to their camp, let alone home, alive.

Leo listened with flattering attention as the tale progressed. Eamon made light of the serious situation and played up the three men's banter as they strove to escape.

"You blew up the Frenchies?" Leo gasped when Eamon ended with the black powder exploding, confusing the soldiers that were almost on top of them.

The blinding smoke had let him and his two friends slip through, both he and McCormick half carrying Wolfe between them.

"I don't know if we actually blew up anyone," Eamon said. "But it disoriented them. They thought they were under attack by an entire platoon. One French officer even shouted at us to join the line, because the damned—er, the rotten—British had broken through. McCormick, who can speak French like a native, said, *Oui, oui, on arrive,* and started cursing out Wellington in vivid terms. It was all Wolfe and I could do to keep from falling about in laughter."

That had been a tense moment. If the well-armed officer had seen through the smoke that Eamon and his companions wore the colors of their British regiment, he and his soldiers would have shot them dead.

Eamon met Caro's gaze above Leo's head. He read in her eyes that she knew exactly how lucky the escape had been, how close Eamon had come to not surviving at all. Also, he saw her gratitude for understating the danger for Leo's sake. Eamon sensed that Leo was a tougher nut than Caro realized, but mothers worried for their sons.

Leo bounced on his toes. "What else happened, Captain? Were you shot?"

"Leo," Caro said, aggrieved. "A battlefield is a terrible place. I am pleased Mr. Stone was not hurt."

Before Leo could become too crestfallen, Eamon broke in. "I wasn't injured, no, except for minor cuts and bruises. Wolfe, though, took a ball through the leg. He was furious. Laid him up a long time."

"He must be jolly brave," Leo declared. "I wish I could have been at Waterloo."

Eamon expected his mother to admonish him, but she nodded, her eyes sparkling. "They were indeed very brave," she agreed.

Eamon wished she did not look so beautiful when she said this.

"It was an adventure." Eamon waved away the fear, the tense moments, the certainty they'd feel bullets in their backs at any moment. "Here, lad, let me show you." He retrieved a few books from the shelves and carried them to the table that held the bust of Vespasian. "We'll say the Roman emperor here is Wellington." He laid large tomes along the floor in front of the table. "Here is the river Sambre, and here is how Boney lined up his men."

He seized more books, organizing them by color, red to represent the British forces, and blue to represent the French, brown for the Prussians poised to attack from the woods. Leo dove in to help, arranging the books where Eamon directed. Eamon hadn't known where his own platoon had stood at the time, but McCormick and other officers at their veterans' club had refought the battle on maps many times since.

Three very small tomes became himself, Wolfe, and McCormick. "My friends and I were here," Eamon explained as he and Leo set them between encircling lines of blue books. "A very tight spot."

"You have to tell me again what you did," Leo said, eyes shining. He didn't command as a haughty duke but an excited child.

"Of course." Eamon hunkered down next to the books, and Leo joined him, arms around his small knees.

Eamon went over every word of the tale, embellishing it with more details, moving his props as necessary.

He was not so engrossed that he didn't spy Caro give them a little smile and silently glide away, leaving them to it.

———

"THE DUCHESS OF AYLESMORE," A TALL YOUNG MAN, resplendent in powdered wig and satin livery, announced into the Princess of Osagard's opulent drawing room the next afternoon.

A fine rain fell outside but no damp would dare penetrate the warm elegance of the Portman Square home. Caro had let the coziness of the house embrace her as she entered then followed the footman up the grand flight of stairs to the first floor.

She'd hoped for a quiet visit, but the drawing room was crowded, morning calls in full fervor. One of this year's debutantes was pounding out a rather heavy-handed minuet by Mozart as her mother proudly observed her.

The young ladies and matrons in the room came alert when Caro was announced, feathered headdresses bobbing like a startled flock of colorful birds. Caro strove not to cringe as quizzing glasses rose to train on her.

The rare occasions Caro paid calls these days subjected her to many a stare, ranging from delighted surprise to barely concealed hostility. When the nobody Miss Arnott had landed herself the Duke of Aylesmore, she'd made enemies overnight of people she'd never met.

The hostess of the drawing room, a tall, middle-aged woman with a turban that rose higher than any of her guests', came to her feet in welcome. Her pleasure in beholding Caro was genuine, though the dignified lady would never reveal such a thing.

Her daughter, on the other hand, sprang up with a squeal of gladness and rushed across the room.

"Caro, my dearest darling." Princess Josephine Anne-Marie Sophia Vollen of Osagard flung her arms around Caro and crushed her in a pink-and-cream silk embrace. "You ought to have warned me you were coming. I'd have had Mason lay on a feast."

"Nonsense." Caro kissed Jo's cheek when her friend released her. "The only feast I need is seeing you."

The other ladies in the room witnessed this display with a fluttering of fans and a few whispers, but when Jo led Caro across the room and placed her in the seat of honor—a comfortable armchair nearest the fire—many stares, though not all, became ones of grudging acceptance.

Josephine's father, Prince Rupert, was no longer welcome in his tiny kingdom on the Austria-Bohemia border, but he'd been instrumental in providing money and a squadron of men in the recent battles with Napoleon, which had won him respect and honor.

In addition, Prince Rupert might any day be restored from his exile, when the ancient king who'd pushed him away years ago finally expired. The ladies and gentlemen of London cultivated the approval of Josephine's prestigious family, just in case.

Jo's friendship with Caro, and her parents' approval of her, had gone a long way to ease Caro's entry into society as the new Duchess of Aylesmore.

Caro hadn't been out much since Leopold's death, but today, she'd very much wanted to speak to her friends.

Jo dragged a chair close to Caro's and gazed at her as though she hadn't seen her for months.

Princess Jo was a beauty, a fact so many misses tried and failed to despise her for. She had the golden hair and fair complexion common in northern European climes, her eyes a crystalline blue. Ladies whispered that Jo must secretly rub buttermilk on her skin and rinse her hair with lemon juice, but Caro knew she'd simply inherited the coloring of her parents.

The kingdom of Osagard had been settled by Northmen a thousand years ago, at about the same time those marauders had made their way into northern England, Scotland, and Ireland, as well as Normandy and what was now the great empire of Russia. The small kingdom had managed to survive the machinations of the Holy Roman Empire and retained its autonomy to this day.

Young ladies of society found they couldn't dislike Jo, however much they tried, because she was sunny-natured, kind, and generous. Any debutante terrified of scrutiny, or weeping because the gentleman she fancied didn't notice her, had a sympathetic ear in Jo as well as sound advice to bolster said lady's spirits.

"Darling, it's been an age," Jo gushed to Caro.

"It has been since last Tuesday," Caro corrected her good-naturedly. Jo had called on Caro at the Grosvenor Square house, and they'd had a fine tea with the dowager and Leo.

"Well, it *seems* an age. It is a sad time for me when I do not look upon you every day."

"You're a goose." Caro laughed, Jo easily calming her agitation. "I do admit, though, that I've been languishing for a good gab with you." She tried not to glance around the very full room, but Jo caught her unease.

"It is the height of the Season, my friend," Jo said. "We must all rush around to each other's drawing rooms and stuff ourselves with lemonade, macaroons, and gossip. Fortification for sailing out to evening balls and soirees to do it all again."

"I had forgotten," Caro said with a pang. The year since Leopold's death had passed in monotony, Caro uncertain of her welcome at any gathering not hosted by her closest friends.

"My poor dearest." Jo squeezed Caro's hands, her compassion unfeigned. "I have neglected you. That will change, beginning this instant. I am frivoling, while you have been abandoned in that great, dreary house."

"Don't be so silly. I have plenty to do at home, including raising a son who has more energy than a live volcano." Caro warmed, as always, when she thought of her beloved Leo.

"Where *is* dear Leo this afternoon? In the care of Singleton? The poor man will be run off his feet." Jo grinned, picturing Singleton's discomfiture.

"No, Mr. Stone has rather taken Leo under his wing," Caro said before she thought.

A sharp light entered Jo's eyes. "Mr. Stone? Who is Mr. Stone?"

"No one at all." Caro tried to keep her cheeks from scalding, to no avail. "He works for Cheswell's gallery and was sent to look over a few art pieces I wished to sell. Mr. Stone became interested in the duke's collection and is inventorying it."

Jo's steady gaze was unnerving. She was no fool, and Caro regretted the easy way Mr. Stone's name had tripped off her tongue. Caro had just revealed to Jo that she trusted Mr. Stone with both her husband's artwork and her son.

"I see we *do* need to have a chat," Jo said. "Wait here. I must do my duty and not disappear, but after the crowd has gone, we will withdraw."

Caro had called today to bury the disquieting feelings Mr. Stone stirred in her by listening to Jo rattle out the latest gossip. She hadn't intended to bare her soul, but nothing slipped past the astute Jo.

"Very well," Caro said meekly.

Jo slid away to chat with the other ladies in the room, and Princess Maude, as good-natured as her daughter, made certain that Caro had a glass of cool lemonade to sip.

Princess Maude was nothing like the mother Caro remembered from her childhood, a beautiful lady taken from Caro far too young. However, the dignified Maude always had a kind word for Caro and a reassuring hand on her shoulder when needed.

The callers drifted away more quickly than Caro anticipated, and soon Jo waved at Caro to follow her.

On an upper floor of the house decorated by the Adam brothers, Jo ushered Caro into a sitting room that was no less luxurious than the drawing room they'd left. Gilded moldings surrounded panels that held paintings of soft landscapes and one portrait of Jo as a child, her golden ringlets surrounding a winsome chubby face.

The same eyes and smile from the portrait fixed on Caro as soon as the door shut, leaving them alone.

"Now then." Jo tugged Caro to a rose-and-white striped settee and pulled her down upon it. "Tell me *everything*."

CHAPTER 7

"Everything?" Caro strove for an innocent tone.

"Oh, my friend, I have known you far too long." Jo leaned to her with a brush of lemony perfume. "You did not call today because you craved a bit of society. You barely spoke to anyone and listened less. Who is this man who's come to value your pictures, and why do you trust him to look after Leo?"

"He is not looking after Leo," Caro said quickly. "Singleton and Mama-in-law are there for that. Leo admires Mr. Stone. Natural, I think, since the poor lad lost his father. Mr. Stone was an officer in the war, and Leo is interested. That is all."

"Yes, but who *is* he?"

Jo obviously would not be put off. "He has excellent references." Or so Caro assumed. The haughty owners of Cheswell's gallery wouldn't have hired him otherwise. She could ask to view the letters of reference any time she wished, couldn't she?

Caro would most definitely not tell Jo what the dowager had proclaimed, that Eamon's father had been a charming rogue who'd had a way with the ladies.

A new and younger voice joined the conversation. "You are asking the wrong questions, Aunty Jo."

The door of an ornately scrolled armoire swung open, and a slender girl popped out. Her fashionable pale pink and cream gown was a near duplicate of Jo's, a pink sash separating skirt from bodice. The cloth roses on the sash now hung precariously by a few threads, and the girl's pink slippers were smudged with dust.

"What are you doing in there, impertinent miss?" Jo asked her sternly.

"Eavesdroppers learn much to their advantage," the being returned without shame. "Is that a quote from something, Aunt Caro?"

Caro was not the girl's aunt, but she'd accepted the honorific years ago. Twelve-year-old Meredith Sutcliffe was the daughter of Jo's older sister and a handsome British earl. Young Merry held the courtesy title of Lady because of her father, and under the curious inheritance laws of Osagard, she also retained the title of Princess.

"I'm not certain," Caro said in answer to Merry's question.

"You are very, very bad and won't have any ices," Jo scolded.

"I've already eaten three," Merry chirped. "I know Miss Crone will give me only bread and weak tea when I go home, so I've filled up."

"Her name is Miss Crane," Jo corrected her. "Her new governess," she explained to Caro.

"I don't need a governess." Merry's brow furrowed. "I have no intention of becoming a young lady and catching a husband. What a beastly idea. But we're listening to Aunt Caro tell us about her new young man. She's a widow, so she can have an *affaire de coeur* without censure." Merry's blue-eyed, piercing gaze was much like Jo's. "Confess, Aunt Caro. Is he handsome?"

Caro's face burned to the roots of her hair. She ought to command Jo and her niece to cease this interrogation and mind their own business, and then she'd rise and coolly quit the house.

Which would tell the two ladies all they needed to know.

"Yes," Caro whispered.

Jo and Merry erupted into squealing laughter. They hugged each other, then Merry squeezed her way between Caro and the arm of the settee.

The two proceeded to bombard Caro with questions from both sides. What did Mr. Stone look like? Where did he come from? Why was he examining old paintings if he'd been an officer in a regiment? Did he have any brothers or close friends?

This last came from Merry, with emphasis, as though it was the most important point.

Caro supplied them with every detail she could, knowing she'd never leave this room alive if she did not.

"He did mention two fellow officers," Caro answered Merry. "They were together at Waterloo, trapped behind enemy lines. Mr. Stone made light of it, but from the story he told Leo, I gather it was quite perilous. They were lucky to escape unscathed."

"A dashing officer surviving a dangerous mission," Merry cooed. "Better and better. Ripe for an *affaire de coeur.*"

"You should not even know what that means," Jo said severely. "She is right, though, Caro. It is time you enjoyed yourself."

Caro thought she'd never cease blushing. "My dears, it will hardly come to that. And you should not know of such things either, Jo. You're an unmarried miss."

"Spinster, you mean," Jo said with a grin. "Unmarried, but so very wise. The things my sister has told me about ladies of society would shock you senseless. *You* are a paragon of virtue, Caro, which is one reason they took against you when you married Leopold. They expected you to be a hussy, not an angel."

"I would be exactly that if I follow the path you are suggesting," Caro pointed out.

She strove for indignation, but a sudden image took her breath away. She saw herself entering a bedchamber where Mr. Stone, undressed for some reason, turned to confront his intruder. He'd start at her entrance, but quickly pull her into his arms, stifling Caro's apologies with a scalding kiss.

Heat pooled in Caro's belly, and she inhaled sharply.

Jo and Merry went off into laughter again. "I vow, Caro, you are lost," Jo declared. "I *must* meet this gentleman."

"And so must I," Merry declared. "And his friends." She pointed behind her hand at Jo and mouthed to Caro, *For her.*

Jo ignored the gesture. "Not you, child. Not until I assess him and decide whether he is good enough for our Caro. We must consult Louise as well."

"No, no." Caro said hastily. "Louise has her hands full with her boys. No reason to disturb her."

"Nonsense. I will write her this evening. We'll think of an excuse to bring your Mr. Stone somewhere we can meet him."

"Or we'll simply turn up in Grosvenor Square," Merry suggested. "Calling on our poor, lonely Aunt Caro."

"That is enough." Caro finally dredged up some firmness. "If you three arrive to stare at the man, he'll flee, and I'll never know if there's anything of value among Leopold's things."

"If Mr. Stone survived being penned up on a ridge by the French army, he will stand ladies asking him questions," Jo said. "Merry will either keep silent or shan't be allowed to come." She glared at Merry, who rolled her eyes but subsided. "Why do you say *anything of value?*" Jo asked Caro. "I thought your Leopold's collection was priceless. Enough to keep you in splendor the rest of your days if you and the dowager can bear to part with any of it."

Caro wiped away the rose-tinted dreams of Eamon Stone in a bedchamber and returned to her present circumstances. "Mr. Stone has found some very convincing fakes Leopold's father and grandfather must have been tricked into purchasing. I've written to Mr. Clive about them but have had no answer."

The explanation of Mr. Stone's discoveries started Jo on another series of questions about Mr. Stone, Cheswell's, and how reliable was Mr. Stone's appraisal.

Jo rang for tea and cakes, and the conversation lasted well into the evening, Merry neither growing weary nor uninterested in the topics that so absorbed the adults.

By the time Caro departed, she was both exhausted and exasperated. A hug from Leo, a warm bed, and a good book was what she needed to comfort her, but in all of this, she was to be disappointed.

"Who the devil are *you*?"

An overly well-bred voice spoke in the shadows of the gallery where Eamon was making a sketch of a statuette that might be worth something and might not.

He pulled his attention from the bronze Diana, who was modestly draped—an indication it was probably a modern copy—to find a willowy man in a well-tailored suit and thick golden hair staring at him with icy blue eyes.

The man's frock coat collar was so high that the points indented his soft cheeks, which were adorned with well-trimmed sideburns. He was in his thirties if Eamon was any judge and hadn't done anything harder in his life than ride a horse. Slowly.

Eamon noticed that Leo, who'd been helping him sort books in his mother's absence, had vanished.

"Mr. Eamon Stone, at your service." Eamon supposed he should give the man a deferential bow, but for some reason, his back would not bend. "As you have sprung from nowhere, unannounced, in Her Grace's house, I should ask—who the devil are *you*?"

The blue eyes bulged. "How *dare* you, sir. Are you not beaten enough for your impertinence?"

"No one so far has managed it." Eamon let a dangerous note slip into his answer. "I did not hear Singleton announce you. The lady of the house is out, so I suppose it has fallen upon me to turn away intruders. I'll conclude that Singleton is taking a well-deserved nap, and you somehow managed to sidle in. Your name, sir, before I push you back down the stairs."

The man drew himself up, the collar points scraping his chin. "You are as ignorant as you are foul. I am Rudyard Berridge, heir to the dukedom of Aylesmore. I do not *sidle* anywhere."

"And yet, you walk into a house that is not yours, uninvited." Eamon closed his sketchbook with a loud snap and set it on the table next to the Diana.

Rudyard gazed disdainfully about the dusty gallery and its high windows that let in a modicum of the evening's light. "Uncle let me run tame in this house from the time I was a lad. That was natural, since he had no children of his own. I was his heir."

Then pretty Caro had come along to bear His Grace a healthy son and change all that. This man was still an heir and would become duke if something happened to Leo. No wonder Leo had made himself scarce.

"I assume you've arrived to visit Leo's grandmother," Eamon suggested. "I will call Singleton to take you to her."

Alarm crossed Rudyard's face at the mention of the formidable dowager, whom Eamon had yet to meet. She kept herself sequestered on a floor that Eamon so far had not been allowed onto.

"*Our* grandmother, I am certain, is resting," Rudyard said, a trifle nervously. "I am here to see the mother of my cousin Leo. Though I do not need to explain myself to a servant."

This man could call Eamon a servant or any number of unpleasant names, and he'd take them in his stride. But Rudyard's sneer of *the mother of my cousin* awoke Eamon's fury.

"You mean, Her Grace," Eamon said coldly.

Rudyard snorted. "That title applied to my grandmother and my uncle's first wife, not an upstart chit from the country, little better than a lightskirt."

A dark fog coated Eamon's vision, obscuring everything but Rudyard's symmetrical face and colorless eyes. A gentleman should call out another who'd tarnished a lady's name, avenge the insult in a civilized manner.

Rot that. Eamon was simply going to knock Rudyard to the floor.

Rudyard held out his hand, a coin glinting between his fingers. "Be a good fellow and tell her I'm here."

The idiot had no idea how close he came to death in that moment. Eamon would sweep the man's legs out from under him, crash him to the floorboards, and then break his spine. He made the first step toward Rudyard when a light voice startled them both.

"Rudyard?" Caro stepped off the flight of stairs to the gallery, her eyes flashing anger, a lock of hair tumbling to her shoulder. "You are supposed to write before you call."

"I refuse to adhere to such nonsense," Rudyard scoffed. "I am here to see you, *Aunty*." He spat the word.

Eamon took another step. "I'll show him to the pavement, if you'd like, Your Grace."

For a moment, Eamon thought Caro would happily accept. Then she firmed her lips and shook her head.

"I will speak to him. Briefly." She turned to descend the staircase once more, fingers light on the banister, but Eamon saw the lock of hair tremble. "Downstairs, please. In the blue reception room."

CHAPTER 8

$\mathcal{E}$amon followed Rudyard closely down the stairs as the man scurried behind Caro.

He knew it was none of his business why Caro's husband's nephew had come to call on her. Eamon was, as Rudyard had pointed out, the hired help, not a member of the family or even a trusted friend.

But there was no way Eamon would allow Rudyard Berridge into a room alone with Caro.

He knew a devious bastard when he saw one, and Rudyard was a thorough louse. An especially dangerous one, because he thought himself clever. Like hell Eamon would decorously withdraw and let Rudyard have his tête-à-tête.

Caro glanced at Eamon in surprise as he entered the blue reception room in Rudyard's wake, but she said nothing.

The room was as small and cold as Eamon remembered, with only enough seating for two. Eamon remained standing near the door as Rudyard waited for Caro to sit before taking the blue damask chair next to hers.

Rudyard noticed Eamon lingering and waved his hand. "Be off with you. This is a private affair."

Caro's agitation signaled that the last thing she wanted was to be alone in Rudyard's presence. She wasn't exactly afraid of the man, but she was extremely wary.

Eamon folded his arms and leaned against the doorframe. "I'd be a churl to leave a lady unguarded. Speak your piece. If she says the word, I will see you out."

Rudyard began to rise, but at Eamon's hard stare, he sat back down with a thump. "I will ask again, who *are* you?"

Before Eamon could answer, Caro broke in. "He is Leo's new art curator."

Eamon warmed at his promotion but made no sign of surprise as he watched Rudyard digest the information.

"Oh." Rudyard looked Eamon up and down. "Well, best you get on with it, man."

Eamon settled in comfortably against the walnut doorframe. "It will keep."

"Tell me why you've come," Caro instructed Rudyard. She'd perched on the edge of the chair, her back ramrod straight.

Rudyard regarded Caro in a way Eamon did not like. "I'll not pretend I'm here to inquire about your well-being, or any of that inanity. We both know where we stand with each other. I have come to talk to you about my cousin, Leo."

"What about Leo?" Caro asked, her uneasiness rising. Eamon kept his stance casual but readied himself to haul Rudyard out of there the moment it was necessary.

"This cave of a house is no place for him," Rudyard said. "He shouldn't be in London at all. Leo ought to be in the sunshine, running and playing and riding, as a boy longs to."

"This is Leo's home," Caro informed him coldly. "In June, we will return to Kent, to Mayfield Hall, where there is plenty of room for him to play outdoors."

"And yet, that house is as ramshackle as this one. So many hazards for a boy of fragile health."

Caro stiffened. "Leo's health is far from fragile—"

Rudyard held up a hand. "You misunderstand me. I mean that it's dangerous for so young a lad to dash about a farm that barely functions. I, on the other hand, have a well-run country house with plenty of staff. It would be to Leo's advantage to move there, where he will be comfortably looked after."

Eamon had spent a lifetime learning to read people, sifting out the needs and desires they told no one, perhaps not even themselves. Studying at his father's knee, Eamon had become skilled at understanding how people thought.

It would be obvious to anyone, though, that Rudyard was lying like fury. The man's fingers twitched on the arms of the chair, he shuffled his feet, and his gaze bored into Caro's almost frantically. Any honest man would be struggling not to look his fill of Caro's lovely breasts and the cameo locket that rested between them.

"It is a kind offer, but Leo is happy here, with me," Caro said stonily.

Rudyard lost his false geniality. "You are not one of us, *Aunty*. How can you know what it is to be a Berridge? From one of the highest families in the land? If Leo is to thrive, he must be removed from your care. At once."

Caro was on her feet. Eamon came away from the wall, no longer bothering with nonchalance.

"My husband named *me* as guardian of my son," Caro declared, the words ringing in the small chamber. "Leo remains here, where he belongs."

"Guardian?" Rudyard rose with disdain. "A woman, who is not even of noble birth? You did your duty pushing Leo out, but after that, you need have no connection to him, ev— gah—."

His words choked off as Eamon wrapped his arm around Rudyard's throat from behind and jerked him backward, pressing on his windpipe.

"I believe you should apologize to the lady," Eamon said quietly into his ear.

Rudyard made a few gasping noises, his feet scrabbling. He didn't have the air to speak, let alone apologize, but Eamon was beyond caring.

Caro stood over Rudyard like a goddess of vengeance. "Never return to this house," she commanded. "You are no longer welcome here."

Rudyard's face went puce, and not only because Eamon held him fast. He sputtered a few insensible words, clawing at Eamon's arm, to no avail.

Eamon dragged Rudyard out of the small room into the large front hall. He half-pushed, half-hauled the unwelcome guest into the foyer, where Singleton, who'd appeared from nowhere, calmly opened the front door.

Rudyard struggled, but his soft living had made him no match for Eamon. Singleton held the door open, his stance haughty.

The doorstep was a few feet from the street, where passers-by trudged and carts rumbled. Eamon lifted Rudyard high on his toes, shoved his well-shod feet out from under him, and pushed him from the house.

Rudyard flailed wildly, managing to catch himself by flinging one arm around a stone pillar that held up the portico.

Plenty of people witnessed his undignified exit—servants on errands for their Mayfair lords and ladies, fops in phaetons on their way from Hyde Park, and matrons in landaus who gaped as Rudyard struggled to gain his feet.

Eamon made a show of dusting off his hands. Singleton, as cool as ever, waited until Eamon had retreated into the house before he closed the door, utterly ignoring Rudyard's shouted invective.

Eamon laughed for the joy of it. He'd have slapped Singleton on the back if Singleton would bear the indignity, but Eamon did offer his hand to shake. Singleton clasped it politely without a word, then turned and glided away as though nothing very dramatic had happened.

Caro emerged from the reception room, her anguish crying out to Eamon.

"He will do it," she said in a rush. "Rudyard has many friends and connections, and he is right that I am powerless."

Eamon caught her hands, finding them too cold. "You are the Duchess of Aylesmore. An important woman."

Caro shook her head, ringlets trembling. "I am only the mother of the duke. I ceased to be important in the eyes of the world when his father passed on. And by the quaint laws of England, a mother is not related to her own child. Rudyard *is* related to him. He can take Leo away from me." Her words ended in a half sob.

Eamon tightened his grip. "Caro, trust me—I will never let that happen."

Caro's eyes flicked to him in shock, and Eamon realized he'd addressed her by her given name.

"I beg your pardon," he said, releasing her. "Duchess."

Caro continued to stare at him, her lips parted. Before Eamon could offer another word of apology, she launched herself at him.

Caro's arms went around his shoulders, her warm body crushed against his, and she kissed him frantically on the mouth.

CHAPTER 9

The hot jolt of Caro's kiss wiped away the dark hall, Eamon's anger at the boorish Rudyard, and any worry that Singleton or young Leo might reappear.

Eamon only knew Caro's supple body under his hands, and the thin broadcloth of her gown that allowed him to feel her lithe curves.

More of Caro's hair slid from its pins to brush Eamon's fingers with silk. He wanted to bury his face in her thick tresses, pull it free lock by lock, until it swathed her bare body.

Eamon tugged her closer in the shaking kiss, hand on her back, her skirt not much of a barrier between his thighs and hers.

He felt Caro gasp, her sharp intake of breath on his lips.

In the next instant, she jerked from him, scrambling back until she crashed into the newel post at the base of the stairs. She turned and clutched it as though it kept her from falling, and stared at him through wisps of hair.

"I am so sorry," she babbled. "Mr. Stone, I do beg your pardon. I have no idea what came over me." Her face was scarlet, her eyes moist. "Please say you will accept my apologies, before I faint from shame."

Eamon regarded her with astonishment. What had *she* to be ashamed of?

"My dear Duchess, you have no need to apologize to *me*." Eamon's heart banged thickly, making it difficult to breathe. "I used your name without permission, and I certainly did not push you away." He moved to her, but slowly, as though she were a bird he did not wish to startle. "As kisses are, that was one of the finest of my experience."

Caro's agitation eased slightly, but her blush remained. "I should never have contemplated doing such a thing. I have employed you—you are trusting me ..."

Eamon reached her, relieved she did not flee. "You are a woman, Caro Aylesmore, duchess or no, and I am a man. All of our families, names, titles, and circumstances of birth will not change that. I've wanted to kiss you since I first saw you struggling with that window, and I thank you for making my dream a reality."

"You mistook me for a maid." Indignation flashed in her eyes, erasing some of her embarrassment.

"I did, I will admit." Eamon gently brushed a lock of hair from her cheek. "A beautiful maid who deserved better than drudging in someone else's mansion. I was pleased to find you *owned* the mansion, but not that you were still drudging in it."

"I do not own it," Caro said faintly. "It is leased to the Dukes of Aylesmore, and I am allowed to live here only on Leo's sufferance."

"I doubt Leo will turn out his beloved mama." Eamon dared trace her cheek. "He loves you."

"And I love him." Caro's worry came flooding back. "You know that Rudyard will do his best to take Leo from me."

"As I told you, I will not let him."

Caro gazed at him, her mortification abating. "How can you

possibly prevent it? To Rudyard, you are nobody, as am I. *He* is cousin to the Duke of Aylesmore, and until Leo marries and has a son, Rudyard is unfortunately the heir."

"Exactly. Which is why we cannot entrust Leo's care to him."

"I am well aware of this. What is to prevent Rudyard from letting Leo fall victim to an accident? A ride gone wrong? A fall down the stairs? Leo is resilient, but Rudyard is insidious."

"He'll not have him, Caro," Eamon promised in a hard voice.

This time, he didn't apologize for using her name, but she was too distressed to notice.

"They *can* take my son away, though I will fight it until my dying breath. This has nothing to do with you, Mr. Stone, or the artwork. I'd give the bloody lot of these paintings to Rudyard, if he would only leave Leo alone."

She spoke with vehemence, her anger, fear, and burgeoning desire making her beautiful. Eamon wanted to be her champion, to throw himself at her feet and declare he'd fight every dragon who ever put a claw wrong in her presence.

His friends would laugh and call him a fool, but the need to defend her was strong.

"You might be very surprised what I can do," Eamon made himself say calmly. "I will think on it." He had resources of many and various sorts, both within the law and outside it, and he'd draw on every single one of them to save Leo from the foul Rudyard.

"You are kind," Caro said without much conviction. "You have been good to me and to Leo in the short time we have known you. But I must face this myself. And go to Leo. Rudyard's visits always frighten him—for good reason."

Eamon glanced up the staircase. "Leo vanished when Rudyard appeared, and I was too preoccupied to see where he went. Shall we begin a search?"

Caro's rigid mouth softened into the one that had sponta-neously kissed him. "He will be with his grandmother. Rudyard is not allowed into the dowager's rooms without direct invitation. Come with me? Leo finds your presence steadying."

Eamon wasn't certain why this should be, but he was enormously flattered by Leo's trust. "Of course. Shall we?"

He offered his arm. Caro's smile deepened as she laid her hand on it, her touch no longer feverish.

Eamon led her up the long staircase, which itself was a masterwork of art, polished wood a century old rising around three sides of the echoing foyer. Eamon had noted on his first day the skillfully carved newel posts and the sleek craft of each spindle. The banister was wide enough for a man's large hand, and nearly overwhelmed Caro's slimmer one.

They passed the gallery and the false Diana Eamon had been studying to continue upward. Eamon had never been past the second floor, where he'd first met Caro, but now she guided him two flights higher, into the family's sanctuary.

At the end of their long climb—Eamon reflected that any intruder to this house would need a strong pair of legs and a stout constitution—Caro led him along an echoing corridor to double doors that blocked its end. She opened these doors and ushered him inside.

Eamon entered a chamber that might have been lifted straight from Versailles. The walls were covered by moiré fabric in a soft shade of blue, framed with gilded panels. Columns with Corinthian capitals fit into each corner, and an arched marble fireplace lined with still more gilded wood breathed warmth into the room.

The furniture was from the time of Louis XV, the middle of the past century. If this was all the dowager's father had managed to save when he'd fled France at the end of Louis XVI's reign, what he'd left behind must have been magnificent.

Leo was indeed there, as Caro had predicted, standing on a wooden bench to peer out the window. An older woman sat straight-backed in a chair near the fire, an embroidery hoop in one hand, needle with floss in the other. She had a sharp face that spoke of a once haughty beauty, and her blue eyes held animation.

Leo swung around when he heard Eamon and Caro arrive. Leo grinned at Eamon, no fear on his face.

"I saw you throw Cousin Rudyard out," the lad announced. "He almost fell on his—" He hesitated and shot a look at his grandmother. *"Derrière."*

The dowager set down her embroidery, lifted a walking stick that leaned against her chair, and thumped the stick once on the floor. "Better than he deserved," she said in an icy tone. "Is this Sir Benedict's son, Caro? Bring him to me at once."

———

CARO HAD LEARNED TWO THINGS QUICKLY WHEN HER HUSBAND had first brought her home—one, that the dowager was always to be obeyed, and two, that she had reasons, sometimes kind ones, behind her imperious demands.

Caro sensed Eamon's trepidation, which was normal for anyone meeting the formidable Dowager Duchess of Aylesmore for the first time.

She led him to the dowager's chair, and Eamon executed a courtly bow. "I am humbled, Your Grace."

The stick thumped again. "None of that. I met your father, Mr. Stone, several times. A scoundrel if I ever saw one. But a very charming one."

Eamon rose from his bow, abashed. "He was, indeed, Your Grace. It was often a trial, having a father like Sir Benedict."

"I imagine it was. He enjoyed spa towns, mainly Bath, which was where I encountered him. You must have been a small boy at the time. I don't remember *you.*"

Eamon nodded. "Alas, I was often tucked away in a corner while he … entertained himself."

His light answer couldn't quite mask his flash of pain. Caro, who'd loved her doting parents dearly, wondered how Eamon had coped with being shoved aside while his father had enjoyed luxury and feminine company.

"I see." The dowager's tone softened a fraction. "And now we have hired you to look at our artworks. Are you certain you know what you are doing?"

"*Maman,*" Caro said quickly. If Eamon took offense, he might decide to depart, never to return.

"I have studied art all my life," Eamon assured the dowager. "Have learned the techniques and history of the great masters. I'd not be trusted by Cheswell's, who have a fine reputation, if I did not know my Canaletto from my Cosway."

The dowager did not appear to be impressed. "Cheswell is a greedy man. Some dealers love art for its own sake, but *his* first love is guineas. What sort of man are you?"

She pinned him with the gaze of her Celtic ancestors, who'd so terrified the mighty Roman armies.

"I do love art," Eamon said, his tone respectful. "No matter what we must face in this life, a beautiful painting or piece of sculpture from the past can be soothing. It has endured centuries of war, hardship, and sorrow, yet still remains, like a mountain that watches over a city or the sea's unchanging depths."

"Very poetic," the dowager said. "How long have you rehearsed that speech?"

Eamon flashed her a grin. "Since I was a boy, Your Grace. I was left to my own devices much of the time. I learned to draw and paint to pass the hours, and I became interested in historic art. I'm not talented enough to be a great artist myself, but I can restore damaged paintings, find artworks for those who want to purchase them, and assess and catalog collections."

"I suppose you encountered plenty of paintings in the houses your father dragged you to." The dowager's statement was less abrupt, as though he'd provoked her sympathy.

"I did indeed. Meandering through the galleries at Chatsworth and Wilton House provided me an excellent education."

Eamon spoke without regret, but Caro pictured a lonely boy wandering dark and empty corridors, set aside and forgotten. Had he entertained himself by gazing at the paintings until someone finally remembered to fetch him?

"I will not inquire about your actual schooling," the dowager continued. "Public schools and universities churn out vapid young men fit for nothing. My husband was one of those, but fortunately he had enough shrewdness to forget everything they tried to beat into him. My son, on the other hand, became a dreamy recluse."

Caro's rose to his defense. "Leopold was very learned, *Maman*."

"I daresay he was. Never did him much good that I could discern. I know you were fond of him, Caro, but it is the truth." The dowager focused on Eamon once more. "You are going to find all the paintings worth something and sell them for us, are you not?"

Eamon made her another bow, this one subdued. "I will do my best, Your Grace."

"See that you do. Now, about you tossing Rudyard on his, as Leo terms it, *derrière*. That will cause a scandal, I wager. How many people witnessed it?"

"A good number, I am afraid," Eamon confessed.

Caro had kept herself well away from the open front door during the incident, but at this time of day, there would have been plenty of passers-by, as this side of Grosvenor Square was a thoroughfare to Hyde Park to the west, New Bond Street to the east, and Oxford Street to the north.

"Rudyard will complain," the dowager said. "What do you

intend to do about it? Caro must not be touched by scandal. The *ton* can be brutal, and she does not have the high birth to withstand it."

Caro did not wince at the dowager's blunt words, because they were only the truth.

Eamon glanced at Caro, and she read compassion in his eyes. She did not like how much that warmed her.

"Her Grace could always sack me," Eamon suggested. "Be outraged at me for the manner with which I behaved toward her cousin."

"Ha," the dowager snorted. "Not what I'd recommend."

"I have no intention of dismissing you, Mr. Stone," Caro said stoutly. "That is exactly what Rudyard would want."

"What Rudyard wants is the dukedom," the dowager said. "The title, the power, the seat in the House of Lords, and the envy of his friends. He knows there's no money in the estates, but he cares nothing for that. His father, Rudolph, rest his soul, was much cannier about the blunt, as the English say, so it is not a fortune Rudyard is after. The foolish boy craves the glory, without understanding the work that being an aristocrat entails."

Leo listened to all this with rapt attention. The dowager never curbed her speech or avoided serious subjects in his presence. Leo was a duke now, the dowager contended. Better he learned the harshness of the world early and be prepared for it.

"Rudyard does not see behind the trappings of power," Eamon said, nodding. "It is a common failing among the Upper Ten Thousand, if you'll pardon me, madame. My father was able to worm his way among them by making those he targeted fix on those trappings."

"I am not surprised," the dowager said. "Sir Benedict flattered them with great skill, from what I recall. You do not offend me, young man. I have the advantage of being somewhat of an outsider. Though French aristocrats were almost as foolish, which is why they fell. Napoleon and the Republic may be gone now, but all those aristocrats will never lift themselves again." Her expression took on a faraway light before she waved it away. "But never mind. We must decide how to protect Leo and Caro."

"Leo *is* the Duke of Aylesmore, and Ca—the duchess—is his mother," Eamon said. "That should count for much."

"You would believe so," the dowager said wisely. "But in our world, ladies have no real power at all. Oh, we wield it—there are those who would not dare to oppose us—but we do it with the force of our personalities. Caro has no force. She is too kind."

Caro flushed. *"Maman."*

"Do not argue, my dear. You *are* kind. It is refreshing, and why I did not kick up a fuss when Leopold chose to marry you. I understood his reasoning perfectly, and I have become quite fond of you. But you do not have the strength to oppose wealthy men in their counting houses scheming to take the world away from you."

"I agree," Eamon said, with a glance at Caro that made her flush deepen.

The dowager fixed her hard gaze on Eamon. *"You,* on the other hand, are the son of a swindler. I am certain you learned a few tactics from your father about how to wrap the *haut ton* and all their men of business around your fingers. You *will* find a means to keep Rudyard from having his way, and you will keep Caro from scandal. You cannot afford exposure either, can you? Or else Cheswell's will cease to employ you, and so will the aristocrats who hire you to find art for them."

Eamon withstood this onslaught without flinching. Caro knew her mother-in-law was not threatening to betray Eamon's origins but simply stating harsh truths. If Rudyard discovered who Eamon's father had been, he'd use that fact to convince every solicitor in the land that Caro lacked judgment and force her to hand over her son to Rudyard.

"You have my word that I will assist you to the greatest extent," Eamon said to the dowager. He turned to Leo, who'd stayed by the window, a sturdy lad in trousers and frock coat that he'd gotten plenty dusty. "In fact, I will pledge myself to you, Leo—Your Grace." Eamon bowed to him and remained bent from the waist. "I promise to be your protector, to make certain you will never be taken from your family, especially not to live with your odious cousin Rudyard. Will you have me, my liege?"

The duchess frowned at Eamon's sudden solemnity and overblown language. Caro said nothing, letting Leo respond on his own.

Leo studied Eamon's bowed head in a mixture of perplexity, awe, and delight. Then he walked to Eamon and rested a small hand on his shoulder.

"Rise, Sir Eamon," Leo said in as serious a tone as Eamon had used. "I accept your pledge and will take you for my knight."

Eamon came out of his bow but went down on one knee. "Thank you, my liege. I will ever be in your debt."

The dowager's brows furrowed further, as though she did not know what to make of this play, but Caro turned quickly away, so no one would see her eyes fill with sudden tears.

———

No letter from Mr. Clive waited for Eamon when he returned to Cheswell's. Likewise, none had been delivered to his lodgings in Oxford Street when he reached it that night.

Eamon had sent Clive several missives requesting a meeting to discuss the duke's artworks, but he'd received no word back. He'd gone over Clive's ledgers that Caro had given him, finding them masterworks of obfuscation. The man used codes of his own that Eamon had yet to decipher.

"Nothing from Mr. Clive, but you do have a few other letters," the landlady told Eamon at his inquiry.

Mrs. Temple was a willowy personage who wore billowing caps but dresses of so straight a line she resembled nothing less than a snowy egret with a head plume. She handed him three folded and sealed letters as they stood in the cold downstairs hall.

"One from your Scottish friend, Mr. McCormick, and one from his lordship. Oh, and this one is intriguing." Mrs. Temple turned it over in her hand. "It has been franked by the Prince of Osagard. My, my. Someone knows someone in high places. The Prince and Princess of Osagard have become very fashionable, you know, since they gave all that money to defeat Napoleon. The prince wanted to form his own regiment and fight, but of course, he couldn't, being foreign." She added this last in a confiding tone.

Plenty of foreign princes had thrown together to fight Bonaparte, but Eamon knew what Mrs. Temple meant. Though the Prince of Osagard was in exile in London, he could hardly raise a regiment that might be turned against the British Crown once his men had bested Napoleon. Eamon doubted the prince would want to do such a thing, but the theory that he *could* was what counted.

Eamon reached for the letters. "Interesting. Thank you, Mrs. Temple."

Mrs. Temple, who was clearly curious, released the papers with reluctance. "I've got a bite set on the board in the dining room. Mind you take some food. You work hard all day and then pour over them books all night. You'll waste away, lad."

Mrs. Temple's "bite" usually consisted of several meat pies, large hunks of bread, piles of boiled potatoes, and three different kinds of tarts. She served these on a long table in her dining room, which was often filled with gentleman boarders as gossipy as she.

"Thank you, Mrs. Temple." Eamon had purchased and eaten a hand pie from a cart on his way home, not eager to chat with those who'd want to pry information from him about the Duchess of Aylesmore and her family. "I'll retire, but if I grow hungry, I'll come down."

Mrs. Temple shook her head. "Waste away, I say. You need a nice lass to look after you."

At her words, the intense memory rose of Caro's kiss—her lips beneath his, her trembling shock when they pulled apart, the taste of her filling Eamon better than any feast.

Eamon tamped down the vision with difficulty. "Alas, I am a man scratching for his living. No woman would be foolish enough to take me on."

Mrs. Temple waved this away. "You're charming enough to convince any lady to be your helpmeet. That's the best sort of marriage, you know—true partners in life who can sort out anything thrown your way. Mr. Temple and I were such a pair." She paused, her eyes growing misty. "Rest his sweet soul. Now, off you go to read your letters. One from a friend of the Prince of Osagard, just fancy. I wager that between whoever that friend is and Lord Dominic, you can find a lady who has a few coins to rub together."

Eamon raised his brows. "I thought I was to marry a true and equal friend. Partners against the world."

"Yes, but a bit of blunt doesn't hurt, my boy. You read the letter franked by the prince first. It is likely the most important of all."

Eamon did not recognize the handwriting on the direction, and he had to admit he was as curious as Mrs. Temple. He did not intend to open it and read it in front of her, however, as she obviously wished.

Eamon thanked her again, bade her goodnight, and started

up the stairs. Mrs. Temple didn't hide her disappointment, though she returned his farewell cordially enough.

Mrs. Temple remained in the hall, watching Eamon climb the wooden staircase all the way to the third floor. He waved at her when he reached his landing, and only then did she finally turn away.

Eamon entered his rooms, which were well fitted for a man of modest means. He had a sitting room and a bedchamber, both paneled in soft golden wood, their furniture comfortable if aging. He had a desk large enough for his work in the front room and a warm bed in the rear one.

Mrs. Temple was generous with fuel and candles—as long as one paid one's rent in a timely fashion—so the rooms were warm and light.

Others at Cheswell's congratulated Eamon for stumbling onto such pleasant lodgings, but Eamon hadn't found this house by luck. He'd learned from his father how to discover the most agreeable places to live for the least possible expenditure.

Eamon opened the franked letter first, his inquisitiveness as healthy as Mrs. Temple's.

The letter wasn't from a friend of the Prince of Osagard, as Mrs. Temple had speculated, but from the Prince himself.

Mr. Stone,

I am extending an invitation for you to attend my wife's supper ball at our home in Portman Square, Wednesday the twenty-second of May, at ten o'clock in the evening. We will expect you punctually.

Yours in friendship,

Rupert Vollen HRH

Osagard

*E*amon read the invitation several times over, but the information remained the same.

The Prince of Osagard, for some reason, wished Eamon to attend a gathering in his home tomorrow night.

Eamon sank to the chair at his desk, mystified.

Did the prince want to consult Eamon about art? Had he heard that Eamon was looking through Aylesmore's collection and decided that Eamon would do? But, in that case, why not write to Cheswell's and request his services?

A more sinister thought occurred to him. This might be a ploy of annoying Cousin Rudyard in his adamance to gain control over Leo. Perhaps he'd decided to entice Eamon to a society ball and corner him there. To do what? Threaten him with violence, or more likely, legal action?

Well, there was only one way to find out.

Eamon found a clean scrap of paper, dipped his pen into ink, and wrote out his acceptance to the supper ball.

When Eamon entered Cheswell's auction rooms in Regent Street the next morning, Cheswell himself intercepted him.

"You must hie to Bedford Square, my boy," the man said in his breathy voice. "Immediately. A gentleman at number 7 has a Guido Reni he wishes to sell. He's waffling between using Cheswell's or Christie's, and we must win him over. The commission on a rare Reni is nothing to sneeze at."

If the request had come a few weeks ago, Eamon would have rushed to Bedford Square without question. Today, he couldn't be less interested. The anticipation of seeing Caro every morning made him wake with excitement in his heart and stride through London with lightness in his step.

He wanted to tell Caro about his invitation from the Prince of Osagard and speculate with her about what it might mean. He'd stand close to her while he did so and perhaps entice another kiss from her while Singleton was occupied elsewhere.

"The duchess will be expecting me," Eamon said, striving keep his voice calm.

"I will send word to the duchess." Cheswell bodily turned Eamon around. "This gent in Bedford Square is a stubborn one, and you are the only man who can convince him. Ingratiate yourself and get us that Reni. Make haste, dear boy, make haste." He all but shoved Eamon out the door.

Eamon resumed his hat with stiff fingers as he stepped into the street. He could resist Cheswell's instructions, but Cheswell would want to know why. He'd argue, rightly so, that Eamon had found nothing in Caro's house that was of interest so far, and that the Reni was an opportunity not to be missed.

He could also resign his post instead of obeying but for two things—Eamon needed the salary Cheswell paid him, and he'd not have an excuse to hurry to Caro's home every day if he gave his notice.

He found himself turning his steps to Bedford Square, grumbling under his breath.

Eamon spent the entire day in a cramped and dusty townhouse filled with intriguing artworks owned by a white-haired gentleman with a sour disposition. In the course of their multiple conversations, the gentleman changed his mind a dozen times about sending his Reni painting to Cheswell's. He might not sell it at all, he declared more than once.

Eamon brought forth all his powers of persuasion even as he inwardly cursed the man. He would much rather be entertaining Leo, keeping an eye out for treacherous Cousin Rudyard, and scheming to be in a situation where he could kiss Caro again.

She was worth kissing. And touching …

Simply being near her made Eamon feel more alive than he had in years.

By the time Eamon departed Bedford Square, with the Reni and several other paintings packed in a cart that he accompanied to Cheswell's, it was far too late to call at Grosvenor Square. The streets were already dark, and by the time he reached the gallery, Cheswell was ready to shut up shop.

Cheswell was delighted that Eamon had acquired not only the Reni but the few smaller paintings that would bring in a fine commission. Cheswell locked away the paintings, shook Eamon's hand, and sent him home.

Mrs. Temple opened the door of the boarding house before Eamon reached the front step. "Good heavens, Mr. Stone, you scarcely have time to put on your finest clothes. You will be late, and what will His Highness think of you?"

Mrs. Temple had wheedled the contents of the prince's invitation out of Eamon when he'd paused for breakfast this morning. She'd been greatly delighted and honored that a guest in her house had been asked to a prince's supper ball.

"It is fashionable to be late, Mrs. Temple," Eamon reassured her. In truth, he was agitated about the meeting with the prince and feeling the need to hurry.

"For the nobility, yes." Mrs. Temple shooed him up the stairs. "But for the likes of you and I, we must attend when we are called."

How damnably true that was.

Eamon ran upstairs with a pace that won Mrs. Temple's approval and stuffed himself into the fine suit he'd robbed his savings to purchase upon his return to London last year. The tailor, who was Wolfe's, had forgiven much of the price when Eamon pointed out that making a hard-up gent look like a rich one might persuade other such gentleman to use his services.

Now Eamon muttered about stiff collars and the lack of assistance to tie his cravat. He refused to imagine Caro doing it, her slim fingers brushing his chin as she fixed the knot, her smile one of encouraging fondness.

"Damn and blast," Eamon whispered as he gave the cravat a final tug into place.

Rapidly enough to satisfy Mrs. Temple, he was out the front door and into a hackney, which he hoped would keep mud from his clothes the short distance to Portman Square.

Eamon descended a little way from the house and walked through the crush of carriages unloading the creme de la creme of London society at the prince's front door. His invitation was scrutinized by a cool footman in a powdered wig who admitted Eamon without question.

A good landscape by Jan van Goyen hung in the foyer, and a Rubens held pride of place on the first staircase landing. The Rubens was nothing too dramatic and didn't display much flesh, a tasteful painting one could display for guests.

Another impassive footman took Eamon's greatcoat and directed him to the long row of connected ground-floor rooms, whose inner doors had been opened to create a ballroom and supper room beyond.

This house was not as large as Caro's abode in Grosvenor Square, but its light and airy style made it seem grand. The foyer and public rooms were filled with the most modern furnishings Eamon had ever seen gathered in one place, the enameled and gilded tables enhanced with objets d'art by Canova and Vulliamy.

Prince Rupert of Osagard and Princess Maude, his wife, greeted guests at the head of a long line that snaked through the ballroom. No one was being announced, and groups stood chatting informally—everyone seemed to know one another. Eamon recognized gentlemen and ladies he'd met in passing either through Cheswell's, the war veteran's club, or via introduction from Wolfe. Some greeted Eamon with obvious surprise at his inclusion tonight, but they all remained polite.

Eamon was very well acquainted with the two men who stood uneasily near a pillar that held a priceless Ming vase. He dodged through the line and headed for them.

"Is this your doing?" Eamon asked Wolfe when he reached his friends.

Wolfe was resplendent in a black suit that emphasized his muscular handsomeness—not that the man would realize this. He had absolutely no vanity about his appearance.

He knit his brows at Eamon's question. "I supposed it must be yours. You are good at insinuating yourself into such situations."

McCormick, his shaggy red hair tamed into an old-fashioned queue, listened with interest. "You mean neither of you is responsible for our invitation? My curiosity rises."

"I assumed I'd been invited to look at artwork," Eamon said. "Or you might have had me come for some unfathomable reason, Wolfe."

"We thought it was you." McCormick pointed a thick gloved finger at him, his tall, broad body ill at ease in his tailored suit. "We couldn't resist attending to find out what you meant by it."

Eamon studied the filling ballroom. "Well, *someone* knew how to entice us out of our holes."

"Ah." Wolfe stilled, his gaze becoming fixed. "I believe I have discovered who."

Eamon turned to see what had caught Wolfe's attention, and froze.

Caro stood in a corner of the large room, framed by a garland of spring flowers draped over an arch. She was speaking animatedly to the two young women beside her, her face alight, eyes sparkling.

Her gown tonight was the color of rich cocoa, trimmed with lighter braids and ribbons. Eamon kept himself cognizant of the latest fashions, and that gown could have been made yesterday. Not for Caro—his trained eye observed where it had been modified here and there, and it was slightly too short, though only a keen eye would catch this.

He suspected the gown had been created to fit the slim, blond woman at Caro's side and altered for Caro's taller and more curved form. Skillfully altered. Eamon saw the work of a talented dressmaker in it.

A lady's maid must have dressed Caro's hair, which was coiled into a tight knot. As Caro's hair wasn't meant to be contained, the coiffure already drooped and locks dangled, intensified by the vigorous way Caro nodded when speaking to her friends.

So intent was Eamon with taking in her whole being that he almost missed the glittering diamonds that encircled her throat. The modest necklace lay subtly on her covered bosom, sparkling softly against the dark gown.

Even at this distance, Eamon suspected that either the diamonds weren't real, or she'd borrowed them from the same friend who'd lent her the dress and lady's maid. A family trying to sell off its paintings to clear debts had probably run through its jewels long ago.

The third woman in the trio had hair darker than Caro's, and her participation in the conversation was more subdued.

The cut of her dark violet gown was simpler than those of the other two, but no less elegant. The frock hung on her easily, as though she could go for a brisk walk if she chose.

Her muted colors indicated that she, like Caro, was a widow. Their fair-haired friend, on the other hand, dressed in bright pink, was obviously an unmarried miss.

The pink-clad lady rapped Caro on the arm with her fan and indicated Eamon and his companions, who were all staring intently at the three women. Caro started, her eyes widening.

Did Caro's surprise turn into delight, she happy to see Eamon? Not at all. She mastered herself after her slight jump and bathed Eamon in a disapproving frown.

"Is that your duchess?" McCormick asked with great interest.

"Not *my* duchess," Eamon corrected him. "At least, not yet," he finished under his breath.

"They seem to be debating about whether to speak to us," McCormick said.

Eamon had no intention of waiting until the coy choreography of a society ball let him meet with Caro as if by chance. That might take an hour or more, and he didn't have the patience.

"Let us settle the question, shall we?" Eamon said. "Are you with me?"

"Not the thing to approach ladies uninvited," McCormick answered, though he did not sound alarmed at the prospect. "Even I, a rough-hewn islander, know that."

"We haven't been introduced," was Wolfe's tight-lipped contribution.

"I know the duchess, and I can make your introductions," Eamon said. "Fortune favors the bold, gentlemen."

"It favors *you*," Wolfe muttered.

McCormick nodded. "Aye, every time you say something like that, Stony, disaster follows. But lead on."

Both men fell into step behind Eamon as he began his journey across the ballroom.

Caro's countenance did not grow any more welcoming as they approached. Her polite expression became fixed, but her eyes held vast annoyance.

Caro's friends, on the other hand, turned interested gazes to Eamon and his companions. Sizing them up, Eamon understood. Caro must have told the ladies about him, possibly even including their frenzied kiss. Eamon warmed at the memory, but Caro looked full of regret.

He halted courteously in front of the three ladies, and McCormick and Wolfe moved to flank him. Preparing for battle, even in a ballroom.

"Good evening," Eamon said with a formal bow. "Please forgive my forwardness, but I wished to greet Her Grace."

"Mr. Stone." Caro's voice evoked a chill she must have learned from the dowager duchess.

Eamon pretended to be undismayed at her coolness. "Allow me to present my friends, Mr. Hayden McCormick, who originally hails from the Shetland Isles, and Lord Dominic Wolfe, who kicks about Berkshire when he is not in London. We were thrown together as lads and now continue the habit."

McCormick bowed his tall body, while Wolfe favored the three ladies with a stiff nod.

Caro returned their greetings with a brief nod of her own. She could play the haughty duchess when it pleased her, Eamon saw. He only wished she weren't pleased to do it now.

"Lady Heyford and Princess Josephine of Osagard." Caro indicated the dark-haired lady and then the princess in turn with a flick of her fan in an elegantly gloved hand.

The two ladies made brief curtsies, and the gentlemen bowed once more. How agreeable they all were.

Eamon cleared his throat, unnerved at its dryness. "And how

is His Grace?" he asked Caro. "Did Leo find anything intriguing while burrowing through the books?"

Caro became still more frosty. "My son expected you at every moment, all through the morning and the afternoon. Was most unhappy when you did not appear."

A look into Caro's eyes told Eamon she did not mean *she* had been waiting anxiously for him all day. She spoke the truth that it was Leo who'd been upset, which suddenly explained her unforgiving demeanor.

"Damn it all," Eamon said with feeling. As Caro's friends fluttered fans and his companions stared at him, he went on quickly, "Cheswell promised he'd send you word. He packed me off on another mission which took all blasted day. Please send His Grace my abject apologies."

Caro drew back slightly at the explanation, as though she wanted to soften, but she held steady. "Leo made you his knight."

"He did. I should have made certain Leo knew of my detainment today and never left it to Cheswell." Cheswell had obviously not thought sending a message to Caro important. "I do most humbly apologize, Duchess—I mean, Your Grace."

The other two ladies listened to the exchange with interest, and Eamon felt the same from his friends, even Wolfe.

"Well." Caro's wall of ice thawed slightly but not completely. "I suppose you could make it up to him."

"I will, indeed. Please tell me what I can do."

Eamon had mouthed such words before, especially in his school days when he sought to lighten punishment from his tutors. Against the pain and anger in Caro's eyes tonight, Eamon's offer was the most sincere it had ever been.

Before Caro could answer, the princess spoke up.

"You can request a dance, Mr. Stone," the golden-haired woman said. "There is a set forming even now."

CHAPTER 11

Caro bit back her dismay. Easier to trust herself around Eamon if she kept him at a distance, more difficult if they were gliding together, hand-in-hand, up and down the ballroom. She wanted to remain angry at him for Leo's disappointment, and she feared he'd charm her into forgiveness too rapidly.

"An excellent suggestion, Your Highness," Eamon stated, as though Jo was the most brilliant woman he'd ever met. "Your Grace? I have some small skill in dancing. Perhaps I can entertain you for a moment or two."

He held out a hand, strong in a fine glove.

The quartet around them had no qualms about staring, waiting to see how Caro would respond. Even the aloof Lord Dominic regarded Caro with interest.

Whatever Caro's feelings about the matter, Jo had put her on the spot. Acceptance would imply some forgiveness for Eamon, and refusing might send him away forever. How would Leo feel about that? Fleeing the ballroom was tempting but would provide even greater fodder for gossip.

Scandalmongers watched the tableau, some of whom already

believed Caro wasn't lofty enough to be friends with ladies like Jo and Louise. The matrons of the *ton* mistook Caro's shyness for coolness and labeled her a haughty chit who'd married above her station.

Rebuffing Eamon might imply to the gossips that Caro would only dance with dukes. The disapproving matrons would enjoy such a thing.

Caro drew a breath for courage and made her decision. "Of course, Mr. Stone." She laid her hand in Eamon's.

Eamon's eyes held understanding, as though he'd followed her inner debate. He closed strong fingers over hers and pulled her hand to the crook of his arm.

"I am enchanted, Duchess. I will endeavor not to tread on your toes."

Caro could think of nothing in reply. She tried not to enjoy the sensation of Eamon's hard arm under her fingers, his coat's thin cashmere letting her feel his strength. He led her out, Jo watching them go with glee.

A line of ladies and gentlemen had formed in the center of the ballroom, the first set of the evening. Eamon ushered Caro to a spot in the middle of the line, gliding into place opposite her.

The gentleman next to him glanced at them, and his eyes widened. "Captain Stone? Is it you?"

Eamon, with a smile of greeting, extended his hand. "It is, indeed, Colonel Harper. Though I am a civilian once more, rendering me plain Mister."

"I am the same." The former colonel shook the offered hand. "My dear," he said to the lady with him. "This is the man I was certain we'd tragically lost after I sent him off to find out what was happening on a foggy ridge at Waterloo. I'd given him up, and then he jogs out of the smoke with his two companions, looking very pleased with himself."

"You have told me the tale." Mrs. Harper regarded her

husband with an indulgent glance that hinted she'd heard the story many a time. "I am happy to see you well, Mr. Stone. Your friends are also in good health?"

"Good Lord, they are here." Colonel Harper stared past Caro to where Mr. McCormick and Lord Dominic stood. "Well, well. We might have a chat this evening, if time allows it." The colonel's gaze went to Caro, and he bowed, flushing. "Good heavens, my manners. Good evening, Your Grace. How delightful to see you again."

The Harpers were two of the few people who had not condemned Miss Caroline Arnott when she'd agreed to marry the Duke of Aylesmore. The amiable Harpers had long been friends of Jo's parents, and Caro had always admired their comfortable but caring marriage.

"Colonel," Caro ducked her head in response. "Mrs. Harper."

"Please give my regards to the dowager," Colonel Harper said. He raised his voice over the music that had begun. "You ought to pay a call on us, Stone. Bring your friends, and we will have a lovely time."

"I'm certain they would be happy to," Eamon said with sincerity.

"Excellent. We must fix a date—"

"Cease your chatter, husband," Mrs. Harper admonished amiably. "We are beginning."

"Yes, indeed, my dear." Colonel Harper laughed at himself as the dance commenced. "Afterward, Stone. I shall keep you to it. That is an order."

"We are finished with orders now, *Mr.* Harper," Eamon said. "But yes, let us certainly fix a date."

Around them, gentlemen were giving bows to their partners. Eamon executed a graceful one to Caro, and she shakily curtsied in return.

Colonel Harper was Caro's partner in her corner, so she

took his offered hands after she and Eamon had passed around each other and back to their place in line.

The country dance was lively, and the nature of it did not lend itself to conversation. Caro continually returned to Eamon to link arms and promenade or to catch hands to spin to the opposite point in the line.

Caro's nervousness eased as the dance went on, each couple making their way down the floor in the pattern. The music, played by one of the best orchestras in London, was vibrant, and reminded Caro how much she loved to dance.

Leopold hadn't been one for it, as he'd no longer been able to move very swiftly, and Caro had stayed quietly by his side at gatherings such as this one. It was heavenly to glide once more with the music, to spin and step, catching the tempo.

Eamon possessed more than the little skill he'd boasted of. He moved with controlled athleticism, never missing a step. He smiled charmingly at his corner partner and beamed an even brighter one on Caro.

Caro had to keep reminding herself how annoyed she was that he hadn't turned up today, upsetting Leo.

She hadn't admitted, even to herself, her own disappointment. She hadn't liked the way she'd constantly watched out of the window for a hackney to roll up and discharge Eamon, or for him to come walking around the corner to the square with his buoyant stride. Hadn't liked the sting in her heart when hackney after hackney passed without halting, and no gentleman glided out of the fog. Caro had accomplished little that day, and she was vexed at herself.

When she'd seen Eamon enter the ballroom, her heart had leapt with gladness, and she'd had to strive to remain put out with him.

His explanation relieved her more than she cared to admit. Of course, Eamon was at Mr. Cheswell's beck and call, and he logically would be sent to examine other art collections. She also believed his claim that Mr. Cheswell had promised to send word but neglected to do so. Not Eamon's fault.

Still, she couldn't appear to be too eagerly forgiving. Eamon might draw the conclusion that Caro was giddily happy to see him. Which she was. She'd feared that Eamon had already tired of his daily visits and would cease them.

Her relief made her effervescent, but it would never do to show such a thing.

Caro also had to decide whether to forgive Jo. Jo hadn't been in the least surprised when Eamon had strolled in, which meant she'd orchestrated Eamon's invitation and likely that of his friends. Caro needed to have a long and serious talk with the interfering minx.

For now, Caro let her cares fly away and danced. Her worries dissolved on the lightness of the music and the pleasure of movement. She'd been still for too long.

The room blurred, becoming a bubble of color and sound. Eamon's strength anchored her, his smile warming her through.

It had been an age since such awareness had taken hold of Caro, and for this hour on this night, she decided to enjoy it.

When Caro and Eamon reached the top of the line, they separated to promenade to the bottom. Caro glimpsed Jo and Louise still standing near the garland of hothouse flowers that Princess Maude loved, watching Caro with very pleased expressions on their faces. Eamon's gentlemen friends sipped ratafia and appeared uncomfortable, Lord Dominic much more so than Mr. McCormick.

Eamon bowed to Caro when they met again, and she curtsied. Her shakiness had vanished, and she couldn't stop her smile answering his.

Something raw flickered in Eamon's eyes, and Caro's body heated like a flame.

Eamon shielded his expression as he passed Caro again, their left hands touching as they went by. The contact was a mere brush, but the spark that jumped between them made her knees weak.

She calmed herself by taking the hands of the kind Colonel Harper, her corner partner once more. When she returned to her place, the orchestra finished the piece, and the dancers halted, breathless and flushed, applauding.

Before Caro could decide what to say to Eamon as they walked from the floor, Colonel Harper appeared at her side.

"Might I escort you to a seat, Your Grace?" he asked.

Of course—it was proper for the older gentleman to ensure that a younger and higher-ranking lady was looked after. Caro could only nod and agree.

She saw Eamon smoothly move to Mrs. Harper without missing a step and offer the same to her.

"I am pleased to see you out and about, Your Grace," Colonel Harper said as they strolled to the edge of the ballroom. "If you'll forgive me my blunt observation, you are young, with much of your life ahead of you. Do not stifle it in that mausoleum of a house. Captain Stone is a fine young man. He will take very good care of you."

Caro started, then rapidly fanned herself, pretending the dance had overheated her. "I am barely acquainted with Mr. Stone, Colonel Harper."

Colonel Harper's gaze turned knowing. "I met my Felice only weeks before we wed. You will have plenty of time to grow familiar with each other, my dear, through your life together. I am not saying you ought to rush into marriage, but if you decided to, Stone would not be a bad choice. His upbringing was a tad rough, but that is not his fault, and he's smoothed his edges splendidly."

"I have no wish to be courted," Caro said, flustered. "I have a son to look after."

Colonel Harper patted her hand. "Forgive me, my dear. I am an old man, and I want everyone to find the happiness I have had. Stone is an honorable fellow, in spite of what some believe. If you rebuff him, at least be gentle when you do. He's too much alone, the poor lad."

The poor lad was now gallantly presenting Mrs. Harper with a cup of punch and sharing a lively chat with her.

"I will remember your advice," Caro managed to say.

They'd reached a line of gilded, ivory damask chairs. "If you will sit, Your Grace, I will rush away and bring you refreshment." Colonel Harper indicated the chairs with a sweep of his glove.

"Thank you, but I will return to my friends." Caro nodded to where Jo and Louise waited. "You have been kind, Colonel Harper."

Colonel Harper squeezed Caro's hand. "If you ever need someone to talk to, my dear, please remember that my wife and I are at your service." He released her and bowed before Caro could express her gratitude for this offer. "Good evening, Your Grace."

"Good evening, Colonel." She gave him his title still, and his eyes twinkled.

Colonel Harper politely waited for her to reach her friends before he returned to Mrs. Harper, who was still speaking with Eamon. He entered their conversation, which became animated, as though Eamon had wanted nothing more tonight than to converse with his former commander and his wife.

Jo's smile to Caro when Caro gained her side was too broad. "You are quite flushed, dearest. Dancing agrees with you."

Caro resumed her agitated fanning. "I have not scampered about so in quite a while. I must be out of form."

"You seemed to enjoy it," Louise observed, her dark eyes knowing.

"She did indeed," Jo said. "Such a lively set. The orchestra is fine tonight."

Lord Dominic, who had remained at their side, cleared his

throat. "Perhaps you would care to join the next, Your Highness? I dance stiffly, but I can still manage it." He held out a broad hand.

Jo's smile wavered, and her tone turned almost pitying. "Oh, that is kind, your lordship, but I am afraid I must decline."

Caro understood why, and it had nothing to do with Jo's opinion of Lord Dominic. Jo's mother and father, though warm-hearted people, strictly regulated who could and could not make overtures to their daughter. Their decision came not from snobbery but from the fact that they were royalty in exile.

Jo's father had to take care that the gentleman who showed his daughter attention had neither ambition to put Prince Rupert illegally on the Osagard throne nor to assassinate him, as sometimes happened to princes of Osagard. Every gentleman had to be vetted by Prince Rupert, Princess Maude, and their trusted advisors before said gentleman could even dance with Jo in their own ballroom.

Lord Dominic nodded, as though unoffended, but Caro saw his annoyance. He turned to Louise.

"My lady?" Lord Dominic extended the offered hand to her.

While Jo had showed embarrassment at having to refuse, Louise met Lord Dominic's gaze coolly. "No, thank you, sir."

Lord Dominic's gray eyes flared with even more irritation. This could be a dangerous man, Caro sensed, in a different way than Eamon was.

"I see," he said stiffly. "Is there a reason why not?"

"Steady, Wolfe," Mr. McCormick said at his side. "A lady doesn't have to give you an excuse. Maybe she's afraid you'll tread on her slippers. You do have a large foot."

While Jo relaxed into a chuckle, Louise continued to fix Lord Dominic with her steady stare. Lord Dominic met it with grim determination.

"I am still in mourning for my husband," Louise informed him.

Lord Dominic looked her up and down, taking in her finery in its subdued hue. For a moment, Caro thought he would argue with her, but he must have realized how gauche this would be, because he gave her a tense bow.

"I understand."

He continued to stand before Louise, however, their gazes locked in some sort of battle. Jo leaned closer to Caro, her fan waving slowly as they observed the drama.

Mr. McCormick clapped Lord Dominic on his cashmere-clad shoulder. "Come along, Wolfe. We've been rebuffed. We must take it on the chin and leave these ladies in peace."

Lord Dominic started, ending his rude stare. Caro thought he'd let out a growl, like the wolf of his namesake, but he swallowed it and also managed not to punch his friend.

"As you say." Lord Dominic made another bow, this one a bit churlish. "Good evening, ladies. Your Grace."

Mr. McCormick also bowed, but much more good-naturedly. He put both hands on Lord Dominic's back, guiding him into the crowd. Lord Dominic shrugged him off with a scowl after a few paces, and Mr. McCormick turned to flash a grin at the three ladies.

Jo began waving her fan hard enough to stir her hair. "Well," she said, a bit breathlessly. "Your Mr. Stone has very interesting friends."

"Arrogant," Louise stated. "At least his lordship is. Mr. McCormick seems much more friendly."

"Well, the Scots are, aren't they?" Jo asked.

Louise dragged her gaze from Lord Dominic's tall form and rested it on Jo in surprise. "I don't think it has anything to do with his being Scots."

"He is from the Shetland Isles," Caro corrected them. "Perhaps they are a friendly people there."

"The Shetland Isles, yes." Jo's fan moved still faster. "How very interesting. I must obtain a book about these islands, and discover whether the inhabitants are, in fact, more friendly than Englishmen."

Jo had spent her entire life in Britain, but she could play the curious foreigner when it suited her. This time, though, her curiosity was tinged with agitation.

"Read away," Caro said. "It will give you something to do when I have shunned you for inviting Mr. Stone tonight. I know you caused it to happen, Jo, so do not pretend innocence with me."

Jo's nervousness evaporated. "Of course I did, my friend. When our previous conversation was so full of Mr. Stone, Louise and I agreed we had to know more about him. To meet this person and decide what to make of him ourselves."

"*You* made the mistake of speaking of his army friends," Louise put in. She'd regained her usual composure, but Caro noted her stealing a glance across the ballroom to Lord Dominic. "Jo discovered their names from Colonel Harper and decided the two gentlemen needed to attend as well."

"I told Mama everything," Jo admitted. "I didn't need to coax her much at all to have Papa send them invitations. Papa and Mama were most curious as well."

"Does all of London know I've hired a picture man?" Caro asked in consternation. "Is it being whispered throughout society that a gentleman waltzes though my house each day, going over every book and painting with a fine-toothed comb?"

"Not all of London," Jo assured her quickly. "Only my family. And Louise and her family. That is all."

"So, about twenty people then," Caro stated. Louise had two sons, parents, and brothers who had wives and children of their own. "Jo, how could you?"

Jo shrugged. "Do not make your information so interesting and at the same time so cryptic that we *must* know. Is Mr. Stone truly waltzing through your house each day? He is a fine dancer,

I could not help noticing. The pair of you were quite graceful together."

Caro's face went hot. "This is absolute nonsense. Jo, you must apologize to those gentlemen for dragging them here."

"Pish tosh." Jo brushed away Caro's objections. "They could have turned down the summons. They were obviously as curious about us as we were about them. Very polite and handsome gentlemen they are too."

Jo, while not overtly flirtatious, had no hesitance about looking over a gentleman with enjoyment. She knew none would come near her without passing the rigorous tests of her parents and their adjutants, so she indulged herself in admiring them from afar.

"Somewhat forward gentlemen," Louise observed coldly.

Jo softened. "They could not have known, darling."

Louise had not been simply inventing an excuse to avoid dancing with Lord Dominic when she'd claimed she was mourning her husband. Louise had grieved deeply when the Earl of Heyford—Geoffrey—had passed away of a sudden illness four years ago. Louise had nursed him to his last hour and had been inconsolable for a very long time.

Louise was still devoted to him. Caro had been very sad at Leopold's death, and missed him, but she always felt a twinge of guilt that she didn't mourn as intensely as did Louise.

"Mr. McCormick, we agreed, is sunny natured," Caro said into the awkwardness. "Not forward at all."

"That is true." Louise adjusted her gloves as she admitted this. "I suppose his lordship vexed me, is all. He is conceited, like so many of his kind."

Caro and Jo exchanged a glance, Jo raising her brows.

"*Of his kind?*" Jo asked Louise. "What kind is that, my dear friend?"

Louise's cheeks grew pink. "Second sons who have no idea

what to do with themselves. From what I hear, his brother, the Marquis of Cheltenham, has no use for him."

"Perhaps that should engender our pity," Jo said. "More than our condemnation."

Louise stopped short of rolling her eyes. "I've met such gentlemen before, my sweet Jo. They know I am a widow of some fortune, and therefore, I must be in want of a husband. Or a lover, on whom I will lavish fine gifts that they will then turn and hand to their much younger mistresses. They flock like vultures."

"So cynical." Jo shook her head. "My poor darling, to have men falling over themselves to be next to you must be a terrible fate. Yes, some will be after your fortune, but a few likely want to gaze upon your beauty, listen to your dusky speech …"

"She is romantic," Louise said disparagingly to Caro. "One day, unhappily, she will be disabused of these notions."

Jo laughed, in no way worried. "Speaking of romantic …" Jo pointed with her closed fan at Eamon, who had departed from the Harpers and was slowly making his way back toward Caro. "I imagine he wishes another dance. How splendid."

Caro's heart beat rapidly. In panic? Embarrassment? Joy?

"Well, I do not wish another dance," she said hastily. "One was enough to keep everyone from believing me haughty. Two would be quite improper. Excuse me, please."

As Eamon neared the group, Caro spun and walked rapidly away, as though she urgently needed to seek a withdrawing room. She used her knowledge of Jo's home to open the nearest door to a private passageway and vanish into it.

CHAPTER 12

$\mathcal{E}$amon halted a step to watch Caro pointedly turn and hurry away from him.

What to do? Change direction and pretend he hadn't been making for her? Pause to speak to those he passed? Or rush after Caro like a lovelorn swain?

Eyes were upon him. Though Eamon was acquainted with more than half the people in this room, he was a newcomer in the prince's circle. The guests scrutinized him, wondering at his sudden inclusion.

If Eamon charged after Caro, tongues would wag, and wag hard, which would do Caro no good.

He changed his falter into a deliberate stop to acknowledge a group of gentlemen he'd met at gaming hells, some of whom regularly dandled ladybirds on their knees. Tonight, they were pretending to be virtuous, honorable gents for the Prince and Princess of Osagard.

"Stone," one of them said awkwardly.

"Good evening," Eamon said, but to their relief, he soon moved on.

Instead of continuing toward Princess Josephine and the

countess, he gave them a nod as he strolled past to casually move through the crowd. He halted to chat now and again with knots of guests, as though this had been his intention all along. He felt the two ladies observe him, their eagle-like stares most unnerving.

Wolfe and McCormick were now engaged in conversation with the prince himself. None of the three noted when Eamon slipped out of the ballroom through its main doors.

Eamon drew a breath of relief when he reached the front hall. A footman immediately advanced upon him, ready to direct Eamon somewhere, or fetch him something, or perhaps boot him out of the house entirely.

"Seeking some air, my good fellow." Eamon adopted the tones of a twit-about-Town. "It is damnably close in the ballroom."

The footman eyed him in some suspicion but bowed and returned to his post at the front door.

Eamon eased through the hall as though he was simply taking in the prince's sumptuous house. It was, Eamon had to admit, well-appointed, with art displayed to best exhibit each piece.

The mansion was narrow but deep, with a long staircase on one side and wide rooms on the other that reached a long way back into the property. Another room or set of rooms likely ran the width of the building in the rear.

Caro could be anywhere. Eamon doubted she'd fled the house—she'd wanted to avoid *him* but not be rude to her friends.

"Psst."

Eamon stilled, glancing about until he determined that the noise came from above. He stepped to the staircase and peered up into its shadows.

A golden-haired girl with a pixie-like face and a sharp pair of blue eyes gazed down at him through the balusters. When

Eamon fixed on her, she frantically gestured for him to ascend the stairs.

Eamon gave this command careful thought. The girl much resembled Princess Jo and therefore must be a member of the prince's household, no one Eamon should be near. He hesitated, but his curiosity as to why the lass signaled to him won out.

The young woman watched him climb to her, hands on hips. She was about twelve, Eamon judged, and wore an ivory silk gown as frilled and laced as that of any society lady in the ballroom.

"*This* way." She made an imperious gesture as Eamon gained the landing. "If you want to speak to Aunt Caro, come with me."

Eamon followed, keeping a few yards between himself and his summoner. He had no need to ponder how the devil this waif knew he sought Caro. In his own childhood, he'd easily discovered the secrets of the host and all guests of the house into which his father had cajoled entry. No one paid any attention to a lad, or in this case, a lass.

The girl scurried lithely up another flight of stairs then leaned over the railing to glare down at Eamon.

"Hurry, before anyone sees you." She raised her eyes heavenward. "Honestly, I do not know why I bother."

Eamon smothered a laugh and continued his ascent, again keeping a respectable distance between them when he reached her. "Lead on, my lady."

"Your Highness," the girl corrected him. "I am Princess Merry. Or Lady Meredith—but I hate it when anyone calls me Lady Meredith. Sounds so stuffy. Princess Merry is much more fun. Of course, everyone in my family is Princess This or Prince That, so it isn't really remarkable. Aunt Caro is in there." Princess Merry pointed to a door recessed into a paneled wall. "Staring out the window, last I checked, though there's nothing to see in the dark."

Eamon's heart beat faster. He imagined Caro gazing at an

unseen world with the remote beauty that had already captured him.

"What makes you believe she won't push me out of said window if I go in there?" Eamon asked.

Merry put her head to one side, looking wise. "Because she hasn't been in a flutter about a gentleman in a very long time. Since before she was married, Aunt Jo says. And that was years and *years* ago."

Ten years, according to Wolfe. A lifetime to a mite of a dozen summers.

When Eamon only contemplated the polished door, Merry made an impatient noise. "Well, are you going inside, or not?" she demanded.

"A scandal for a lady and gentleman to be alone in a room together," Eamon answered in a light tone.

"Nonsense. She is a widow, not a debutante of eighteen. She is much older now, and you're a retired officer. It doesn't matter so much anymore."

Eamon bit back his amusement that Merry viewed both Caro and himself as elderly, and therefore unimportant in the eyes of the world.

He knew, however, that what they did still mattered. Caro caught alone with Eamon would humiliate her and be fuel to those in the ballroom waiting for her to step one beaded slipper out of line.

"Will you stand by and warn us if someone comes?" Eamon asked her.

Merry's nod was tinged with exasperation. "Of course. Now, off you go, before she hears you and runs away again."

Eamon plucked up his courage and moved to the door. He drew a breath, turned the handle, and quietly entered the small chamber.

The white-paneled room was lit by two sconces, their wax

candles announcing the prince's wealth. Only a very rich man could afford to let candles burn in a room no one might use.

Caro was indeed staring out the window to what must be the garden behind the house.

Candlelight reflected her in the window's glass, her hair trickling from the careful coiffure, the borrowed diamonds shining softly against her gown.

So deep was her contemplation that she did not hear him enter. Only when the draft from the hall made the candles flicker did she abruptly turn.

"What are—?" Caro's exclamation died, and she stared at him in dismay.

"I am pleased the window is closed," Eamon said as he quietly shut the door behind him. "Or you might truly push me out of it."

"It is too cool to have it open," Caro said, her words stiff.

"No denial that you'd drop me from it, I see." Eamon advanced slowly but halted in the center of the room. He'd not go too close unless she invited him. "Why did you run? I speak to you every day in your own home, where you don't dash off the moment I pause to say good morning."

Caro's dark brows rose. "Why did you suppose I was fleeing *you?*"

Eamon took one step forward. Caro did not move, to his relief. "Well, let me contemplate. I headed toward you in the ballroom, and you turned and rushed away."

Caro's color rose. "I was rude. I apologize."

Eamon moved a few more steps then decided to halt before his luck ran out. "You were quite civil while we danced. I enjoyed it."

"I enjoyed it as well." Caro frowned, as though regretting the confession. "I meant I was rude when I twitted you about not sending word today. I understand now that it was not your fault."

"But it was my fault." Eamon's anger at himself returned. "I should not have trusted Cheswell." Cheswell, the idiot, had decided Caro wouldn't bring the firm much money and so had forgotten all about her. Hadn't thought sending word to her important.

"I worry for Leo, you see," Caro said in a rush. "He has grown very fond of you."

"I have grown fond of him." Eamon realized the sincerity of his words. "He's an endearing little chap. Clever too."

Caro shook her head, ringlets dancing. "I'm explaining poorly. Leo lost his father. Then most of our household deserted us—footmen and lads in the stables he'd come to believe were his friends. Most didn't even bother to say good-bye. We still have Singleton and our cook, but no coachman and groom, because we were forced to part with the horses, which Leo also loved. We have a few more staff in the country house, but they are too busy to pay as much attention to Leo as they once could." Caro ceased her outpouring and simply looked at Eamon. "In the past year or so, Leo has lost almost everyone he's cared about. When you didn't turn up today, he thought he'd lost you too. The look in his eyes broke my heart."

"Oh, Duchess." Eamon threw aside his caution and went directly to her. "I am sorry." He cupped her face before he could stop himself, her skin silken beneath his hands. "Caro, I am so sorry. I never meant to hurt either of you."

"He should not expect you to be loyal to him," Caro said. "Neither should—" She broke off, swallowing.

Damnation. In the past, Eamon had walked away from plenty of people, believing himself lucky to escape before they caught on to what a fraud he was.

This time, he cared.

Eamon's heart burned with the new knowledge. He cared.

He cared too much.

Caro's breath brushed his fingers, igniting him. Eamon, an

expert at controlling every situation he was in, surrendered to the inferno.

In an instant, he was dragging Caro closer, skimming her body with his touch, finding her pliant curves. He brushed a kiss to her lips, then another, then another, each one deeper.

Eamon expected her to shove him away, but Caro's hands came up to his chest, not to push him off, but to close around the lapels of his coat and hold him there.

Eamon let her. He deepened the kiss as he explored her body, cupping her hips, palms gliding over her waist, fingertips catching on the sharp facets of her diamonds.

He abandoned the kiss but only to take his mouth to her cheek, her chin, then to nip her fragrant neck.

Caro let out a faint groan, a woman awakening to passion. Eamon nibbled again, enjoying her raw response.

Her gown was so very prim. A fichu enclosed her to her neck, when every other woman's bosom in the ballroom had been bared for all to see.

The diamonds that lay on it were indeed real, Eamon had noted while they were dancing, but he knew they weren't hers. They didn't go with his duchess, somehow. Probably pushed on her by the same friends who'd enticed her into this gown.

Hooks on the gown's back held the bodice closed and the fichu in place. So easy to undo a few clasps, letting the front of the gown sag enough that Eamon could press a kiss to the hollow of her throat.

"Eamon," Caro whispered.

The sound of his name on her lips changed the spark into wild need. Eamon shoved the fichu out of his way, the diamonds now lying on bare flesh. He kissed her there, the stones catching in his teeth.

Caro's heart hammered beneath his mouth, and she began to explore him in return. Hesitantly at first, and then bolder, as though reveling in newfound fascination. Her hands slid under his coat then his waistband, his shirt loosening.

Eamon lifted his head as she wormed her way beneath the fine linen, at last finding his skin under too damned many layers.

"Vixen." Eamon cupped her face, smiling into their next kiss.

Caro pulled him closer, her warm fingers on his bare back the most exhilarating thing he'd experienced in a long time.

Eamon's desire, suppressed too long, surged, and he felt the answering need in her kiss. He caressed her cheek as he stepped against her, her body against the length of his.

Caro started at the contact. She must be able to feel how much he wanted her, but she didn't shy away, didn't flee.

He had to continue this. Here, now. Eamon was certain his life would be empty and colorless if they didn't.

Merry was outside the door, and they were in another man's house. Eamon's lodgings were close by, but women were forbidden there, and Mrs. Temple was a dragon. The Grosvenor Square house was tall and empty, but the pair of them would never slip past Singleton and the dowager, who were equally dragon-like.

Maddening.

Or they could hide in here, kissing, touching, learning each other. There were plenty of ways to find pleasure besides the most basic act. Caro, opening her lips for his kiss, her hands roving further, indicated she would welcome the simple pleasures, even craved them.

Eamon had just decided that the thick-carpeted floor would do for the next steps, when a noise outside the door penetrated the fog in his brain.

Caro jerked back, quicker to understand what the sound was.

In the corridor, Princess Merry had coughed.

Eamon recognized a cough of warning when he heard one.

He had Caro turned around and was re-hooking her bodice before she could express alarm.

"Good evening, your ladyship," Merry said loudly outside the door. "If you seek a withdrawing room, there is one on the floor below."

"What are you doing wandering the house, young lady?" came a stentorian voice. "In my day, we shut ourselves into the nursery when our family held a ball and didn't stray a step."

"Oh, no," Caro breathed in dismay. She was enticing, with her hair hanging limply, her fichu askew, the diamonds glittering against a tangle of translucent fabric. "Lady Carmichael. She's the worst gossip in all of London."

CHAPTER 13

"No," Eamon whispered back, his fingertips tingling where he brushed her skin. "I imagine she's the *best* gossip."

Caro glared at him. With her hair mussed and lips reddened, she was angelically beautiful. A naughty angel, perhaps, which made her all the more delectable.

Eamon had met Lady Carmichael in his boyhood days and shared Caro's concern. Comfortable in the knowledge that she'd never broken a social rule in her life, Lady Carmichael loudly condemned those who even skirted the boundaries. The French regiment that had pinned Eamon and his friends on the ridge in Belgium would have fled from Lady Carmichael's advance.

"What is behind this door?" Lady Carmichael demanded. "Are you hiding someone in there, child?"

"Oh, Lord, she will burst in here any moment," Caro hissed.

"Rub your eyes," Eamon said in a low voice.

"Pardon?" Caro's glare turned to bafflement.

"Rub your eyes until they're puffy. Then walk out the door, yawning. Don't overdo it. Tell her you stepped in here for a rest, because being in society again has exhausted you. Explain that Merry was protecting you."

Caro regarded him in worry. "What about you?"

"I will slip away once you are downstairs. Never fear, my love." Eamon touched her lips. "I am an expert at intrigue. Go."

After another frozen moment, Caro nodded and turned away from him, pressing the heels of her hands to her eyes.

Eamon quickly concealed himself behind the large Egyptian-style couch, like a lover in a farce. He stretched out on the floor and observed, around the sofa's legs, Caro's pretty ankles and slippers hesitate then move toward the exit.

The door swung open before she could reach it. A large personage, who must be Lady Carmichael, barged inside, while Merry danced in agony behind her.

"Good heavens, it's Caro Aylesmore," Lady Carmichael announced in her sergeant-major tones. "What on earth are you doing in here?"

Lady Carmichael tried to push her way around Caro to scan the room, but Caro, Eamon's lovely lady, marched purposefully out of the chamber, all but forcing Lady Carmichael to back out with her.

"Having a little sleep, if you must know," he heard Caro say in her best duchess tones. "I haven't been to a gathering this large since poor Leopold ..." She faltered with a perfection that Eamon wanted to applaud.

"Oh." Lady Carmichael sounded both sympathetic and disappointed. "You poor darling. Come with me. We'll find a withdrawing room and put you to rights, then I will take you under my wing. No one will overtax you this night, I promise."

Commanding her thus, Lady Carmichael led Caro away, their footsteps fading into the distance.

Eamon let out a breath, relieved the lady hadn't insisted they use *this* room to straighten Caro's hair and clothing. He remained on his back behind the couch, emotions racing through him faster than he could remember them doing in a long while.

Footsteps pattered into the chamber. "She's gone," Merry announced in the loudest stage whisper he'd ever heard. "Mr. Stone?"

Eamon thrust his arm up and waved over the back of the sofa. "Go on, lass," he instructed. "Don't give me away."

Merry let out a satisfied giggle and retreated.

Once it was quiet, Eamon told himself to rise and make his way downstairs and out of the house. Better to disappear altogether than for others to notice that he and Caro had both been out of the ballroom for the same length of time.

But Eamon's mouth tingled from her kisses, and his limbs held fire. His longing manifested itself in other ways, as well. Though the bare wood floor behind the sofa was cool, he remained still for a very long while, wishing Caro was there to warm him.

"I am a dreamer," he told himself sternly, but his imagination did not care one whit.

———

CARO FOUND HERSELF LADY CARMICHAEL'S CAPTIVE. THE WOMAN quite literally took Caro under her wing, linking arms with her so firmly Caro could not stray a step from her side.

Caro was still aflame from Eamon's fierce kisses, and her equally fierce ones in return. The sensation of his mouth on her bare flesh wouldn't fade, igniting reactions she'd never experienced in her life.

Leopold had been a polite lover, cautious and gentle, as though he feared every touch would hurt her. Caro had appreciated his tenderness, but Eamon had given her a taste of what passion could be.

She shook from it and could scarcely focus on Lady Carmichael's commands.

Lady Carmichael took Caro to a withdrawing room on the ground floor and instructed her own lady's maid to restore Caro's hair. The maid was only partly successful, distressed when Caro told her that more effort would be in vain.

Caro, however, became grateful for Lady Carmichael's attentiveness when they reentered the ballroom. The lady shunted away questions of where Caro had run off to and what she'd been doing, telling anyone they encountered to leave the poor woman be.

Lady Carmichael even turned aside Jo and Louise, who were both agog to know if Caro had encountered Eamon again. Caro was not ready to discuss so intense an experience, when she wasn't yet certain of her own feelings about it.

Lady Carmichael also prevented other gentlemen, young and aged, from seeking a dance. Though Caro and her son were in straitened circumstances, Leo was still a duke, and many a gentleman would be interested in forging a connection to him. Lady Carmichael deflected them all with a flip of her fan, keeping both ambitious dandies and middle-aged, heirless gentlemen away.

When Caro murmured that she wished to leave, Lady Carmichael loudly declared that the poor duchess was growing weary and should retire home.

"Thank you," Caro said to Lady Carmichael with sincerity when the prince's coach, which the family had lent her for the evening, rolled to the door to collect her. "You have been very kind."

"Nonsense, my dear," Lady Carmichael returned. "I well remember what it was like to reenter society when I was newly widowed. Most people mean well, but the hounds do come out of the woodwork. They wish to use you to influence the young duke for their own benefit. You must take care who you let near your dear Leo."

"I agree." Caro thought immediately of Rudyard, though she knew Lady Carmichael would also warn her against Eamon.

"Good girl." Lady Carmichael kissed her cheek, bathing Caro in a wash of French perfume. "Greet your mother-in-law for me. I must call 'round and have a grand chinwag with her."

Caro promised to pass on Lady Carmichael's regards and climbed into the carriage, assisted by one of the prince's correct footmen.

The short ride home did not give Caro a chance to sort out her thoughts. They were jumbled with images of the ballroom and so many watchers, the pleasure of seeing her friends again, shock when Eamon arrived, the joy of the dance, and the wild desires stirred by his kisses.

When she arrived home, still agitated, Singleton told her that the dowager was already asleep, and Leo tucked up in bed. Caro climbed to the nursery at the top of the house, wanting to at least smooth Leo's hair and whisper a good night.

She found her son sitting up, awake and brimming with the energy of small boys. Caro seated herself on the edge of Leo's bed and explained to him why Eamon hadn't arrived that day. She conveyed his profuse apologies—Caro had seen that Eamon truly felt wretched about it.

"He'll come tomorrow?" Leo asked with dismaying eagerness.

"He told me so. But tomorrow is already *today*, my little scamp. It is past midnight. You should be asleep."

"Couldn't," Leo said. "I'll try now. Good night, Mama. You look pretty."

Caro's heart warmed with his offhand compliment, delivered before a yawn nearly swallowed him. The bewilderment and confusing emotions of the night dissolved beneath her son's unquestioning love.

She kissed Leo's cheek, straightened his covers, and then descended to her own chamber. The dowager's maid came out of a doze to help Caro from the gown and necklace that Jo had so graciously lent her.

Even with the calming effect of her chat with Leo, Caro did not sleep well. She was restless, Eamon's fiery touch lingering on her skin as did the heat of his mouth on hers. Her heart sped into wild paroxysms every time she let herself think on it fully.

She worried in between her bouts of elation whether Eamon would escape the prince's house without notice. She had no doubt he'd finagle it somehow or talk himself out of the situation if he was caught, but she'd feel better when she saw him again.

Caro's eyes were sandy when she at last rose, dressed, and descended the stairs to the green morning room where they breakfasted.

The dowager, an early riser, was already seated at the table, munching on toast spread with peach jam made last summer from the Aylesford orchard at Mayfield. At least they had the peach trees, Caro thought as she slid into her chair across from her mother-in-law. Perhaps they could do something with them to bring in funds.

"Lady Carmichael sends her best wishes," Caro dutifully reported.

The dowager snorted. "That busybody. How is *ma vieille?*"

"Quite well." Caro would never have dared refer to Lady Carmichael as "the old dear," but the dowager, of an age with her, had no qualms. "Thank you, Singleton," Caro said as the butler slid a plate in front of her and lifted its lid. The lid was pewter—all the silver not part of the entail had already been sold.

Cook had prepared an egg and a few potatoes along with the slice of bread and jam. Mrs. Mulligan could do wonders with paltry supplies.

Singleton laid a sealed letter beside the plate. "Arrived with the morning post, Your Grace."

"Mm." Caro, hungry, already had a mouthful of toast. The jam was quite wonderful.

Caro did not recognize the handwriting on the thick folded paper. It was not Jo's exuberant pen or Louise's more sedate one, though they might have asked a maid or butler to address it for them. Nor was it Eamon's rather spare and precise hand—she'd seen it in the notes he was making about the collection.

"You will never know what is inside unless you open it," the dowager observed.

"That is a point." Caro laid down her toast and licked blobs of jam from her fingers. She lifted her knife, broke the plain seal, and unfolded the letter.

To the Duchess of Aylesford, greetings. I hope this missive finds you well.

Please be advised that Rudyard Berridge, nephew of the late Duke of Aylesford (sixth of that title), has begun proceedings to gain the guardianship of the current Duke of Aylesford (seventh of that title). Berridge is the current duke's closest male relative of guardian age and will extend his right to take custody of his cousin.

All correspondence about this matter will be carried out through the offices of Messrs Morgan, Brooks, and Monroe.

Your assistance will make the transition a smooth one, and any hindrance is liable to be taken to the courts.

Your most humble servant,

T. Morgan, Esq.

CHAPTER 14

The previous night

𝓔amon had learned discreet ways out of every sort of house, thanks to his father, who'd had an uncanny sense of when he'd worn out his welcome. Once Eamon convinced himself to rise from his place of refuge, he quietly slipped out of the chamber and down the stairs.

A coin to the cool footman still lingering in the foyer had his hat and coat fetched. Eamon handed the lad another half-crown and walked out of the prince's house through a side passageway to the mews, turning up his collar against the damp. Wolfe and McCormick would tax him with his disappearance, but he'd put up with them to keep speculation away from Caro.

He had many things to do, in any case. Eamon left Portman Square behind and sought a hackney. He paid more coins to the rain-soaked driver to take him, not to his nearby lodgings in Oxford Street, but to the Strand.

From there he walked north to Maiden Lane, near Covent Garden, and ducked into a tavern. The locals glanced up as he entered, assessing him to decide whether he was a threat or someone they could cheat out of whatever money he carried.

In the very depths of the tavern was a narrow inglenook that other patrons avoided. A table had been placed in front of one of the benches surrounding the stone fireplace, and it was this table Eamon made for, halting at the foot of it.

The man seated on the bench observed him without a word. He was on the small side but solidly built, with dark hair and light brown eyes. He sported a cauliflower ear from his days as a prize fighter but was otherwise whole.

The man pinned Eamon with a shrewd gaze while the others in the tavern stilled to watch, holding their collective breaths. Well they might. Sam Noble was a dangerous man.

Sam continued to give Eamon his stare until he abruptly broke into a wide grin.

"Stone!" he bellowed. "Me old china. How are you?"

He pushed himself off the bench, wrung Eamon's hand, and clapped him on the back with a force that could have pushed down a wall. Eamon manfully kept to his feet and tried to match Sam's strong grip.

"I am doing well," Eamon told him. "Can I stand you an ale?"

"Make it brandy. The ale here is horse piss."

The landlord, who'd been heading over to ingratiate himself to a friend of Sam Noble, scowled.

"Brandy it is," Eamon said congenially to the landlord. "And one for yourself, good sir." He handed over several coins.

The landlord's sour expression cleared, and he beetled off to fetch a small cask from behind his counter.

Eamon rubbed his hand once Sam released it. "Brandy is also more expensive, my friend. You could fleece the greatest miser."

Sam stood a head shorter than Eamon, though his barrel chest was wider. Eamon remembered looking *up* at Sam as a boy, gaping in wonder at the seeming giant.

"'Tis a talent," Sam said modestly. "Sit down and gab with me, lad. Never think of saying no."

"Wouldn't dream of it." Eamon waited for Sam to take his seat at the back of the inglenook, nearest the fire—not only the warmest place in the room, but from whose vantage point Sam could survey the entire tavern.

Eamon sat next to him and nodded at the landlord when the man brought them goblets of brandy. The landlord hovered, as though hoping Eamon would order some other item of expense, then drifted away when Eamon only smiled at him.

Eamon lifted his goblet. The brandy inside was potent, its odor alone making his eyes water. "Your health," he said to Sam.

"Thank ye very much." Sam raised his glass, and both men drank deeply.

Eamon bit back a cough at the strong liqueur. "An interesting vintage," he wheezed.

"The best that can be smuggled to the Norfolk coast. But trust me, lad. 'Tis better than the ale."

"I will take you at your word."

They drank in companionable silence for a few moments, while the other patrons went back to their drinks, games, or low-voiced conversations. More than one man shot a glance at them, clearly wondering why the villainous Sam Noble had suddenly turned so friendly.

The answer was a long tale concerning Eamon's father, Eamon's quick thinking that had taken both Sam and Sir Benedict out of a situation where the Runners would have nabbed them both, and Sam's fascinated interest in a boy who could out-cajole even his father.

After that adventure, Sam had declared himself Eamon's life-long mate. Sam hadn't felt the same kindness toward Sir Benedict, who he'd labeled a right bastard and a terrible father.

"Where have ye been keeping yourself, lad?" Sam asked

Eamon. "Haven't seen ye since ye donned a red uniform and ran off to Spain."

"Mucking about, here and there," Eamon answered. "Trying to paint pretty pictures and failing at it. I'm no good unless I'm copying someone great."

"Aye, you'd have made a grand forger, me lad. A grand one." Sam took a long sip of brandy in regret.

"Sadly, I am too honest to deceive," Eamon said good-humoredly.

And too proud, he added to himself. He'd prefer to be known for his own paintings. If Eamon sold his copies of Canalettos or Caravaggios as genuine, he could never have the recognition for what he'd done. The forgers he'd met did not care—they were happy to take the money and be pleased they'd fooled their marks. Eamon's vanity would give him away.

He did not admit to Sam that he'd started making original sketches again. When he opened his notebook in the evenings, his pencil drew lines of a woman's face, untamed locks of hair wisping across her cheeks. Diamonds glittered on her bosom, and her smile could melt the hardest heart.

"Strange you are so honest, recalling who your father was." Sam broke into Eamon's thoughts. "A blessing that he fell off his perch, I will tell you the truth. He'd have had you churning out your drawings and daubs to sell off to gullible punters by the bucketful."

Eamon knew this to be true. Even as a boy, he'd realized that Sir Benedict had exploited Eamon's winsome manner, small stature, and agility to help him swindle his way into comfortable situations. He'd have done more and more as Eamon grew, until Eamon would have had to battle his way free.

Eamon sipped more bad brandy, willing the past to remain in the past. He had more important issues to face here and now.

"I didn't only come to have a gossip with you, Sam," Eamon began.

"Didn't fink ye did." Sam nodded. "You need good old Sam Noble's expertise. What are we stealing?"

"Nothing. Yet." Eamon liked that Sam turned his full attention on him. Sam had been one of the few of his father's colleagues to take Eamon seriously. "Do you know of a bloke called Clive? Styles himself a curator of paintings. Had a post with the Duke of Aylesmore before said duke gave up the ghost."

Sam's brows knit. "You mean Hieronymus Clive?"

"Is that his name?" Eamon asked in surprise. "Like Bosch who did all those bizarre paintings in the 1500s? Allegories and such."

"Wouldn't know about that. But yes, if it's the Clive you're thinking of, he has that moniker. Don't trust the man." Sam squinted at him. "What are you asking me for? You're a perfectly fine judge of a bloke. What do *you* make of him?"

"I've never clapped eyes on him. Only seen his ledgers and heard his name. The Duchess of Aylesmore doesn't know much about him. Her husband worked with Clive—I imagine neither man found any reason to discuss their business with a woman." More fool they.

"He's a fence," Sam said without hesitation. "Takes pieces of art, silver, gold plate, bits and bobs, and asks no questions. Sells them on without a qualm."

"A receiver?" Eamon sat back, disconcerted. "He was turned loose in that house in Grosvenor Square, where he might have found treasures unimaginable."

"He probably imagined them just fine. But he's no thief. Won't soil his precious hands. If he has any treasure from Aylesmore's hoard, they were handed to him. Don't mean he wouldn't take something home for cleaning or appraisal, with the owner's permission. But what he brings back won't necessarily be the same thing he took away."

"He'd replace them with forgeries." Eamon turned his glass on the table. "Does he make the forgeries himself?"

"You'd have heard about him before this if he did. No, he hires them, same as he hires a thief to steal to order for him or his clients. As I say, he won't soil his own hands."

Eamon glared at the blackened brick wall opposite him. "How the devil did he get hired on by Aylesmore? Surely the duke, or his man of business, would have asked for references?"

"Clive would have them," Sam answered. "From what I hear put about, the Duke of Aylesmore was several planks thick. Most of these aristos are. Their heads are messed about by breeding too close to the bloodline. Happens in horses too."

"Bloody idiot." Eamon refrained from hurling his glass against the wall to hear the satisfying crash. It wouldn't be wise to burst out with sudden violence in this place.

"Aye," Sam agreed.

"Thank heaven Clive quit the place as soon as the late duke was laid to rest," Eamon said. "Probably had picked it clean by then. I hate to think of a man like that roaming the house, and Caro there without protection."

Sam's brows climbed his broad forehead. "*Caro*, is it? Is that the duchess you're meaning? Lad, run far from such things, before ye find yourself too deep. What did I just tell ye about aristos?"

"She isn't an aristo," Eamon said impatiently. "Not in that sense. She was born a plain Miss, a gentleman's daughter. Her family were on the same footing as mine." Sir Benedict, though he'd finagled his way into his knighthood, had at least been gentry born.

"Even so, she's one of them now. Not for the likes of you and me, I'm thinking."

Eamon fell silent, not intending to argue. In this world, a person's background and breeding counted for far more than how clever he was or even how wealthy he was. Nabob's daughters were sought for their father's money but never really accepted by the old blood. A self-made man was regarded with deep suspicion.

Eamon fell into no category he knew, but he'd comforted himself that he and Caro had arisen from much the same stock.

However, Sam was right. Caro was now the mother of one duke and the widow of another. Her mother-in-law was definitely aristocratic and guarded Caro fiercely. Caro's friends, likewise, were lofty.

If any of them wanted Eamon out, he'd have no recourse.

Did that mean Eamon was giving up? Far from it. If he could do nothing but save Caro from a crafty swindler and the duke's vindictive cousin, then save her he would. His reward would be watching her and Leo live a safe and happy life.

He repeated this to himself with vehemence.

"Where can I find Hieronymus Clive?" he asked Sam.

"Has a shop in Cheapside." Sam huffed a laugh. "Pretends it's a proper business, a secondhand place and a pawnbrokers. His real work he keeps hidden, probably in the back or a cellar, or in his attic. Somewhere the Runners and the bailiffs won't work too hard to find."

"Or he pays them to look the other way."

"He could do." Sam and Eamon shared a look of distaste, both more repelled by corrupt men of the Crown than outright thieves.

"I will call upon him," Eamon said. "Ask why he's not answered my letters."

"Because he's afraid you'll find him out." Sam saluted Eamon with his cup. "Which you will, lad. I have no doubt."

"I'll have a bloody good go at him," Eamon promised.

And if Mr. Clive had been cheating Caro and her son out of Leo's rightful inheritance, Eamon would make the man pay dearly.

"Good for you, lad," Sam said. "If you need me help, you give me the nod. I'm here most nights."

Sam had the reputation for making problems disappear—permanently. Not someone a sensible man would join forces with, but Sam had always been a loyal friend, no matter his reputation.

Eamon thanked him and they imbibed a while longer, Sam reminiscing about the adventures they'd had in the old days. Eamon listened and tried not to think of Caro and her kisses, or picture her curled up in bed in her grand house, damp from sleep. The visions would not depart, however, no matter how much brandy he drank.

———

IN THE MORNING, EAMON ROSE EARLIER THAN HE'D HAD SINCE HIS army days and took a hackney to Cheapside. His head was fuddled by the foul brandy, but he forced it to clear as he rode along in the rather smelly coach.

The eastern parts of London were already alive with activity. The markets began early, and every cook, chef, and provider knew that the best bits went to those who arrived first. Each market he passed was bustling as Oxford Street became Holborn and then Newgate Street.

Eamon turned his face away when the coach passed the grim wall of Newgate Prison. His father had never ended up there, thank the Lord, but he'd spent days in the Fleet, with five-year-old Eamon to keep him company. Not an experience Eamon ever wished to repeat.

Newgate Street took a jog near St. Paul's, its great dome rising through the fog, and merged into Cheapside.

The shop Sam had indicated lay near the turning to Milk Street. Eamon instructed the coachman to pass it and let him down near Poultry, with its view of the great Bank of England and Mansion House. No sense rolling up in front of Clive's door, giving the man a chance to flee out the back.

Eamon paid the hackney driver, then took his time strolling back toward Milk Street.

Businesses were already open, with owners displaying wares on the pavement. Eamon paused outside a secondhand book-shop to thumb through a few tomes. He selected a pocket-sized volume on medieval manuscripts, marveling that a printer could tuck so much information into such a tiny book.

The bookseller wanted to chat about the weather, the crowds on the street, and every other topic he could think of, but Eamon paid over a tuppence for his purchase and gently pried himself away.

Clive's business was located a few doors down from the booksellers. An unpretentious black painted door led Eamon into a small shop that held a jumble of secondhand goods displayed in a haphazard fashion. Polished cups and plates of middling quality stood next to wicker sewing baskets, and pewter candlesticks mingled with vinaigrettes and brandy flasks.

The very thin young man who looked up from behind a walled counter when Eamon entered could not be Mr. Clive. He was fifteen at most.

The counter closed off shelves that displayed more expen-sive items: watches and fobs, thick gold rings, gold snuff boxes, cameos and lockets, and a few tiny pictures of painted single eyes, the sort exchanged between lovers. Presumably those who pawned them could no longer bear to have their ladylove giving them a one-eyed stare, or else someone had inherited the trinkets and hadn't known what to do with them.

Eamon put on the stuffy, blue-blooded accent he'd learned so well from his father and addressed the young man.

"A fine morning to you, sir. I hear this is where I can inquire about buying some pictures. Some *good* pictures, you understand."

The lad grinned and leaned through the counter's window. "*French* pictures, sir? Have those in the back." He winked.

Eamon drew himself up. "Certainly not. What do you take me for?"

The youth immediately straightened, flushing. "Beg pardon, sir. We get all sorts in, don't we? Wanting all manner of things."

"Well, I am not all sorts. When I say *good pictures*, I mean those of quality. I have heard that Mr. Clive is one to provide them."

"Right." The young man hesitated, uncertain, before he bounded like a rabbit through a wooden door behind the counter, slamming it shut.

Eamon was left to meander about the shop, wondering if Clive would appear or if the youth had given him warning to escape.

He idly opened a jewelry box that held an assortment of necklaces and bracelets that must not be worth anything, or else they'd be locked behind the counter. Nor would Eamon have been left alone in the shop with them.

He had no intention of buying the cheap gewgaws, but they inspired an idea of finding a diamond necklace for Caro. She deserved something of her own instead of having to borrow from her friends.

Eamon let himself imagine standing behind her while he lowered the glittering necklace to her throat. Caro's warm hair would brush his fingers as he affixed the clasp, and she'd turn and smile at him.

My duchess in diamonds, he'd whisper before kissing her cheek. *As you should be.*

The interior door banging open once more tore away these pleasant thoughts.

The man who stepped through the opening must be Mr. Clive. He was of middling height, with a paunch for a stomach and a head of thick, graying brown hair.

His face was broad but had strength, his dark eyes holding a flintiness he tried to hide behind a beaming smile as he came out from behind the counter.

"My dear sir. I beg your pardon for keeping you waiting." Clive had a loud voice, not deep, but one a person could hear across a crowded room. "What sort of artworks did you have in mind, Mr. ...?"

"Wolfe," Eamon extemporized. "Dominic Wolfe."

He wasn't certain why he'd invoked Wolfe's name, but he'd learned to go with whatever popped into his head. Wolfe would understand. Eventually.

Clive's eyes widened. "I am honored, my lord."

The man must have memorized Debrett's *Peerage* if he recognized Wolfe's name, but it was clear he did not know what Wolfe looked like.

"Quite," Eamon said gruffly. "I'm here to view paintings, not exchange pleasantries." He imitated Wolfe's arrogant bark well, he thought with some satisfaction.

"Yes, yes, of course. Would you care to follow me?"

Clive strode swiftly to the very back of the shop, beyond the tables of wares. Eamon passed an eight-foot-tall torchiere, wonderfully carved and gilded, ready to hold one of the silver candelabras locked behind the counter.

Mr. Clive led him through a door in the shop's rear, which gave onto a small corridor ending in yet another door. Clive unlocked this and ushered Eamon into a warehouse of sorts.

Bookcases and shelves lined three walls of the vast room, each holding still more valuable things than those displayed behind the shop's counter. The fourth wall was hung with a large collection of paintings—the floor below these were stacked with canvases five or six deep.

Clive swept his arm to encompass the hung artwork. "What strikes your fancy, my lord? I have many quality pieces here, both from the great masters and more recent artists who have started to be in demand."

Most of the paintings were very good copies, Eamon could see. Rubens was prevalent, as the man had produced mountains of artwork in his long life. A few faux Titian paintings and Mantegna engravings hung among them, next to vague landscapes and still lifes that could have been painted by anybody.

There was true art among the dross. Eamon could feel it pulsating, calling out in distress.

He feigned a sneer. "Is this all?"

Clive blinked in surprise before he gave Eamon another once over. "Ah, I see you have discerning tastes, my lord. Perhaps this is more to your liking?"

Clive moved to the canvases on the floor and seized three from the middle of a stack. He removed the cloths that protected them, turned them around, and leaned them against a rare empty space of the wall.

One was a genuine Rubens, featuring a large, golden-haired woman in flapping draperies, another, Guercino's almost serene depiction of Cleopatra's death, a painting Eamon had last seen in a country estate in Yorkshire.

It was the third picture, however, that seized Eamon's attention.

The aging face of Rembrandt van Rijn, his small eyes peering over his bulbous nose, regarded Eamon with frank interest from the canvas. The painting was an undisputed masterpiece, and an excellent copy of it now hung in the gallery in the Duke of Aylesmore's home.

CHAPTER 15

*E*amon gazed at the picture for some time, while Rembrandt regarded him from under his drooping beret. Eamon didn't realize he was holding his breath until his chest began to burn.

The copy Caro had shown him was almost identical. Barring the few gaffes that only an expert would notice, Caro's painting was uncannily like what Eamon viewed now, except that this one glowed with the authenticity of its artist's brush.

Forcing himself to breathe again, Eamon stepped back. "Provenance for this one?" He gestured at the Rembrandt, striving to sound immensely skeptical.

"I have plenty of documents, my lord, if that is what you mean, all the way back to the 1600s. The Duke of Aylesmore acquired it in 1780, from a Frenchman, I believe."

Interesting that Clive would tell a stranger the truth about who had actually owned the painting. The notation for it in Clive's ledger had a cryptic code next to it, but Eamon recalled the 1780 date.

"And the duke sold it to you?" Eamon asked.

"Not directly." Clive sounded smug. "It came into my possession."

An answer as cryptic as his ledger entry.

Eamon decided to continue feigning ennui with the entire procedure. "I will give you five hundred for it."

Clive sent him a look of amazement. "Five hundred? That is a paltry sum, even in guineas. My price is five *thousand*."

Eamon languidly waved a gloved hand. "You are a madman. Seven hundred at most."

"My lord, you insult me."

"Not at all. What is to say that is not a copy?"

Now Clive became outraged. "I have told you. It has provenance, and it belonged to a duke."

Eamon sniffed. "If you present me with these papers, and my man of business looks them over, I might be able to make you a better offer. *If* the painting proves to be genuine, that is."

"I assure you, my lord, I would not have shown it to you if it was not."

That was probably true. Clive had thought he'd at last met a discerning member of the nobility and was now protesting that *this* painting, at least, was real.

"Mm." Eamon paused, as though considering. "Very well. See that the papers are sent to my man. He is Mr. Kennedy, in Lombard Street." He named Wolfe's man of business, who sometimes acted for Eamon.

"I will do that," Clive assured him.

He seemed very confident. Either he truly did have the provenance or was certain that the forged paperwork would stand close scrutiny.

Eamon gave him a condescending nod. "I will take my leave, then."

"Do the other paintings interest you?" Clive asked quickly. "If you do not want anything so large, I have a lovely miniature by Holbein. Also, some nice Roman bronzes."

"No, no." Eamon brushed the offers aside. "The Dutch fellow will do. I look forward to him regarding me from my mantlepiece."

The elder Rembrandt, who'd seen much hardship in his life, studied Eamon as though he understood his struggles. Eamon gave the painting a friendly nod and a haughtier one to Clive before turning to depart.

Clive hastily bounded to the door ahead of him, opening it to lead him out. Clive steered Eamon resolutely toward the shop, which made Eamon wonder what else was stored back here that Clive didn't want him to see.

The innocuous passageway ran a long enough way from the shop that Eamon suspected he'd been in the building behind the one on Cheapside. Clive might have rented more rooms in that building that held other treasures.

The youth in the shop bowed with more respect when Eamon emerged into it. The young man's fingers twitched as Eamon passed him—no doubt hoping for a coin.

Eamon disappointed him. He settled his hat, bade the two a good morning, and swept out. Instead of seeking another hackney, he strode off along Cheapside, his head high. Wolfe was known to eschew carriages to walk, even with his injury.

The brisk wind dispersed clouds and chimney smoke, actually letting in a bit of sunshine. Eamon slowed his walk after passing St. Paul's, tipping back his hat to enjoy it.

He looked forward to telling Caro what he'd found.

He was interested enough in what sort of papers Clive would produce that he'd not rush away to find a magistrate and report a stolen painting. Also, there was the possibility that Caro's late husband—or his father—had actually sold Clive the bloody thing to make ends meet, without telling anyone.

If Eamon could pry that painting from Clive's hands, even if he had to sell everything he owned and touch his friends for funds to do it, he'd return it to the Aylesmore family, and Caro could sell it on. He'd make certain a reputable dealer gave her a good sum, which would help Caro and her family enormously. The thought cheered him very much.

Eamon sought a hackney when he reached the Strand, and rolled into Mayfair, lowering the window to bask in the tolerably good weather.

He rapped cheerily on the front door at Grosvenor Square. Singleton, within seconds, pulled it open.

One look at Singleton's dour countenance made Eamon's good spirits evaporate.

"What happened?" Eamon demanded.

Singleton's expression remained grim. "Her Grace received bad news from His Grace's cousin."

Rudyard. Damn and blast the man. "Where is she?"

"The green morning room, sir. On the fourth floor, at the very top of the stairs."

Caro and the dowager took breakfast there, Caro had told him, but Eamon had never seen the place. The only chamber he'd entered on the fourth floor had been the dowager's drawing room.

Singleton's worry propelled Eamon up the stairs. He tapped on the door Singleton directed him to but heard no reply.

He pushed the door open and peered inside. Caro was there, alone, Leo and the dowager nowhere in sight.

The chamber's Wedgewood green walls, so fashionable in the last century, held plaster reliefs of jars of trailing plants, silhouettes of women in Greek-style dress, and geometric designs. The remains of breakfast lay on a square table with upholstered chairs drawn up to it, while other seats invited a person to relax with a cup of coffee, tea, or chocolate after the meal.

Caro paced in the midst of this elegance, fists clenched, tendrils of hair loose. She'd donned a white lace cap, but it had sagged to hang from the back of her head, its pins barely holding it on.

Eamon closed the door with a hard thump, and when that did not make Caro cease glaring at the carpet as she marched, he cleared his throat.

Caro swung around, and Eamon found himself facing Medusa in all her rage. Caro's eyes were wild, her face flushed, her breathing ragged.

"Duchess?" Eamon addressed her gently as he approached. "What is it?"

Caro emitted a noise between a shout and a scream. She thrust a much-crumpled piece of paper at him.

Mystified, Eamon took the page, smoothed it and read.

The letter from Rudyard's man of business was short and to the point. Eamon read it through twice, rage boiling inside him to match Caro's own.

"Devious prick," he stated.

Caro nodded, joy flaring in her eyes that Eamon shared her fury. "He will not have my son."

"No, he will not." Eamon dropped the letter to the breakfast table and took Caro's clenched hands. "We will fight this, my love."

Caro did not seem to notice the endearment. "That is what my mother-in-law said. She is busily writing letters to everyone she knows, including the queen." She managed a faint smile. "I am certain the queen has more to concern her than my paltry troubles."

"Separating a mother from her son is hardly paltry. Her Majesty will likely understand your anguish, as a mother herself, the Prince Regent notwithstanding. She has other sons she must love."

"Do not try to make me laugh." Caro jerked from his grasp. "I wish to be angry, because it will save me from despair."

Eamon took her hands once more, this time soothing them open.

"There will be no need for despair."

Caro's eyes blazed, but she did not pull away. "No, because I will fight for Leo, no matter what I need to do."

Determination flared from her like the halo of a smiting angel.

Cousin Rudyard likely thought Caro would easily give way to his threats, crumpling like gossamer, but if so, the man was a fool. What Rudyard didn't understand was that gossamer was actually quite strong, and nothing was fiercer than a mother protecting her child.

"I will fight alongside you," Eamon promised. He traced her cheek, and when Caro softened, leaned to her.

She pressed her hand flat against his chest. "No, please do not kiss me."

"Oh." That stung. Eamon lifted his head. "I beg your pardon, Your Grace."

"I mean no offense," Caro said quickly. Her touch turned to a light caress. "When you kiss me, I can think of nothing else."

Eamon's ache eased. "Mm, I do like that explanation."

"It is not amusing. I have been befuddled since the day you walked into this house."

"I likewise have been befuddled, Duchess. That started as soon as I saw you."

Caro's gaze held heat that seared Eamon's body. "Eamon, I—"

The door to the room burst open, and a small figure barreled in. "Mr. Stone! You're back! I found something."

Eamon turned from Caro, surprised at the delight that infused him. "There's my lad. I mean, my liege." He turned his impulsive reach for the boy into a courtly bow.

Leo grabbed Eamon's hand, ignoring the play. "It's in the gallery. Come with me."

Eamon let himself be towed away. When he looked back, the smile Caro beamed on them made every hurt from his past life dissolve and flow away.

———

LEO EAGERLY DRAGGED EAMON DOWN THE FLIGHTS OF STAIRS, not releasing him until they'd reached the gallery floor.

The boy raced through the long room, sliding to a halt at the table that held Vespasian. He seized a small book he'd left the Roman emperor to guard and slammed it into Eamon's hands.

"It's old," Leo stated, dancing from foot to foot. "Smells like it too. Is it worth a lot of money?"

"Give me a chance to look at it, lad."

It was always confounded dark in the gallery in spite of the tall windows, even on this fine day. Only one candle burned in the candelabra, and Eamon used it to light the other three. Singleton would swoon at the waste, but Eamon would risk his wrath.

The book was about seven inches by five with a leather-tooled binding, which must have been very nice when it was first purchased. The leather was cracking a bit, more so where it had been exposed to the air than where it had been squeezed between other books.

Inside, Eamon found printed pages, which was a pity, because hand copied books were far more valuable than those churned out by a printing press.

It was a book of hours, in Latin. The title page held a picture of the Virgin and child in an embellished oval, with the name of the Italian publisher beneath it. The date was listed as MDCCLX.

"Very nice," Eamon said. "The condition isn't bad. Published in 1760, so about fifty or so years old. I'm not an expert on books, but I am guessing this would fetch about twenty-five quid to the right collector."

"Is that a lot?" Leo asked in hope.

"It would buy more candles, that's for certain." Eamon snuffed out the extra two with his fingers to save Singleton apoplexy. "Well done, Leo. This is the sort of thing we need."

The book wasn't worth very much in comparison to what the duke's collection should have brought in, but Eamon wasn't going to sadden the boy by telling him so. And anyway, it was a start.

Leo drew himself up proudly. "I'll keep on looking. There's bound to be more."

Without waiting for Eamon to answer, he ran for the bookcases and swarmed up the steps. Eamon enjoyed watching him solemnly pull out a tome, examine it, shake his head and replace it, then move to the next one.

Eamon balanced the small volume in his hand. If this had been a medieval illuminated book of hours—for keeping track of saints' days and daily, weekly, and yearly prayers—it would be worth a fortune. This one had been churned out by printers by the hundreds to sell to the faithful about fifty years ago. The binding and good condition of the paper inside made it sellable, but only if someone wished to purchase it. Otherwise, it could be torn apart and used for fuel.

Damn it, there had to be *something*.

Eamon gazed upon the rows of copied paintings, some of them better than others, and up at the full bookcases, anger rising.

He was furious at Caro's husband for not noticing that his collection was worth damn all, and at her father-in-law, or whoever it had been, for selling off the Rembrandt and probably more of the best paintings and then squandering the money. Both dukes had left their wives, not to mention their heirs, in near poverty, while the world expected them to keep up grand houses and move among the loftiest of society.

Eamon thought of Caro in the borrowed and altered frock, wearing diamonds lent by her friend the princess. Caro had graced both gown and jewels with her natural elegance, but she should be in silks, with diamonds dripping from her. The rest of the *ton* ought to be bathing in the glow of her greatness instead of pitying her or mocking her.

Now their idiot relation, Rudyard, was trying to control the young duke, to keep himself the sole heir or maybe speeding himself into the dukedom.

Eamon would stop him. He leaned against the long table, one eye on Leo, who was nimble on the ladder. Eamon wasn't certain exactly how he would best Cousin Rudyard, who had money and position behind him. Plus, unfortunately, the law that said he was a more important relation to Leo than Caro.

But he would think of something. Eamon hadn't grown up surrounded by confidence tricksters without learning a thing or two from them. Not that he'd do anything fraudulent to keep Leo at home—the solution would have to be honest and legal, so none could reverse it.

Rudyard might have money and be the heir to a dukedom, but Eamon had friends and connections all over London, many of them lofty, some of them, like Sam Noble, from a shadowy world. He knew they'd back him, especially when they saw what was at stake.

Eamon would keep Leo with Caro no matter what he had to do, even if it meant bowing out and never seeing her again.

That would put a hole in his life he'd never fill, but if that was what it took for Leo and Caro to remain safely together, he'd do it.

If Eamon told himself this often enough, he might even believe himself capable of the sacrifice.

———

"A Mr. McCormick has come to call, Your Grace." Singleton's stiffness as he announced this in the drawing room signaled his vast disapproval. "I believe he is Scottish."

Caro turned from the desk where she'd been writing an indignant letter to her husband's—now Leo's—man of business, telling him he must help her deal with Rudyard's demands.

The trouble was, Caro had the feeling the duke's man of business might take Rudyard's side. Mr. Forsythe preferred to deal with gentlemen, not mothers, and he might agree that Leo was better off with a male relative.

It was frustrating and frightening.

"He is from Shetland," Caro told Singleton. Mr. McCormick felt it important to make the distinction, so Caro would oblige him. "He is a friend to Mr. Stone. I believe Mr. Stone is consulting him about some of the books. You should show him to the gallery."

"He said he wishes to speak to *you*, Your Grace," Singleton continued with hauteur.

"Oh." Caro had to wonder why, unless he was here to ask to be Leo's tutor, as Eamon had mentioned. She'd have to turn him down, citing lack of funds. "Second-floor drawing room, then."

"Yes, Your Grace."

Poor Singleton. Ever since Eamon's arrival, he'd been beleaguered by the sudden shifts of protocol.

Caro slid her letter into the drawer of her small writing table and followed Singleton out and down the stairs. She rehearsed in her head a gentle way of explaining that she couldn't possibly hire Mr. McCormick.

Mr. McCormick had been left in the lower hall while Singleton consulted Caro. The tall man was pacing there but halted and gazed up the stairs when he spied Caro descending. He bowed to her, his red hair bright in the dim light.

"Forgive my impertinence, Your Grace. I happened to be passing."

Before Caro could answer, or Singleton could admonish him for speaking, someone banged on the front door, then pushed it open.

A footman had done the heavy knocking, but the young woman who skirted past him and into the house was no servant. She wore a light blue frock with a fetching darker blue spencer that matched her bonnet, from which golden ringlets peeped. Jo always looked as though she'd stepped out of a fashion plate, bless her.

"Good afternoon, Singleton," Jo chirped in her friendly way. "Tell Caro I've come to call. Oh, there you are, darling."

She sped toward the stairs, and because her eyes were on Caro, she never noted the red-haired gentleman in her way, until she ran straight into him with an ungainly *thump*.

CHAPTER 16

$\mathcal{M}$r. McCormick deftly caught Jo before they both went down in a mortifying tangle of limbs. He turned the collision into a brisk dance, steadying Jo on her feet.

Jo gaped, for once speechless. Mr. McCormick returned her shocked look with a warm smile as he released her.

"I beg your pardon, miss." He gave her a modest bow.

"Her Highness, Princess Josephine of Osagard," Singleton announced wearily as he came off the stairs. "Might I take your wrap, Your Highness?" He glared at Mr. McCormick, silently berating the man for his gaffe.

Jo didn't respond to Singleton's question. She gazed at Mr. McCormick as though she'd never seen him before, never mind that she'd chatted readily with him at her mother's ball.

"Do you often linger like a boulder in other people's front halls?" she demanded.

Caro recognized that Jo was embarrassed and flustered, the only situation that would make her rude.

"Do you often run pell-mell into other people's homes?" Mr. McCormick countered.

"Caro is a very dear friend," Jo said icily.

"Aye, a kind young woman, which is why I've come to speak to her. I was here first, Your Royal Highness, which you might have seen if ye'd opened your eyes."

"Not *Royal* Highness, just Highness," Jo corrected him. "In Osagard, no one is Royal Highness except the heir, which is my father."

"Thank ye very much for reminding me of both my manners and your position," Mr. McCormick returned.

Singleton took a step forward, as though ready to show Mr. McCormick the door, but Caro put a light hand on his arm and shook her head. Singleton's heavy brows furrowed, but he subsided.

Neither Jo nor Mr. McCormick seemed to note Caro's and Singleton's presence. They fixed on each other, Jo's cheeks bright pink, Mr. McCormick stiff-backed and annoyed.

"You're welcome," Jo said with lofty sarcasm. "I believe you need the instruction. Perhaps you ought to schedule a few lessons."

"With you?" Mr. McCormick opened his blue eyes wide. "You'd like to tutor a rude Scotsman, would you?"

"I believe you said you were from Shetland. And of course I would not presume to teach you. That would be highly improper. I meant to leave you at Singleton's mercy." Jo jerked her attention from Mr. McCormick and returned it to Caro, but Caro sensed she did so with reluctance. "Might we go up, Caro? The hall is a bit crowded."

Mr. McCormick's face was as red as his hair now, but he bowed and backed away as Jo swept past him toward the stairs. Jo seized Caro's arm in passing, turning her around and half dragging her up the first flight of steps.

Caro called down from the landing. "Singleton, please show Mr. McCormick to the gallery, where Mr. Stone is. I will speak to him later."

She nearly missed Singleton's unhappy, "Very good, Your

Grace," because Eamon had appeared from the shadowy gallery, capturing her attention. From his amused expression, he'd witnessed the entire exchange below.

Eamon gave Jo a polite bow then shot Caro a good-natured grin that flashed heat through her, before Jo's determined stride pulled Caro up the next flight of stairs.

Jo's anger receded the higher they climbed, and she was her usual chipper self by the time they reached the fourth-floor drawing room.

"Where Mr. Stone is," Jo repeated, mimicking Caro's cool tones. "Such richness, my friend."

"Such prickliness between you and Mr. McCormick." Caro closed the door in the empty room, the dowager in her own chambers writing her letters. "The poor man came here to ask for a post, I believe."

"A post?" Jo untied the ribbons on her bonnet and pulled it off, blinking as though she'd never heard of such a thing.

"Yes, a post." Caro gestured her friend to the sofa. "A paying job. Did you think I meant a pillar?"

Jo plopped down in a flutter of skirts. "Why on earth would he ask you for a post?"

"I imagine he needs the money." Caro sat more gently next to her. "He was with Mr. Stone in the army, and none of them had a bean when they left it."

"You say that so airily, as though money doesn't matter."

"It doesn't. Not really. It is very useful for paying one's bills and buying potatoes, but one doesn't need riches to have kind friends. I've discovered that one knows very quickly who one's true and dear friends are as soon as we are in straitened circumstances. Such as you and your family and darling Louise and her sons."

"And now you've made me feel frivolous and shallow." Jo balled her hands in her lap. "I apologize, dearest. I am behaving abominably. I didn't see the wretched man until he was very solidly in my way." She rubbed her shoulder. "I meant it when I called him a boulder. Mr. McCormick is quite strong." Her voice lost irritation and admiration crept in. "And rude," she added quickly.

"He did not expect to be dashed into by a princess," Caro said. "An adorable one, at that. I imagine you flustered him."

"Perhaps," Jo conceded.

Caro hid her amusement. Jo wasn't used to gentlemen like Mr. McCormick, who didn't fawn over her or try to ingratiate himself with excessively courteous sentiments.

Mr. McCormick hadn't been awed by the grandeur of the Portman Square house or daunted by the lofty company he'd found himself in, either. He was a plain-spoken man, from what Caro had seen, who wouldn't scrape and bow if he did not believe the person in front of him deserved it.

Caro found him refreshing, but Jo apparently did not know what to think.

"What did you rush into the house to tell me?" Caro asked. "It must be important, to risk Singleton's ire."

"Singleton is a sweet man, and we both know it." Jo's dimples returned as she scooted closer to Caro and locked her arm through hers. "I came to find out what happened when you disappeared with your Mr. Stone last night. Merry told me," she explained when Caro drew a startled breath. "I didn't have a chance to speak to you after Lady Carmichael took you as her prisoner."

"I was grateful to her," Caro said. "She spared me much unpleasantness. She is another friend I now know is true."

"You are evading the question with your usual adroitness. Tell me *everything*. Merry said she led Mr. Stone to the room where you were hiding and that you were alone together in there for quite some time."

Caro's face flamed so fiery hot that Jo burst into peals of laughter.

Caro knew Jo would not release her until her curiosity was fulfilled, so she tried to sketch what had happened in that room in a few short sentences while revealing as little as possible. In the end, however, she found herself leaning on Jo's shoulder, confessing the elation that had seared her at Eamon's touch.

"I am glad, darling." Jo stroked Caro's hair. Caro's lacy cap, which she'd neatly pinned on this morning, had come all the way loose and now lay in her lap. "You deserve some passion in your life. Will you have an *affaire de coeur* with him, as Merry suggested?"

The question was put quietly, with no eagerness, a friend asking what decisions Caro would make.

Caro popped her head up. "An affair? It was only a kiss. Hardly worthy of an operatic drama."

"Mr. Stone is a man," Jo said in a reasonable tone. "A handsome one, yes, but a man all the same. A gentleman either wishes to marry a woman or be her lover. As Mr. Stone is not wealthy, he likely will not propose. But he might agree to a liaison."

"You are very cool." Caro regarded her friend in surprise. "When Leopold courted me, you couldn't contain your excitement, saying you knew he'd marry me. He was in straitened circumstances as well."

"Yes, but Leopold was a duke, and you were an unmarried miss. Now you are a widow, and Mr. Stone is an intriguing but penniless gentleman."

"He has made no mention of a liaison," Caro said, flustered. "It sounds quite temporary, in any case. What would be left of my reputation if he made me his lover and then disappeared?"

The practical part of her mind said this, but the emotional side was all aquiver. To be Eamon's lover would be astonishing, glorious, a brief moment of happiness in Caro's drab life.

"Nonsense," Jo said with adamance. "We both know lovers

who have been devoted to each other for years and years. There is Lord Carew and Mrs. Watkins, for example."

Jo named two prominent members of the *ton* who, both widowed, had been together for so long that everyone thought of them as married, though they were not. They'd met when very young, had been forced into different marriages by ambitious parents, and still managed to be together in the end.

"They are in their eighties," Caro reminded Jo. "It was more permissible in their day to carry on outside of wedlock."

"They weren't always in their eighties." Jo grinned. "Mama remembers them from when she was a girl. They were quite naughty, she says, and I say, good for them. Then there is the Prince Regent and Mrs. Fitzherbert."

"Who are highly scandalous," Caro argued. "And the Regent has taken other mistresses besides her. Even though he's married to poor Princess Caroline."

"But they were still devoted, at first." Jo waved gloved hands. "Never mind. I am trying to explain that a liaison needn't be temporary. You could live out the rest of your life surrounded by admiration and passion, doted on by a handsome gentleman with very blue eyes. They are quite nice, his eyes."

Jo's tone turned appreciative, and Caro felt a puzzling dart of jealousy. Why should she mind if Jo thought Eamon attractive?

"This is all building castles in the air." Caro pretended to revert to her sensible self. "It was one kiss. Well, a series of kisses."

Jo's smile deepened. "So you said. My question is, what are you going to do about it?"

"Nothing at all. What do you expect me to do? Follow Mr. Stone through the halls and entice him into more kissing?"

Caro's imagination took flight even as she spoke. She pictured herself coming upon Eamon as he poured through a dusty book in the shadows of the gallery. He'd smile his warm smile, set aside the book and encircle her in his arms. His skilled lips would caress hers, and his hands would find the laces and catches of her bodice, as they had last night, his touch burning her once more.

Caro sucked in a breath, forcing herself back to the cool blue room and Jo's knowing gaze.

"Ah, you *are* thinking of it." Jo nodded. "Why not?"

"When have you become such a coquette?" Caro lifted her cap and fanned herself with the thin fabric.

"I have always been. But I am not allowed liaisons or flirtations or even a dance to satisfy my heart." Jo's words turned bitter. "I must live through you and Louise, and Louise is not likely to have a liaison for the rest of her life, she has retreated so far into her shell. So, you must enjoy yourself, because we cannot."

"That is ridiculous." Caro sprang up to pace. "Anyway, I cannot enjoy myself. I must be an upright, perfect mother to Leo, because his cousin will take him away from me in a heartbeat if I am not." Her voice broke in the end, her worry crashing into her once more.

"What?" Jo rose, her levity falling away. "What has the diabolical Rudyard done now?"

Caro could not stop herself from pouring out her fears to Jo, her body tight, her throat aching. Her friend listened, as indignant on Caro's behalf as she had been excited for her a few minutes earlier.

"We will not let him." Jo moved resolutely to Caro and slid an arm around her waist. "I will tell my father, and he and my mother will rally behind you. Papa will find you all the legal advice you can possibly stomach."

"You are kind." Caro sagged into Jo's half embrace. "I will do everything I can to stop Rudyard, but I am so afraid. If Leo is taken from me, I don't know how I will stand it."

Caro had borne up stoically when her parents had died a few

years after her marriage, and she had borne up again when the *haut ton* had scathingly disapproved of her marrying he Duke of Aylesmore. She'd also remained strong when Leopold had breathed his last, and again when the creditors had descended, and the staff had deserted her.

But if Rudyard had the courts snatch Leo from her, Caro would never survive it. Nothing would mend her heart if she lost her little boy.

Jo was sweet to offer help, but while Prince Rupert was a powerful man in his own way, he wasn't British, and the haughty judges in the courts might pay no attention to him or his solicitors.

Eamon said he'd help as well, but again, Caro had little conviction that he could. Not against the might of the judiciary, combined with Rudyard's family connections and standing.

She laid her head on her smaller friend's shoulder and let Jo try to comfort her, squeezing her eyes tightly against the tears that threatened to shatter her.

"It's a mess, isn't it?" McCormick said bluntly.

Eamon and his friend surveyed the massive bookcases, from which Eamon had pulled volumes here and there, shaken out pages, and perused books that appeared interesting. He'd tried to keep the stacks neat, but that had proved impossible. This corner of the gallery looked as though it had been struck by a very small tornado.

Leo, who'd been responsible for some of the chaos, had gone upstairs to study, reluctantly, at his mother's insistence, conveyed through Singleton.

McCormick had come to cast his practiced eyes over the books. Though he'd intended to speak to Caro beforehand, to ask her permission to invade her house, Caro hadn't reappeared. He and Eamon had made a start while the ladies remained upstairs.

"Any book might be valuable," Eamon said. "The duke's organization was, shall we say, haphazard. Cheap junk next to nice tomes that might fetch a quid or two from a decent bookseller. The man didn't know the difference. The duchess says he bought what he liked without understanding what he'd obtained."

"I meant the entire situation." McCormick leaned against a long table. "Piles of this stuff, most of it worthless. A lifetime of being swindled."

"The Aylesmore dukes weren't wise, no," Eamon said in some frustration.

"More like bloody fools. Dukes are supposed to be wealthy beyond measure. How does all of that slip away?" McCormick glanced down the long gallery to the massive staircase in wonder.

"It happens if they make unwise investments," Eamon said. "Or neglect to go to court to retain rights over certain lands. Not all land and personal property is entailed, and entails can be broken or not renewed."

McCormick blew out a breath. "Too complicated for me. Math should be pure numbers, not mucked up with money and law."

"Pure numbers." Eamon grinned at him. "That's why you taught the artillery about trajectories and Wellington how to strategically move his men and equipment."

"Different altogether," McCormick insisted. "What did you want my opinion on?"

"I'm not as versed in rare books as you or Wolfe. I don't want to miss anything in the dross that might bring Caro some needed cash."

McCormick's brows climbed. "*Caro*, is it? You've moved on from *Duchess*, have you?"

Sam Noble had said much the same thing. Eamon's cheeks warmed at his slip, but he shrugged. "She's a real person, not the sort who waves her status in one's face."

"Which means she's kinder to you than you deserve." McCormick chuckled. "If you're still on about that wager, I advise you to look elsewhere. Leave the poor lass alone."

"Shall we change the subject?" Eamon's voice cooled. "I'll not pursue her because of a wager, don't worry. She is worth far more than that."

"Mm." McCormick watched him with more understanding than Eamon liked. "Her Grace is very close with the lively princess, is she?"

"Very dear friends." Eamon lost his annoyance. "If you're thinking of winning our wager in *that* direction, you are more deluded than I am."

He had the enjoyment of seeing McCormick grow uncomfortable. "Never crossed my mind."

McCormick was a brilliant man but a very bad liar. Eamon knew he was a fool to show interest in Caro, but Josephine of Osagard was royalty without doubt, far out of the reach of a gentleman farmer's son from the remote north.

Eamon joined McCormick at the table, leaning next to him and folding his arms.

"There might be a gem in that stack of muck," Eamon said, gazing at the books around them. "Maybe we'll be as lucky with that as we are at love."

McCormick shot him a dark look. "In that case, we'll never find a bloody thing."

Eamon had to laugh at his cynicism, but he secretly agreed. It hurt that McCormick was right, but Eamon was unfortunately used to living with pain.

———

CARA ACCOMPANIED JO DOWNSTAIRS WHEN SHE TOOK HER LEAVE. The two had visited with the dowager, who was very fond of Jo, and then Leo, happy for the respite from his studies. Caro relented at Leo's downcast face and told him he could rejoin Mr. Stone after he read three more pages.

Mr. McCormick must have gone, because Caro did not see him in the gallery when she and Jo descended past it. Jo, Caro noted, craned to peer into every corner as they went by.

Eamon stood in the gallery alone, studying a book that lay open on the long table before him. He gave them both a polite nod, and Caro hurried Jo along.

"Goodbye, dearest." Jo kissed Caro's cheek after Singleton had opened the front door and signaled for Jo's coachman to approach. "I promise that Papa and I will rally 'round and keep Rudyard from the door."

"You are too good to me." Caro returned the kiss, pressing her friend's hands.

Jo skimmed across the three feet of pavement between front door and coach, to be assisted into her carriage by two footmen, one who'd placed a stool on the ground for her to step on.

The footmen shut Jo inside, gathered up the footstool, and nimbly sprang to their posts on the coach. Caro waved as the carriage clattered away.

"Tell Mrs. Mulligan a light supper will do for tonight," Caro told Singleton as he shut the door. Her emotions had been spent today, and she believed she could eat no more than a thin soup. Mrs. Mulligan always sent up something tasty, however, so that resolve might change.

"Yes, Your Grace." Singleton hesitated. "Shall I have her prepare something for Mr. Stone? He often works on his notes until well after dark."

Caro had been aware that Eamon lingered in the gallery until late—she'd heard the front door shut and watched out of her window as he'd walked away around Grosvenor Square, heading for Oxford Street in the dark.

Singleton must approve of Eamon if he was offering to bring him a repast.

"If he requires it," Caro said. "Thank you, Singleton."

Singleton gave her his butler's nod and departed for his demesne.

A squeal of laughter above her made Caro hurry to the staircase.

She looked up to see her son, seated on the wide banister high above, sliding swiftly down toward the gallery. Eamon leapt lightly down the steps next to him, hands outstretched to steady him. Leo spied Caro below and waved wildly at her.

He teetered, lost his balance, and pitched forward.

CHAPTER 17

*C*aro shrieked and dashed up the staircase. Before her heart could burst from her chest, Eamon was there, catching Leo in his strong arms.

Leo laughed with delight and hugged Eamon before Eamon set him gently on the carpeted step.

"Mama!" Leo raced to Caro, seizing her hand and dragging her to Eamon. "Look what Mr. Stone taught me."

"I saw." Caro tried to put a stern note into her words. In spite of her jolt of panic, though, Leo's joy was wonderful to hear. "Mr. Stone should not have. It is too dangerous, do you not think?"

She directed the last words at Eamon, accompanied by a glare.

"He caught me," Leo said without worry. "I knew I wouldn't fall. Want to see me do it again?"

Leo prepared to charge to the next floor, but Caro held him back. "Maybe later, love. Why don't you go down to the kitchen and ask Mrs. Mulligan for some bread and jam? It will be some time before supper."

Leo gave a little hop of delight. "Mrs. Mulligan always gives me heaps of jam," he informed Eamon. "With scones, too. All I want. She says I need them because I'm growing so fast."

"Indeed, you are." Caro noted every month that her boy was a bit taller and a bit stronger. It gave her pride but also a little wistfulness.

"Go on, then," Eamon said. "Scones and jam are not to be missed."

Leo turned impulsively to Eamon, gave him a brief hug around his knees, then scampered past Caro and down to the ground floor. The backstairs door banged, Leo's hurried footsteps sounding on the wooden stairs below it.

Caro faced Eamon. She hadn't missed his surprise when Leo had hugged him, plus the gratitude mixed with melancholy that had flitted across his face.

"The lad was in no danger, I assure you," Eamon said before Caro could speak. "I'd never have let him fall."

Caro believed him. Eamon had shown so far that with Leo, he was gentleness itself.

"Sliding down the banister?" Caro arched her brows, trying to sound severe.

"Yours are perfect for it." Eamon patted the railing that led to the next floor. "Wide and flat, for a swift, smooth ride. Unlikely you'd fall." He grew serious. "I promise you, I had hold of him all the time, Caro. I'd never let him be hurt."

Again, Caro believed him, and it gave her a cozy feeling that she could.

"Why on earth did he want to do something so bizarre?" Caro demanded. "Leo's never shown a longing to use the railings as a means of descent before."

Eamon's cheeks reddened. "Because he saw me do it first."

"Oh?"

She enjoyed watching his discomfiture. Eamon tried to look dignified but dissolved into shamefaced laughter.

"I was a champion banister-slider as a boy. As I said, when

my father dragged me to various country houses, I had little to do. I could only read or look at paintings so long." Eamon shrugged. "No one was about once McCormick departed, and I thought I was unobserved. But Leo saw, and he begged me for a lesson. I couldn't say no."

"You could have tried," Caro said.

Eamon shook his head. "Impossible. He makes such a sad face when he's disappointed. It breaks my heart."

"I know." Caro found it difficult to resist Leo anything when he was crestfallen. The dowager claimed he'd be spoiled beyond redemption. At the same time, the dowager slipped him an extra bit of cream in his tea or a penny from her pocket when she thought Caro wasn't looking.

Eamon opened his hands in a helpless gesture. "He had me cornered. I had to surrender."

"Show me," Caro said on impulse.

Eamon's eyes widened. "Pardon?"

"Show me how you were a champion banister-slider. You shouldn't make such claims unless they are true."

Eamon stared at her, then sent her an impish grin before he dashed up the stairs to the floor above.

He lifted the tails of his coat, giving Caro a view of a trim backside and muscular thighs in close-fitting trousers, before he hopped to sit on the banister, his right leg crooked over it.

He glided down with grace, picking up speed as he descended. Just before he reached the newel post at the flight's end, he leapt off, landing agilely on his feet next to Caro. Eamon executed a bow, and she applauded.

"I admit, you do it grandly," Caro said.

Eamon drew a deep breath, hands on hips. "I am out of condition. Going soft, taking my ease after army life." He gestured to the railing. "Try it."

Caro started. "Try what? Taking my ease after army life?"

"You amuse me, Duchess. I mean sliding down the banister."

Excitement tingled through her. Caro hadn't felt such an impulse since her debutante days, when life stretched before her, all things possible. Before the *ton* had censured her for marrying above her, before life had taken away the illusion of stability in which her husband had cloaked her.

"I could not," Caro said, but hesitantly. "I am a widow, elderly and dignified."

"You are a young woman who confines herself too much. Your visitors are gone, Singleton is downstairs with Leo, and the dowager is upstairs. Who is to see?"

"What about the gentleman we hired from Cheswell's gallery?" Caro asked. "He is here before me. What would he think?"

"He'd be happy you were at last taking some pleasure in your life." Eamon held out his hand. "I will steady you all the way, as I did your son."

A wave of daring washed over her. Caro hadn't done anything so audacious since she'd danced with a handsome dandy soon after her debut, against her mother's wishes. Her mother had been right, of course, as the gentleman had turned out to be a capricious philanderer, but the brief sensation of the forbidden had been heady.

But no, she'd been plenty audacious at the ball, dancing with Eamon in front of half of polite society instead of remaining decorously against the wall. She'd been audacious when she'd not fled from the sitting room where Eamon had found her, when she'd let her fingers explore the fascinating planes of his body.

That abrupt need for wildness took hold and would not release her. Caro put her hand in Eamon's, swallowing a wash of yearning as he closed his over it.

Eamon did not seem to notice her sudden elation. He led her up the stairs to the next landing and patted the railing. "Your chariot awaits, my lady."

Caro eyed the wide banister, which, if truth be told, she'd pictured herself riding down on more than one occasion.

"I cannot possibly leap up there as you did," she said. "I did not rush about ridges in the war, leaping streams and evading soldiers."

"No streams were leapt." Eamon's voice rumbled tantalizingly close. "My wet boots and cold feet attested to that. But no fear, Duchess. I will assist."

Before Caro could argue, Eamon closed his hands around her waist and lifted her easily to the banister.

Caro clung to his shoulders as she sensed the empty air behind her. "Perhaps this is not such a good idea," she said quickly.

"I'll not let you fall, my duchess."

Caro gazed at him, standing so close, his eyes deep blue and holding mysteries. His hands on her waist were strong and sure. They'd been thus in the upstairs chamber in Jo's house, when he'd kissed her …

"I know you won't," she whispered.

Eamon's eyes darkened, a spark of desire in their depths. He'd kiss her here and now, she sensed. Caro wouldn't stop him— she'd hold onto him and kiss him back with all her might, never mind that Singleton or her son might reappear at any moment.

Her heart stung when Eamon retreated slightly, though he didn't release her.

"Off we go, Duchess."

His hold loosened, but only enough to start her sliding along the railing, her skirts fluttering. Caro whooped as she picked up speed, torn between terror and delight.

Eamon steadied her all the way. He descended the stairs beside her, hands on her waist, guiding her down to the newel post. When they reached it, Eamon quickly lifted her off the banister and set her down, unhurt and exhilarated.

Caro laughed out loud, her merriment ringing through the stairwell. She tried to pat her loosened hair into place, her hands shaking.

"Can we go again?" she heard herself ask.

Once ought to be enough. Caro should put her skirts to rights, beg Eamon to tell no one of her indignity, and retreat upstairs to her correspondence.

"Of course," Eamon answered readily.

He took her hand, and they ascended the stairs at a run. This time, Eamon hopped onto the railing first.

"We'll go together. Shall we?" Eamon held out one arm, encouraging Caro to step into its circle.

Without hesitation, Caro did. Eamon lifted her the short distance to his lap, steadying her with his enclosing embrace and wrapping a strong leg around hers.

It was an intimate position, and one that should embarrass her, but Caro felt only exhilaration.

This was followed by a burst of alarm as they hurtled down the railing, but Eamon kept them secure. Caro shouted for the joy of it.

Even with Eamon guiding them, the newel post came up very fast. Caro yelped as they neared it, only to find Eamon lifting her off the railing at the last second.

They both lost their balance, feet tangling as Caro fought to remain upright. Eamon grabbed for the post, but their combined weight took them down.

The gallery's carpeted floor rushed toward her, then Caro found herself falling onto the strong body of Eamon, he cushioning her fall.

One stunned moment of silence followed, and then they both burst into laughter.

Lying on Eamon's chest, feeling his body shaking with mirth, released something in Caro. Nothing mattered in this instant but the silliness they'd engaged in, and the knowledge that Eamon had caught her as he'd promised.

It felt only natural to kiss him.

Their laughter abruptly ceased as Eamon's arms came around her. The hall went still, the only sound the rumble of carriages outside the high windows and the rushing in Caro's ears.

The giddy passion that had swept through her in the small room in Portman Square returned as she deepened the kiss, tasting his mouth. Their tongues tangled, Caro's need, too long suppressed, breaking forth.

She surrendered to it. She traced Eamon's face with shaking fingers, skimmed them through his thick hair. His heart banged beneath hers, and their legs were entwined as they'd fallen, only the clothes between them keeping things decorous. Caro felt the strength in his thighs, and the hardness that meant he was as aroused as she was.

There was no chance of fulfilling their longings in the middle of the gallery's landing, but wicked ideas formed in Caro's head of how it might be done.

For now, they were gloriously alone. She would hear Singleton or Leo returning from below stairs in plenty of time to avoid disgrace, and the dowager rarely descended below the fourth floor.

Caro could lie here and kiss Eamon as long as she liked, for no other reason than she enjoyed it.

Eamon skimmed his hands up her body and caressed her neck, loosening her already straggling hair. He nipped at her tongue, smiling when she pretended to elude him, then tugged her back down for a deeper kiss.

When their lips eased apart again, Eamon traced her cheek.

"You are beautiful, my duchess."

"I am a mess." Caro touched his face, liking the rough bristles that brushed her fingertips. "I've never been tidy, as a girl or a matron."

"You don't need to be." Eamon kissed a dangling lock. "Beauty doesn't come from neatness. It comes from here." He placed his hand between her breasts, right over her thumping heart. "It beams from you, Caro."

"You are very flattering." Caro let herself be bold. "And quite handsome, if you must know."

"Ah, she approves of me." Eamon kept his hand where it was. "The time I spend at my toilette has repaid me."

"Don't be silly. You are hardly a dandy. Not immaculately coiffed and in a suit that barely lets you move, thank heavens." Caro drew her fingers over Eamon's lips, their smooth contrast to his whiskery face pleasing. "I prefer a person to look like who they truly are."

"I could look like no other than myself," Eamon said softly.

"I am glad." Caro kissed the tip of his nose. "I prefer you exactly as you appear, Mr. Eamon Stone. Truly handsome, and more kindhearted than you know."

Eamon stilled, something darkening in his eyes.

"Oh, Duchess," he said softly. "I believe I'm falling in love with you."

Caro jerked in surprise, and she drew a sharp breath. "In love …"

The words shocked her at the same time they bathed her in incredible joy. To have such a man look at her with heat in his eyes and declare that he loved her …

She had no idea what to say or do. Caro could only stare at him in stunned silence, unable to form words to respond.

Eamon went rigid under her, a scowl obliterating his warmth. "Damnation." He heaved himself out from under Caro, pulling her to her feet at the same time he rolled to his. "Damn it all to hell."

Caro parted her lips to apologize, or whatever she ought to

say, but Eamon advanced on her swiftly, quieting her with a fierce, hard kiss.

The kiss bruised, commanded. Caro sought breath and couldn't find it, but it didn't matter. The kiss shattered her, even more than his declaration had, her body on fire.

Eamon broke the kiss as abruptly as he began it. He fixed her with a hard gaze for a long moment before he turned away and stormed down the stairs. Singleton had hung his things in the lower hall, and Caro watched over the banisters as Eamon snatched these up and disappeared into the foyer, shrugging on his coat.

She hurried to the front window of the gallery, reaching it in time to see Eamon burst out of the house and tramp away, settling his coat and clapping on his hat as he went. He moved northward around the square, soon lost to sight behind trees, carts, and wagons.

Caro hung onto the windowsill and watched him go, the tear in her heart growing wider with every one of his strides.

CHAPTER 18

Damnation, damnation, damnation. Eamon berated himself with every step as he made for Oxford Street.

Of all the stupid, ill-conceived, miscalculating things he could have said, Eamon had to let the word *love* slip from his lips.

Caro had stared at him in utter shock. So still had been her face that Eamon couldn't determine if she'd been pleased, outraged, or just surprised that the man literally beneath her feet had been presumptuous enough to fall in love with her.

Eamon, priding himself on reading people within a few seconds of meeting them, hadn't been able to discern her thoughts at all in that terrible moment.

He'd found himself a soft job in a comfortable house with a vast collection and the pleasure of conversing with Caro and her son while he assessed it. All Eamon had to do was comb through the chaff and find a few pieces of art worth flogging. He'd sell the things, hand Caro the money, receive his commission from Cheswell, and be done.

Instead, he'd danced with Caro in a crowded ballroom,

kissed and touched her, and then declared himself like a fool in a ridiculous melodrama.

Eamon couldn't decide whether she'd been about to slap him or call Singleton to show him the door, so he'd saved her the bother of both.

Cheswell could send someone else to finish cataloging the artwork, and Eamon would bow out. He'd do something about that Rembrandt he'd found in Clive's warehouse to help Caro and Leo, but stay far, far away from the pair of them.

Any more time tumbling Caro's hair, kissing her mouth, or even being in her presence would destroy him.

He'd pretended to his friends that the asinine wager, made in a moment they all thought they might die, drove him to pursue her, but that had been an excuse.

Caro had delighted him from the very first, when he'd found her struggling to open that damned window. Eamon had told Wolfe he'd assumed her an upstairs maid, but he'd known she was not—his powers of observation weren't so far gone as that.

No, he'd pretended Caro wasn't a lofty duchess, far out of his reach, so that Eamon could indulge his senses and be close to her. He'd let the fact that her father and his had occupied the same class comfort him into believing they were alike.

But they were not. Eamon's father and Caro's might have shared the same level of birth, but Caro's father had been a respectable gentleman, while Sir Benedict had turned into an outright charlatan. He'd no more deserved his knighthood than the lowliest criminal in the streets of St. Giles.

Caro needed someone in her life who would comfort and bolster her as well as be a good father to Leo. She didn't need a man who was little better than an art forger and a confidence trickster himself to pull her into the gutter.

A connection with Eamon might ruin Caro utterly.

He also knew his virtuous thoughts about taking himself away from Caro for her own good was bollocks. Eamon had fled the house because he knew he'd not be able to stop himself if he stayed in there with her.

He wanted Caro with a madness he'd thought he could suppress. As a lad, his youthful passions had been difficult to manage, but war and maturity had conquered them, or so he'd told himself.

Caro had proved Eamon wrong about that. He'd only been numbed by war and survival, convincing himself that *he* suppressed his basic needs at will.

That was before he met Caro.

Now Eamon could think of nothing but her, dreamed of her in the night when he wasn't awake, longing for her. He wanted Caro in his bed, and in his life.

What underhanded deeds would Eamon undertake to get her there? Already the wheels Sir Benedict had oiled in him were turning, suggesting scenarios where Eamon would conquer Caro and bring her running to him.

Best for everyone that he stayed the hell out of her life.

"Damnation," he said again, this time out loud and explosively.

Passers-by on Oxford Street stared, but Eamon ignored them and strode on, awash in his own pain.

———

FOUR EXCRUCIATING DAYS LATER, EAMON RAN WOLFE TO GROUND at Gentleman Jackson's boxing rooms, where Wolfe regularly went to exercise his injured leg. The limb had healed enough for him to walk with only a slight limp and dance in a simple country set if it wasn't too vigorous, but he needed a training regime to keep his muscles hard.

"Where the bloody hell have you been?" was Wolfe's greeting to him.

In shirtsleeves and light-colored breeches, Wolfe braced

himself on a bench, repeatedly lifting his left leg, which had an iron weight strapped to it.

"Tearing about London like a madman, trying to fix things." Eamon plopped onto the bench next to Wolfe and accepted the pot of ale an attendant brought him.

In the center of the room, two spindly, middle-aged men tried to master jabs under Jackson's tutelage. All attention was on them, leaving Eamon and Wolfe relatively alone at the wall.

"You won't fix anything in this benighted city," Wolfe growled. "I never realized, when I was a boy, what a pleasure it was to ride through the countryside for hours, never seeing another living soul."

"Yes, our childhoods were idyllic." Eamon nodded sagely. "That is why they shut us away in Hallbridge, the school for troublesome lads no one knew what to do with."

"Mm." Wolfe closed his eyes while he continued to lift his leg. He grimaced against the strain. "By the bye, I saw the Viking the other day."

"Oh?" Eamon asked without much interest. Nothing piqued his curiosity these days except who Clive did business with and how, and how much chance Rudyard had to gain custody of Leo. "Is he still enormous and thick-headed?"

"Even more so." Wolfe gave a final grunt and set his weighted foot on the floor. "About ten feet tall and bulging with muscle. He hailed me like a long, lost friend and wanted a chat about the old days. Reminiscing on what fun we had together as lads."

"Strange how fistfights to the near death appear as larks to some, twenty years on," Eamon mused. "I spied a French veteran and an English one in a pub the other night, reliving the battle at Salamanca as though it had been a sporting country outing. Jolly good fun." He finished the statement dryly and took a sip of ale.

"You are in a mood." Wolfe unbuckled the weight and eased

it from his leg in relief. "Where is your ever-chirpy and annoying cheerfulness?"

"In the gutter, with my dignity." Eamon leaned his back against the wall. He knew he could pour out his troubles to Wolfe, who would grumble and growl but listen sympathetically at the same time. However, Eamon was already tired of self-pity. "What do you know about Rudyard Berridge? First cousin to the current Duke of Aylesmore and his sole heir?"

"That little oik?" Wolfe asked in surprise. "What is your interest, besides the connection to your duchess?"

Eamon told him, in a few brief sentences, what Cousin Rudyard was up to. "Can he do it?" Eamon finished.

Wolfe nodded with a scowl. "Possibly he can, unless the young duke's mother can prove the lad is better off with *her*."

"The law will favor the cousin, oik or no," Eamon said glumly. "I've concluded that the best way we can keep Leo at home where he belongs is to make it clear that Rudyard is the worst possible person to care for him."

Wolfe shot him a glance. "We?"

"I need to borrow your solicitor, if you don't mind. My father's could prove day was night if he had to, but he's oily, and I need a gentleman with an impeccable reputation. A judge might believe *your* man if he helps us prove that Rudyard is a terrible person."

"I don't know why you bother asking me," Wolfe said. "My man of business already had an inquiry from an art dealer asking if I could be trusted. Kennedy assured him that I could be, but since I've not spoken to a dealer since before Waterloo, we both concluded that the gentleman being asked about must have been you."

"Kind of Kennedy to recommend me," Eamon said with true gratitude. "I ask you so that your solicitor will answer my questions without turning me coldly away."

"You are a bloody nuisance, Stone." Wolfe shook his head. "My first pact with you got my face bashed in."

"I recall you holding your own quite well." Eamon shook his head. "I can't let Leo go to that idiot. It will be the death of the boy."

"You think Berridge would go that far?"

"I do," Eamon said grimly. "Cousin Rudyard wants the dukedom and has the look of a man who will do anything to get it."

"We won't let him then. My solicitor shall be at your service."

"Good man." Eamon relaxed in relief. "I also need to purchase a Rembrandt. A genuine one. Anything you invest in it will be paid back out of its sale."

Wolfe's look of sympathy dissolved. "What the devil are you going on about now?"

Eamon explained about Clive, his shop, and the Rembrandt in the back. "He wants five thousand, but I can talk him down to something more reasonable."

"You're certain it's the one from Aylesmore's collection?"

"Positive. He diddled them out of it somehow. If I can restore the painting to Leo and then arrange for a proper sale, the Duchess of Aylesmore can pay off some of the family's debts."

Wolfe's eyes narrowed. "The Duchess of Aylesmore? Not *Caro* this time?"

"No." Eamon blew out a breath and drained the rest of the ale. "I am a wretched man, my friend. A wretched, wretched man."

"You must do it," Jo insisted. "Mustn't she, Louise?"

Caro set down her delicately thin porcelain teacup and surveyed her friends. Louise had summoned Caro to her home in Berkeley Square, where Jo had joined them for a repast in Louise's tastefully elegant drawing room.

All things Louise had a hand in were tastefully elegant. One would never guess what a madcap child she'd been, taking her two followers on reckless adventures through the woods of Hampshire. Her father had been the local magistrate, and Louise had not only known where all the poachers and thieves dwelled, she'd befriended them.

There was little of the wild girl in this young woman who held her teacup in fine-boned fingers and observed her friends with serene blue eyes. Her late husband, the Earl of Heyford, had been a subdued man, and Louise had calmed herself for him.

"My dear friends," Caro tried. "If Mr. Stone has no more interest in cataloging the collection, then he does not. He sent a very polite letter to me, and one separately to Leo, explaining that his duties are taking him elsewhere. He suggested I have his friend Mr. McCormick look over the library for valuable books, and I will, if we can agree on a fee."

She strove to hide how much Eamon's missives hurt. Leo was most unhappy as well. Caro had forced aside her own distress to comfort him, explaining that Eamon's time was not always his own.

Caro knew full well why he'd gone, and now Louise and Jo had learned the entire tale.

Jo reached slender silver tongs to the sugar bowl and dropped another ragged chunk of sugar into her tea. She'd done so at least five times already.

"Darling Caro, a man does not declare himself and then simply depart and never return. He must be laboring under the misapprehension that you did not like his attentions." Jo slurped her overly sweet tea, made a face, and hastily set down the cup.

"I believe he immensely regrets saying anything at all," Caro said gloomily.

She'd stared at Eamon as though he'd lost his mind when he'd used the word *love*. He must have concluded he'd offended her beyond forgiveness, and took himself away before Caro could think of a thing to say.

She'd rehearsed her apology to him all that sleepless night, planning to deliver it the next morning, but Friday came and went, and Eamon did not return. On Saturday, she and Leo had both received letters from him expressing his apologies and explaining he'd not be back.

Caro had wavered between rage at him for deserting them and abject pain tinged with emptiness.

She'd written to Louise, telling her of the entire incident, knowing Louise would be discreet. Then came the summons to Berkeley Square. Caro had arrived this afternoon to find Jo already present. Louise had relayed Caro's troubles to her, and the two of them had come up with a plan to bring Eamon back.

"Inviting him to dine, to discuss where he left off his cataloging is natural," Louise said. "Your mother-in-law will be there, because she will want to know his findings as well."

"He left his notebooks," Caro said wistfully. They'd been lying on one of the tables in the gallery, written in Eamon's neat hand, with lists of paintings, small sculptures, books, and objets d'art. Caro had traced the lines of his writing, closing her eyes and feeling his last, furious kiss.

"Then he'll be wanting them," Jo said, breaking into her thoughts. "It is a perfect excuse for you to ask him to explain his notations to you. Alone, after the meal. All very businesslike, is it not? Then you can tell him how much you've been pining for him."

"I will say no such thing," Caro snatched up her teacup. "Pining, indeed." Which was exactly what she was doing, and she knew it.

"Best to clear it all up," Louise said in her quiet voice. "Even if he regrets his declaration, things ought to be easy between you. You need Mr. Stone's expertise, and he needs the post. If nothing else, you should remain friends, especially as Leo is so taken with him."

Jo regarded Louise with disappointment. "Friends? No, no, Caro needs a passionate and deeply satisfying affair. She deserves such a thing, after being a martyr for so long."

"I haven't been a martyr," Caro said in surprise.

Jo heaved an exasperated sigh. "Really, the pair of you. When we were girls, Caro proclaimed she'd marry a handsome devil who swept her off her feet and took her around the world, experiencing one excitement after another. Leopold was a sweet man, and I truly liked him, but he was hardly that. He stayed home and read moldy books."

"He made Caro happy," Louise broke in with indignation. "Having a gentleman relentlessly drag you around the world isn't what makes a contented marriage. Caro would soon have been exhausted and longing for home."

Caro wasn't certain she agreed. With the right person, such a life could be exhilarating.

Why was it Eamon's arm she pictured herself on while they moved through the ballrooms of Paris and the spa towns of Bavaria?

Jo turned to Louise. "*You* planned to disguise yourself as a man and ride from one end of Europe to the other with the gentleman of your dreams. You rode as far as Berkshire, in a carriage, moved into a dark, rambling house, and never came out again."

"Of course I came out again," Louise said in annoyance. "Do not exaggerate. I hosted gatherings, both in Berkshire and London, before Geoff ..."

Louise faltered, and Caro reached to clasp her hand. Geoffrey Collett, Earl of Heyford, had been very much a country gentleman, more interested in running his farm than frivolities. He'd been happy for Louise to indulge in soirees and supper balls while they were in London for the Season, but he'd kept to his clubs, hurrying them both back to Berkshire as soon as he was able.

Though Caro and Jo had found Geoff at bit staid—even more staid than Leopold—Louise had been deliriously in love with him. Geoff had fallen ill and died far too young, barely into his fortieth year. His physicians had blamed his fondness for wandering through marshy ground for hours on end, breathing fetid air, for his final illness.

Whatever had happened, Louise had taken a long time to recover from the blow. She'd been a widow for five years now and hadn't yet put aside half mourning.

"Forgive me, darling," Jo said quickly. "I know you loved dear Geoff and love him still."

"I do." Louise nodded at both Jo and Caro, as though signaling she was well, but Caro knew better. "My point is the three of us talked a lot of nonsense when we were younger. Caro and I discovered that married life is less of a whirlwind than we imagined, but also worthwhile. You will see yourself one day," Louise finished with a glance at Jo.

"Do not cast my spinsterhood up to me." Jo seized her tea and took a gulp. "Oh, dear, when did I put so much sugar in this? I will be alone well into my dotage, and you know it."

"You will not," Louise said firmly. "Your family will one day admit a gentleman past the barriers, as they did for your sister, and he'll be perfect for you. You'll be besotted."

Jo sent her a stare so skeptical it confirmed where her niece Merry had learned the expression. "You are sweet, Louise, but they never will. Sutcliffe was allowed for my sister because he hasn't the imagination to pose any danger to my parents. I have given up forming any sort of interest in a man at all."

Caro recalled Jo's flustered demeanor when she'd dashed into Mr. McCormick and her long gaze at him over the banister afterward and decided Jo's last statement wasn't true.

"In any case, you both are mad," Caro said. "Even if I invite Mr. Stone so that I can apologize and make certain we part friends, he will never come. He is finished with the Aylesmore family."

Jo and Louise exchanged a glance that said much, but to Caro's relief, they finally changed the subject.

———

HOURS LATER, CARO RETURNED HOME, CONSULTED WITH THE dowager, and wrote Eamon a letter. She started and discarded the missive half a dozen times, lamenting at wasting so much costly paper. Finally, she managed a few simple lines inviting him to dine at eight o'clock in the evening on Monday next.

She made herself fold the sheet and address it to Mr. Eamon Stone, care of Cheswell's.

He wouldn't come, Caro told herself once she had sent Singleton off to deliver the letter. She'd hear nothing more of Eamon, and she would have to live with that.

The next morning, however, Singleton brought her a note that had been penned on the bottom of the one Caro had sent the previous afternoon. Her heart beat thickly as she unfolded the paper and read the simple message:

I will be honored to attend.

E. Stone

CHAPTER 19

*E*amon arrived at the Grosvenor Street house exactly on time. He'd debated turning up early, as McCormick suggested, to appear reliable, but Wolfe told McCormick he was an idiot. Eamon should arrive late, so as not to seem too keen.

Eamon claimed they were both idiots and knocked on the front door at the stroke of eight.

Singleton answered it after letting him sweat for half a minute, peering down his bulbous nose at Eamon when he opened the door.

"Is it to be the blue reception room?" Eamon asked as he stepped into the silent house. The hall was dark, though the sun lingered in the late May sky. Being sentenced to the blue reception room would confirm that he'd angered Caro irretrievably.

"The gold dining room, sir." Singleton's tones were chilly. "Third floor."

"Ah, the third floor." Eamon hid his relief. "I haven't ventured there." He'd had so much to do in the gallery that he hadn't made a start on the two floors above that. His plan had been to go through the house room by room, methodically, to discover if the dukes had stashed away anything that Clive had missed, but the gallery alone would take months.

"Second room off the landing, sir," Singleton offered.

"I will endeavor to find it. Thank you, Singleton."

The man bowed frostily. Eamon doubted Caro had confided the tale of his ill-chosen words and her embarrassment afterward, but the man would have noted Eamon's absence and concluded that any rift was Eamon's fault.

Eamon ran lightly up the stairs on his own—Singleton was apparently not going to bother announcing him.

He tried not to stare at the place on the first landing where Caro had fallen onto him in a silken armful, tried to banish his memory of each passionate kiss they'd shared afterward. Eamon's heart had been full, nothing existing in the world at that moment but himself and Caro.

He'd forgotten to ask how *she* felt before blurting out his spontaneous confession. Caro's absolute shock had lanced through him, reminding Eamon that he had no business falling in love with a lofty duchess. He'd been hired to catalog the artwork, and not on a quest to conquer the beautiful lady in the tower.

The house grew darker as he ascended, and Eamon had the sudden sense of being led into a snare. Singleton could have directed him to an unused room, which would shut like a trap, imprisoning him for being so disrespectful to the duchess. His friends would wonder for a time what had happened to the annoying Eamon and then gradually forget about him.

When Eamon reached the third floor, he heard no sound at all. He could barely see to find the second door along, having to grope for the handle when he reached it.

Eamon drew a breath, squared his shoulders, and pushed the door inward.

Light poured out at him. The room was a tall square, the

first half of the walls filled with windows and glittering wall sconces, the top register covered in paintings.

Eamon didn't immediately scan the pictures for any that might be of value, because his attention was taken with the dining table and its occupants.

Every candle in the house must have been brought out for the occasion. The chandelier, the wall sconces, and three candelabras down the table's length were filled with tall, lit candles. Their warm glow danced on the porcelain service laid out on a tapestry runner and crystal goblets, already full of pale wine.

The dowager duchess reposed in state at the foot of the table. She wore a sumptuous velvet gown from the end of the last century, her gray hair surmounted by a tasteful diamond tiara. Eamon's trained eye noted that the stones were paste, but they sparkled richly all the same.

Leo's chair was at the head of the table, where he was propped up by cushions. He wore a cashmere suit that was more up to date than the dowager's ensemble but appeared to be uncomfortable for the lad.

Between them, on the table's far side, was Caro. Eamon wondered a moment what was different about her then realized she'd donned a golden-colored gown with a daring neckline that rode low on her shoulders.

As at the ball, she'd filled in the space that would expose her flesh with a gauzy fichu, but the opaque fabric only made her more enticing. Eamon imagined himself peeling away the fichu while he kissed her warm skin, Caro sighing with contentment beneath him.

Eamon jerked his thoughts from such enticements, reminding himself that those pleasures were not for him.

Caro rose in a stately motion, and Leo leapt to his feet, scattering cushions. The dowager remained seated but gave Eamon a sedate nod.

Eamon made his most formal bow. "Good evening, Your

Grace," he said to the dowager. "And my liege." This to Leo. "Your Grace," another nod to Caro, who regarded him without expression.

Was she pleased to see him? Dismayed he'd actually turned up? Deciding to pretend she barely knew him?

Leo, on the other hand, was unabashedly delighted.

"I knew you'd come," he sang out. "I've been going through all the books, like you said, but I haven't found anything yet."

Eamon didn't like how he warmed at the boy's eagerness. "There are very many books," he said. "One of them is bound to be worth something."

"I'll keep looking," Leo said with confidence and trotted back to his chair.

Eamon waited until Caro resumed her seat, then he restored the cushions for Leo, made sure the boy was settled, and took the place that had obviously been laid for him opposite Caro.

As soon as Eamon's backside touched the chair, Singleton appeared through the door to a connected room, bearing a soup tureen. Singleton carried the large porcelain vessel solemnly to the dowager's side and ladled two substantial portions into her bowl before turning to Eamon, the guest.

Eamon stopped him after one ladleful, noting there was only a small amount of liquid left in the tureen. He noted that Caro took very little as well, so that Singleton could give the rest to Leo.

This needed to cease, Eamon thought angrily as he lifted his spoon. Caro should not have to starve herself for the sake of her son and her mother-in-law. As Eamon was here tonight, he was probably taking much of Caro's share.

He silently cursed Mr. Clive for robbing the dukes, and the dukes for not noticing. The pack of fools had left two women and a child to eke out an existence in genteel poverty.

"Do you not like it?" Leo asked worriedly as Eamon glared into his bowl.

"Of course I do." Eamon hastened to reassure him. He spooned up a large slurp—it would be churlish to waste what little comestibles they had. The soup was creamy with the barest hint of fish and vegetables but managed to be tasty. "Your cook is quite talented," he said to the dowager.

The dowager duchess sent him a haughty glare. "She'll do."

Eamon hid a grin. The dowager must be the sort of aristocrat reluctant to praise her staff too highly to others. One never knew when her rivals would pinch her best servants.

Eamon caught Caro's gaze and found humor in it—she knew exactly how to read her mother-in-law. Eamon smiled in return. Caro flushed and immediately returned her attention to her soup.

As soon as Leo had scraped his bowl dry, the dowager laid down her spoon. The door opened immediately to admit Singleton, who deftly removed the bowls from the plates they'd rested in. He disappeared into the next room for a moment then returned with a covered tray. He deposited the cover on the sideboard and circled the table with the platter, dispensing slabs of poached fish, likely more of what had been in the soup.

The dowager took a large filet, Eamon asked for the smallest on the tray, Caro took the next smallest, and the rest went to Leo.

The lad didn't notice that his elders gave him and his grandmother the lion's share of the food, and Eamon would never tell him. Let the boy live in blissful ignorance for a few more years. He'd be sent off to school soon—if the duke had been wise enough to secure him a place with fees paid well in advance— and Leo would face plenty of austerity there.

Caro noticed, however. She frowned at Eamon as though annoyed with him as she daintily cut up her fish.

Singleton came around with a butter sauce, and Eamon allowed him to ladle a large spoonful onto his fish. They seemed to have a lot of butter, which was probably from one of the duke's farms.

No one spoke as they consumed the course, Leo eating happily, swinging his dangling legs. The lad seemed unconstrained, indicating that being invited to the large dining table must not be a rare occurrence. Eamon had always liked that Caro didn't shut her child in the nursery and pretend he existed only on special occasions.

Again, as soon as Leo finished, the dowager, who'd consumed her fish quickly, laid down her fork.

Singleton did his ritual once more, removing the plates and carrying around a platter of roast chicken with accompanying vegetables. Eamon asked for a small amount, eyeing Caro defiantly as he did so.

Halfway through this dish—which was quite good in its simplicity—the dowager broke the silence in which they'd been consuming the main course.

"You left your notebooks behind last week, Mr. Stone," she said crisply. "Does that mean you are returning to continue your work? Or that we've seen the last of you?"

Eamon cleared his throat. "I am very busy elsewhere, Your Grace. I have asked Mr. Cheswell to send you a replacement. I apologize that he has not yet complied."

The dowager stared at him during this speech while Caro studied her plate.

"You have a silver tongue," the dowager stated. "Just like your father. Has our company grated on you? I see no reason *you* should not continue what you've started. Cheswell can send his other assistants to do whatever he has foisted upon you. I shall write to him and tell him so."

Having said her piece, she lifted her fork and focused her attention on eating.

Caro raised her head, her eyes holding both amusement at her mother-in-law's imperiousness and a hint of triumph.

Why triumph? What was she up to? Eamon's heartbeat sped in anticipation of whatever it might be.

"Do come back, Mr. Stone," Leo said. Could he make his plea any more heart-wrenching? "No one will understand us like you do, and I know they won't let me help."

Caro watched Eamon closely, as though daring him to disappoint her son.

Eamon regarded the pair in dismay, torn between joy that they wanted him and worry that he'd make things worse by returning.

He lifted his hands in surrender, uncertain if he was reluctant or glad. "Very well. I will explain things to Mr. Cheswell, but I must leave the decision to him."

"Nonsense," the dowager said. "Cheswell will do what *I* wish. I expect to find you here tomorrow morning. I have given up the notion that you'll discover anything, but we ought to have everything cataloged correctly."

She returned once more to her dinner, as though the matter was concluded.

Singleton stalked into the chamber as soon as the dowager finished, removed the plates, and returned with bowls of bright strawberries for the sweet. The season for them had begun, so they'd be cheap and plentiful.

Once they'd made short work of the berries, Singleton decanted a bottle of dark wine, the second wine serving of the night. The pale wine that had awaited them in the glasses had been thinned with water, but what Singleton now poured into a small goblet for Eamon was thick and blood red.

Port. From the bits of dust clinging to the bottle on the sideboard, it had been reposing in the cellar for quite some time.

As soon as the port finished trickling into the glass, the dowager rose from her seat.

"Caroline, shall we leave the gentlemen to it?"

This might have been a formal supper for twenty the way

the dowager intoned the command. Caro instantly came to her feet, as had Eamon and Leo when the dowager stood.

Singleton retreated to become a statue next to the sideboard as the dowager moved to the door in a swish of silk and musky perfume.

Caro went to Leo and kissed the top of her son's head. "Singleton will take you up soon, darling, and I will come and say good night. Do not talk Mr. Stone's leg off."

Leo spluttered with laughter at the metaphor and hugged his mother. Caro released him and brushed by Eamon to follow in the dowager's wake.

"Thank you for coming," she murmured to Eamon, then she was out the door.

Eamon resumed his seat, closing his palm over the paper Caro had slipped him as she'd passed. He slid the note into his pocket and waited while Singleton served Leo tea in place of port.

Singleton departed, leaving the decanter within Eamon's reach.

Some gentlemen might be offended by being left alone with a child as though expected to entertain him after such a strange supper, but Eamon was glad of the chance. He'd missed the lad more than he'd thought possible.

At Eamon's encouragement, Leo launched into a tale of what he'd done for every minute since Eamon had left the house the week before. As he rattled on, Eamon palmed the paper from his pocket and held it under the table to read.

On a scrap carefully torn from a larger page, Caro had written, *Fifth floor chamber, in the rear of the house.*

Eamon studied the note, possibilities dancing through his head. His hand shook as he folded the scrap and returned it to his pocket.

CHAPTER 20

Time moved interminably before Singleton entered the dining room and announced, "I will take His Grace to the nursery now. Please remain and enjoy the port, sir."

Singleton seemed determined that Eamon drain the entire bottle, having returned to top off his glass more than once already. Eamon could drink heartily if he chose, but he wanted his head clear tonight.

"Thank you," Eamon said, rising. He bowed to Leo. "Good night, my liege."

"Good night, my knight." Leo grinned at his play on words then seized Singleton's hand to be led out.

Eamon resumed his seat and finished the glass he'd begun to soothe Singleton's worries. He lingered, giving Leo time to reach the nursery and Caro to say good night to him as she'd promised.

She might tarry a while, telling Leo stories or singing to him, or whatever she did when she put him to bed. Eamon poured another half glass of port but pushed it away after a few sips. The fortified wine was good but strong.

Eamon waited another agonizing three quarters of an hour, checking his watch every few minutes, before he decided to risk leaving the dining room.

The house was very quiet, and Singleton was nowhere in sight.

Fifth floor chamber, in the rear of the house.

What was there? Caro? A painting she wanted him to value? A strong bloke ready to beat some respect into him?

Eamon made his way to the staircase and paused to listen. When he heard no noise coming from either above or below, he ascended to the fifth floor.

It was even darker here, and no one was about. Eamon ventured to the end of the hall, where a closed door awaited him.

Caro definitely knew how to entice him. There was no way Eamon would leave this house before he satisfied his curiosity as to what was behind this door. He tapped on it.

He thought he heard the word *Enter*, but it was so faint he wasn't certain. Eamon drew a fortifying breath, turned the handle, and pushed open the door.

Caro had lit plenty of candles inside. Singleton had snuffed more and more of them every time he'd come to Leo and Eamon in the dining room and taken them away, and Eamon now wondered if he'd carried them up here for Caro.

The room was a small bedchamber. A bed hung with warm-looking curtains reposed on the far wall, with a padded bench at the foot of it. Comfortable chairs had been drawn near a compact bookcase, and an armoire stood on another wall. Every fabric, from bed hangings to chair and bench upholstery, held sprays of flowers, as did the carpet, which was soft if worn.

It was a very feminine room, one that was never meant to admit a man. The Duke of Aylesmore had never slept here, Eamon wagered. This was Caro's private retreat.

She stood in the middle of it, her lacy cap gone, her fichu

loosened. She studied him with her brown-green eyes that held clarity and determination.

Eamon closed the door, his heart hammering.

Caro said nothing, did nothing. She remained in the center of the carpet, watching him. Her chest rose with a quick intake of breath, but otherwise, she remained motionless.

Eamon moved to her. "Duchess?" he asked softly when he reached her. "What—?"

Caro silenced him with cool fingers on his lips. Before Eamon could decide what to do, she laced her arms around his neck and covered his mouth with a long kiss.

———

CARO KNEW SHE HAD TO BE MAD. SHE HADN'T DISCLOSED TO HER friends the extent of her plans—her wild decision to slip Eamon the note had come from a place inside her she hadn't realized still existed.

The daring miss she'd been had disappeared long ago, buried under caring for an ill husband and a spirited little boy.

This afternoon, the boldness Caro had lost rose again, making her write the note and, even more brazenly, slide it to Eamon under Singleton's and her mother-in-law's noses.

Eamon wouldn't come, Caro had told herself. He'd be dismayed by her presumption or laugh at her.

When he opened the door and walked inside, she froze, unable to move or speak. He'd closed the door and come to her, and she could do nothing else but kiss him.

After Eamon's initial start, he gently pulled her closer and returned the kiss with increasing fever.

Caro curled her hands on his back, the play of hard muscles enticing under her fingers. Eamon deepened the kiss, as though he liked her touching him.

His hands threaded her hair, pulling it loose until it fell

about her shoulders. Eamon broke the kiss to bury his face in a fistful of it.

Unlike their tryst in Portman Square, Caro didn't dread someone coming in to discover them. The dowager had fallen asleep in her large bedchamber downstairs, and Leo, despite his excitement at Eamon's visit, had quickly dropped off in his nursery. Singleton would never dream of disturbing Caro in the night short of the direst of emergencies.

They were gloriously alone, no ballroom of disparaging guests to face at the end of whatever happened here.

Eamon unwound the fichu Caro had already loosened, letting it fall in a waft of pale fabric. He tilted her head back and pressed warm kisses along her throat before moving to her breasts as they rose above her décolletage.

His scalding breath brushed her skin, and Caro began to shake.

"No, my love." Eamon lifted his head, his blue eyes dark in the candlelight. He cupped her face, caressing her cheekbones as her hair slid over his fingers. "Never be afraid of me."

"I am not. I am—" Caro broke off, unable to explain. So much excitement coursed through her, she might fall to pieces. The sensation was unfamiliar, raw.

Eamon silenced her with his mouth then pressed kisses along her throat once more. Unhurried fingers loosened the catches of her bodice and untied the chemise that was her only layer under that.

Caro's body hummed as Eamon lowered the gold satin gown Louise had insisted on lending her. Her modiste had created this gown for the Season, but Louise had never worn it. Caro might as well, she'd said.

Caro realized that Louise might have chosen this dress because it was easy to take off. It fell to her waist in a crush of warm satin, baring her to Eamon's gaze.

He observed her in admiration, his attention as palpable as

his touch. Then he skimmed his fingers under her breasts to gently lift them.

Caro had never had a man's hands there—well, anyone's hands, except her own, and that only in the bath. She let out a breath, trying to relax, but her inner fires shot even higher at his touch.

"You are beautiful," he said softly. "I've never seen such beauty."

"You must have done," was all Caro could think of to say.

Eamon's smile flashed. "Not until this night." He leaned closer. "Caro, my dearest angel, why did you bring me here?"

To touch you. To have you touch me.

Caro had no idea how to say such things out loud. She put her fingers to his lips. "We should not talk."

Eamon's smile beneath her fingertips turned sultry. "I agree."

He gently moved her hand aside and kissed her mouth.

His previous kisses had been fervent, but this one contained an intensity he'd been holding back. He cupped her breasts, her nipples growing tight as they pressed his palms. The fire of that ignited Caro's excitement to desperation.

Caro grappled with the buttons of his waistcoat, so many buttons. Why were women's garments so thin and flimsy while men stuffed themselves into layer upon layer of clothing?

Eamon laughed softly as she struggled. He released her—though she had a moment of anguish when he ceased kissing her—and helped her unbutton and slide his coat and waistcoat from him. Both fell to the carpet, and his cravat soon followed.

Caro untied the tapes that held his shirt closed, letting out a sigh of satisfaction when his hard torso at last was bare for her.

Caro ran her hands over his chest, fascinated by the planes of it, the dark hair that curled over her fingers, the flat nipples waiting for her touch. Eamon sucked in a breath as she squeezed one between her fingers. It pearled, like her own, and she repeated the action, intrigued. She'd had no idea men responded to such a thing.

Eamon let her play as he loosened the final hooks of her gown, sending it, chemise, and her one modest underskirt to the carpet with his clothes.

Now they were skin to skin, and any lingering coolness fled. Caro had been unclothed with a man before—she'd borne a child after all—but not like this. Not standing in the middle of her chamber, in the flickering candlelight, passion running through her like rivers of flame.

Eamon slid warm hands down her back and over her now-bare hips, drawing her closer into the next kiss. They swayed together, mouths seeking, no more words.

Eamon hooked his arm under her thigh, pulling her leg up to twine his. He still wore skin-tight pantaloons, fashionable for a gentleman's evening suit, but the position opened Caro more than she'd thought possible, letting her feel every inch of the hard ridge behind cashmere.

Just when she thought incandescence would overtake her, Eamon untangled them and lifted her in his arms, carrying her to the bed. He deposited her on top of it, not bothering to draw back the covers.

Eamon gazed down at her, his hair a mess from her fingers. "I'd love to sketch you as you are now. I would treasure such a picture forever."

Caro gulped back a laugh. "It would be extremely shocking."

Eamon leaned over her, his fists coming to rest on either side of her, breath burning. "It would be for no one's delectation but mine, believe me."

Caro hooked a finger on his waistband, the daring in her rising once more. "Perhaps I'd like a sketch of you as well."

Something raw flared in Eamon's eyes. In several swift moves, he stripped her of slippers and stockings, then himself of the rest of his garments.

From the moment his arms had gone around her at the window the day he'd arrived, Caro had wanted this. She hadn't realized it, then had denied it, but she'd wanted this beautiful man bared for her.

"Please," she whispered, as he drew his strong hand down her body.

Eamon made a sound like a moan. He climbed quickly onto the bed and slid over her, supporting his weight on his arms.

"Caro, my angel." His rumbling words coursed through her. "My duchess. My love."

Caro had no words for him in return. She traced his cheek then slid her arms around him, coaxing him to her.

Eamon lowered himself, his blunt hardness landing with precision between her legs.

"Lord, forgive me," he whispered, and then he filled her, his warm weight both comforting and completing her.

*E*amon forced down a groan. As he drew back for another thrust, Caro closed her eyes and tilted her head, passion flushing her cheeks.

This was heaven. Eamon's heart pounded, his body roasting. Caro was beneath him, her arms around him taking away every hurt, every doubt, every lonely moment.

Each stroke into her drove him more wild, every little gasp she made stoking the frenzy higher. Caro lifted her hips, instinctively rocking against him, until Eamon was sighing her name, calling her *sweet* and *love* and *my own*.

There were other words he wanted to use, but she wasn't ready for those, and he'd do nothing right now that would make her push him away.

Eamon wasn't going anywhere, not for a long while.

"Please," Caro gasped. Not to stop, Eamon could tell, by the way she seized his hips and pulled him harder against her.

She liked to plead with him. Eamon didn't mind at all, happy to answer her desires.

He drove into her, the heat of her maddening him. This was

deepest passion, sharing this untamed intimacy with the woman he'd so much wanted and ended up loving.

"Caro." He tasted her name on his lips. "Love. Damn it, *no…*"

Blast it all—he'd wanted to make this last all night. Eamon abruptly slid out of Caro and spilled his seed into the handkerchief he'd dropped next to them for just that purpose.

The suddenness of it made him bereft, cold. Caro dragged in a shuddering breath, the shock of it startling her as well.

Eamon quickly wiped himself clean and returned to her, their next kisses moving from feverishly crazed to satisfyingly sweet to the slow brushes of afterglow.

Eamon tugged a coverlet from under Caro and wrapped it around them both. He burrowed into the cocoon with her, their kisses and touches taking them into drowsy contentment.

———

HOURS LATER, CARO STRETCHED HER TOES AND LET OUT A SOUND almost like a purr. She startled herself, never having heard such a thing come from her throat.

Eamon's smile answered. He caressed her shoulder where it peeked outside the covers, his touch gentle but heated.

They were bundled into the bed, where Eamon had tucked them after the second time he'd loved her. The room had darkened, several of the candles burning out. It was relatively early in the night, however, the treacherous dawn still hours away.

"We *could* have an *affaire de coeur*, I suppose," Caro murmured as she skimmed her fingers along Eamon's strong arm. "If you'd like."

Eamon's laughter vibrated the bed. "Isn't that what we're doing?"

"I mean in the weeks to come. While you are cataloging. We could arrange to meet so that we do not upset Leo or shock Singleton."

Eamon's laughter faded. "You have thought this through, have you?"

"Why not?" Caro touched his lips, shivering when he kissed her fingertips. "I thought you'd be pleased."

A frown creased his face. "Because I professed to be in love with you?"

"That and I missed you too much when you were gone. I don't want you to run away again." She trailed off with wistfulness.

Eamon gazed at her in silence for a time, eyes unreadable. Then he briefly rubbed his forehead. "I've behaved like an ass for the whole of it, haven't I? I am sorry, Duchess. I never meant to cause you so much vexation."

Caro hadn't been vexed—she'd been empty. Eamon not being in the house all day had felt wrong, as though the place was incomplete.

"I'm glad you came back," she said softly.

Eamon snuggled closer to her. "There is much more to do, and to be honest, I don't trust anyone but me to do it. I promise to behave myself this time, Duchess."

That hadn't been what Caro had meant, but she shared a smile as though she agreed with him.

She walked her fingers across his chest. "You are hardly behaving yourself now, Mr. Stone."

Eamon captured her hand. "Outside of this chamber, I mean. Inside, I will let myself be *very* wicked."

Caro feigned disapproval. "Is that so?"

"Indeed. It's enjoyable to be wicked, Duchess. Let me show you."

Eamon lowered himself to her and kissed her, his lips hot and leisurely. Then he abruptly stripped back the covers and moved to kneel between her legs.

Caro held her breath, wondering what he'd do, then

suppressed a squeal as he proceeded to demonstrate what pleasures he could bring to her with his mouth alone.

———

EAMON WAS IN THE GALLERY AT NINE THE NEXT MORNING, studiously going over the notebooks he'd left behind when Singleton appeared.

"Good morning, sir."

Singleton's three simple words held a quantity of meaning. Surprise to find Eamon already here when Eamon hadn't knocked on the door. Curiosity as to how Eamon had gained entrance, and wondering if he wanted to know the answer.

"Good morning, Singleton," Eamon returned without trepidation. "Her Grace lent me the key." He lifted a sturdy ring and jangled it. "This way I can make an early start without disturbing the household."

The key had also let Eamon slip out even earlier this morning and hasten back to his rooms for a wash and change of clothing. Mrs. Temple, his landlady, had not been impressed by his early hours, she'd informed Eamon when he stopped for a quick breakfast.

"Blame my friends," Eamon had told her as he'd gulped down coffee and buttered toast. "They do keep me out all night."

"Funny that." Mrs. Temple refilled his cup as soon as it emptied. "His lordship came around looking for you very late last evening. Was surprised you weren't in."

Eamon suspected Wolfe had wanted to learn how the supper had gone. He clearly hadn't expected Eamon to have spent the night in Caro's arms.

Eamon strove to keep the flush from his face. "I do have other friends than Lord Dominic, Mrs. Temple. Now, I must go and earn some coin."

"A gentleman shouldn't soil his hands making a living, you

know," Mrs. Temple said. "If you want to take a true lady to wife, that is."

"Gentlemen who won't soil their hands slowly starve." Eamon grabbed another slice of toast as he rose to leave. "I prefer to eat." He munched the toast, grinned, and departed, as Mrs. Temple shook her head.

Mrs. Temple had a point, Eamon reflected as he finished the bread, donned his hat and coat, and departed for Grosvenor Square. If he wished to take Caro to wife, they must have something to live on. The townhouse was Leo's, the lease in his name as duke, Eamon's research had told him. Caro and the dowager had use of it for their lifetimes, but the dowager might request her daughter-in-law to leave if Caro decided to marry a reprobate.

Caro would never depart without Leo—and Leo would want to go with her—so what would they do? Let the dowager rattle about the empty house while Eamon leased a flat for them or rooms in a cheap boardinghouse? What a comedown for a duke and his mother, if the duke's men of business would even allow such a thing to happen.

Eamon halted in the middle of North Audley Street with a growl, earning impatient words from those trying to press past him.

The situation was impossible. If Caro were a genteel widow with an untitled son, no one would talk very much if they quietly wed. There would be some disapprobation, yes, but most people would regard it as a sweet romance.

As it was, Caro was under close scrutiny of the world. Many had their opinions on what was good for the young duke, including his odious cousin.

Eamon was in love with Caro, no matter who she was. She could sweep gutters for a living, and he wouldn't care. But she was a duchess, regardless of the state of her son's finances, and the world would view Eamon as the swindler trying to gain control over her son and her properties.

If Eamon truly cared for Caro, he'd disappear and leave her free of gossip. But no, he was a selfish bastard who wanted to drink every drop of his time with her.

She'd suggested they become lovers. Eamon had laughed, wondering if she'd truly understood the implications of her idea. Upon reflection, though, Eamon would take her offer if it was all he could have.

What he *could* do was find a way to shower riches upon her and Leo, not to mention the dowager. Eamon had a talent for prying things out of people, and pry he would.

Then, when he departed to save the last shred of Caro's reputation, he'd know she'd be all right. Eamon wouldn't desert her until she and Leo could stand against the world and put the creditors in their places.

His duchess could wear diamonds again—her own—and astonish the world with her beauty.

Eamon then would have to go and explore the Arctic, or someplace suitably remote, until he forgot about her.

Which would take the rest of his life.

Eamon snapped back to the present moment when Singleton, who'd regarded Eamon steadily as Eamon displayed the keys, gave him a nod. "Very good thinking, sir. Will you require tea?"

"Not just yet, thank you. I want to do as much as I can here before luncheon."

Singleton bowed. "Very good, sir," he said and glided back downstairs.

Did Singleton believe the story about the key—even though Caro had indeed handed it to Eamon? Or did he know what had occurred last night after everyone had retired?

Singleton was a canny old sod, so he probably suspected. The fact that he hadn't herded Eamon out the door was a good sign that he wasn't outraged at him.

Eamon forced himself to focus on his work, his determination to find something valuable renewed. He busily went through his notebooks again, pausing at the few pieces, including the book of hours Leo had turned up, that were worth having valued. There were too damned few items for his comfort, though.

The Rembrandt would help, if Eamon could collect enough money to purchase it—and if Caro would accept it from him. Then he'd have to persuade her to sell it again instead of hanging it on the wall to admire it.

Too many things could go wrong, enough to make Eamon grind his teeth in frustration.

He worked all morning without interruption—to his disappointment. He'd hoped Caro would glide down the stairs and greet him, or Leo would appear with his eagerness to help. Eamon was surprised how much he looked forward to seeing the little lad every day.

As it was, nothing disturbed him until the knocker sounded on the front door, and Singleton appeared from nowhere to answer it.

Eamon tensed as he glanced over the banister, expecting Rudyard to try to insert himself into the house again. He relaxed as a maid preceded a young woman inside and helped remove her mistress's light wraps.

"If you'll follow me, your ladyship," Singleton intoned. "Her Grace will see you in her sitting room."

"Thank you, Singleton." The smooth voice of the Countess of Heyford reached Eamon, along with her light footsteps, mixed with Singleton's heavier tread.

The countess gave Eamon a curious stare as they mounted the stairs. Eamon made her a formal bow, and Louise nodded back at him in frank assessment before she followed Singleton up the next flight.

She knew, Eamon decided. Caro's friends were perceptive

and not fools, even if the princess sometimes pretended to be empty-headed.

Eamon hoped the princess and the countess would become his allies, not his enemies, because if the latter, he knew he'd never stand a chance.

———

"LOUISE, I AM SO GLAD YOU'VE COME." CARO KISSED HER FRIEND on the cheek and led her to the warm chair by the fireplace.

The dowager had retreated to her chamber to write letters, and Leo was upstairs trying to study. He'd demand to join Eamon before long, and Caro would let him, happy they could begin their ritual again.

Louise sank to the offered chair, settling her dark gray broadcloth skirt. Clothing always draped well on Louise.

"Is anything the matter?" Caro asked in concern when Louise sat too long in silence. "Are Harry and Jack all right?"

"Yes, yes, they are fine." Louise's face softened at the mention of her sons, who were currently away at school. "They'll be home soon, and ready to have Leo down to Berkshire to romp and play."

"He'll be happy to come." Louise invited Caro and Leo every year in June. Caro looked forward to the month in the Berkshire countryside, a place she could forget her troubles for a brief interval.

This year, however, she'd have to leave Eamon to join Louise and her boys, something she was not certain she wanted to do.

"Caro, I don't quite know how to tell you this." Louise leaned forward in a rustle of skirts and pressed Caro's suddenly cold hand. "Rudyard is putting it about that you are having a torrid affair with Mr. Stone. He is claiming that Mr. Stone is endangering Leo's safety, and he is bringing suit against him—and you—to have Leo removed from his influence."

CHAPTER 22

aro realized she'd ceased breathing. She tried to draw a breath, but she'd gone numb, her ribs constricting. "How?" she choked out. "How could he know?"

She wasn't sure why this question slipped from her, but Louise's gaze sharpened. "It is true, then? Rudyard isn't simply putting slander about?"

"If he'd said it yesterday, it would be slander," Caro croaked. "Today …"

"Oh, my dear." Louise squeezed Caro's hand, though Caro could barely feel the attempt at comfort. "After your supper? He seduced you?"

Caro's face flamed. "I seduced *him*."

She found herself confessing all, from the note she'd slipped Eamon to helping him steal away in the wee hours of the morning.

Louise listened in sympathy, interest, and some dismay. "This is all our fault. Jo and me, teasing you about becoming his lover. It seemed romantic, in theory."

Caro regarded her in surprise. "Of course it isn't your fault. *I* chose to invite Eamon to my chamber, knowing full well what we'd do there. And it was quite wonderful." She emitted a breathless laugh. "I have no regrets, Louise. I'd do it again. In fact, I hope to."

"I thought Mr. Stone looked rather pleased with himself when I passed him downstairs," Louise said, her good humor restored. "I am glad to see him still here. He didn't simply take what he came for and disappear."

"*Take what he came for?*" Caro repeated incredulously. "You make it sound so sordid." She stilled. "Oh, dear. Is it?"

"I don't think so." Louise bathed her in a rare smile. "Jo and I weren't teasing when we said you deserve happiness, Caro. You've sacrificed so much and ought to be showered with pleasure."

"But I'll have to keep sacrificing, won't I?" Caro rose abruptly. "If I have a dalliance with Eamon, Rudyard will force me to give up Leo." She shook her head with adamance. "I will never, ever let Leo go to Rudyard. But that means I have to give up Eamon." She faltered, her heart hurting.

When faced with the choice, Leo would win, without doubt. But Eamon's absence would put a hole in Caro's life.

"I am so sorry, darling," Louise said in distress. "I did not want to bring you this news, but I preferred you to hear it from me, not Rudyard or someone taunting you with it. Rudyard is being less than discreet."

Caro swung from where she'd paced in her agitation, her anger rising. "Rudyard has already threatened me. He is a horrible man, and I will not let him endanger my son. I will keep Rudyard from Leo, and I don't care what I have to do. I'll sacrifice my entire world, including Eamon if I must, to keep Leo from him." Tears stung her eyes, but Caro held herself stiffly, refusing to give way.

"Excellent." Louise jumped to her feet. "I knew you wouldn't crumple and surrender to Rudyard's bullying. What shall we do?"

"I don't know." Caro put her hands to her head. "When I received the letter from Rudyard's solicitor, Eamon promised to help, but I don't know what he's accomplished. If nothing else, we must work to prove Rudyard would be a horrible guardian. Perhaps you can ask some of Geoff's friends if they've heard any dire rumors about him."

Louise flinched slightly at the mention of her deceased husband, but she nodded. "I'll also call upon the most gossipy wives of our old circle. Jo knows everyone in London—she can pry out information as well."

"I wonder …"

Caro gazed up at the landscape painting of Mayfield Hall, the Aylesmore estate in Kent, near Tunbridge Wells. This picture was genuine, painted by an unknown artist hired by Leo's grandfather, worth little to anyone but the family.

"You wonder what?" Louise prompted.

"So much of our artwork has gone missing, and Rudyard boasted that he ran tame in this house when Leopold was alive. I wonder if Rudyard has been robbing us, little by little, over the years."

Louise's brows rose. "Possibly, but I think Singleton would have noticed if Rudyard had tucked a painting under his coat on his way out."

"I don't mean that, exactly. Though there are smaller items to take—books and little statues, gold boxes and things of that nature. Eamon explained that someone might send a painting to a gallery to be cleaned, and the gallery returns a copy while keeping hold of the original. Perhaps Rudyard suggested to Leopold that he should restore the grimier paintings. Suppose the gallery Rudyard chose did the copying, paid by Rudyard, and Rudyard absconded with the real painting and returned the copy? Leopold wouldn't have known the difference. He was quite trusting, and knew little about the value of what he had."

Louise nodded sagely. "Yes, I can imagine Rudyard taking advantage of poor Leopold that way. There must be records of the paintings being sent out—you or Mr. Stone could discover to which galleries and whether Rudyard had anything to do with it."

"Eamon suspects Mr. Clive of substituting the paintings, but Mr. Clive and Rudyard could have been colluding."

"If Rudyard is to blame, we will have him." Louise's smile became determined. "I am pleased *Eamon* is helping you so much."

Caro flushed. "I meant Mr. Stone."

Louise laughed in delight. "I am teasing you, darling. I am glad to see you so in love."

Caro halted. "Am I in love?"

Of course she was, and she knew it. That was why, when Eamon had exclaimed, *Oh Duchess, I believe I'm falling in love with you,* Caro's heart had beat with wild joy.

Louise softened her tone. "You deserve to be. I know what it is to be fervently in love, and I wish it on you."

"I loved Leopold," Caro said in bewilderment. Poor Leopold. So many believed Caro hadn't cared for him at all.

"You did." Louise nodded. "But this is different."

Caro's regrets floated away as the memories of Eamon's touch, kisses, and the glorious way he'd filled her threatened to drown her.

"Yes," she agreed in a whisper. "It is very different."

She'd give anything to hold on to the sensations Eamon had flooded her with, and the new life they'd surged through her, and never let them go.

———

"The queen has answered my letter," the dowager duchess announced the next afternoon in the fourth-floor drawing room.

They'd finished the midday meal moments before, Leo heading downstairs to help Eamon as soon as he'd set down his fork. Caro and the dowager lingered at the table, sipping tea, the dowager reading through her correspondence.

"Her majesty wrote to you?" Caro pulled her thoughts from where they'd strayed to Eamon kissing her in the gallery earlier today. He'd drawn her into deep shadow and kissed her with slow promise.

The last few days had been filled with such encounters, Caro torn between excitement and shyness. Somehow, she'd invented many excuses to go down to the gallery—checking on Leo, bringing Eamon a receipt she'd found for one of her father-in-law's purchases, or simply to ask how things were proceeding.

Stolen kisses were something new for her, the heat that boiled through her when their mouths met both unnerving and glorious.

Eamon shared Caro's rage at Rudyard, which bolstered her more than she cared to admit.

"Her majesty did, indeed." The dowager dangled a letter from her long-fingered hand. "She is outraged that Rudyard dares think to raise Leo himself. Dear Charlotte detests the man but speaks highly of you."

"Does she?" Caro set down her tea, her attention caught. "I believe I've curtsied to the queen once, but she barely saw me. I wasn't lofty enough to be presented to her personally at my debut."

"She knows of you because I tell her about you," the dowager said. "As we both arrived in England from foreign lands about the same time, Charlotte and I became friends. Neither of us knew much English, and we muddled along together—I speak

German well, and she is proficient in French. I was one of her ladies-in-waiting, you know."

"I did know that," Caro said. The disapproving matrons of the *ton* had made certain Caro understood in what lofty circles she was daring to tread. "But not that you were close."

"It was eons ago, when I was quite young. Charlotte and I learned English together, though her accent is heavier than mine." The dowager paused for a flash of vanity. "I retired from court life when I began having my sons, but we've written to each other ever since. Our correspondence has grown since her husband's illness became permanent, because she needs the distraction, poor lamb."

Caro listened to all this with interest. The dowager rarely spoke about the period of her life when she'd been married to Leo's grandfather, though she loved going on about her upbringing on her father's sumptuous estate in France. Aristocratic life there had apparently been ten times more formal, elegant, luxurious, and entertaining than British aristocratic life could ever be.

"Please give the queen my best wishes," Caro said. "I do feel sorry for her, as I know she is so fond of the king."

The dowager looked pleased at Caro's sympathy. "I shall. In any case, she likes you, even though she regards you as a nobody. Do not be offended—she is a foreign princess, and they believe themselves superior to all other mortal beings, though she was quite a nobody herself when she came here."

Caro wasn't certain how to respond to these observations. "I am glad she approves of me," she managed. "Can she really help keep Leo home with me?"

"I do not know." The dowager sighed. "Charlotte has a large influence on public opinion, so her approval of you means much. She finds you the breath of fresh air that the stuffy dukes of Aylesmore needed. Also, you provided your husband a legitimate heir, which she considers a large point in your favor. But she cannot override the law. The king might, if he was coherent, and the Regent might, if he wasn't such a pompous, self-indulgent ass. Laws are made in Parliament by male creatures, and men stick by men, damn them all."

"Thank you for trying," Caro said, her hopes fading.

"I am not giving up, young lady," the dowager said firmly. "I'll not turn my grandson over to Rudyard. That lad was always a bad one."

"Rudyard is also your grandson," Caro pointed out.

"Humph. He does not deserve the designation. He has let his greed get the better of him, which has turned him against his own family. Rudyard does not care about Leo—he only wants the dukedom, never mind that it's bankrupt."

Likely Rudyard thought he could find a way to turn the estate's hardships around. Caro longed to know where he thought he'd come by the money to do so.

Another avenue to investigate, she decided. Caro had already sent a barrage of letters to those who might be able to help. If she could find enough fault in Rudyard, and enough respectable people to declare in court that he would be a terrible guardian, she might have a chance.

Colonel Harper, who'd shared the dance set with her and Eamon at the ball, was one person she'd approached. Mrs. Harper had sent back a note of sympathy and a promise to do what they could.

Jo's father, Prince Rupert, while he held no political power in Britain, did have influence, much as Queen Charlotte did, as did Jo's mother, Princess Maude. The three of them might not be able to change laws, but people listened to their opinions.

Caro would leave no stone unturned. Her letters had already produced a few results, she'd noted with satisfaction when she'd read her morning correspondence. Hearsay only, so far, but it was a start.

"Thank you, *Maman*," Caro said. "I appreciate you writing to the queen. It could be helpful."

The dowager set down the cup of coffee she'd raised to her lips with a firm click.

"Caro, you are a fine and kindhearted young woman. Too kindhearted for your own good, I've always thought. But the moment I saw how happy you made Leopold—and you have no idea how *un*happy he'd been—I decided to like you. Since then, I've grown to love you for yourself. You make Leo an excellent mother, no matter what the resentful snobs outside these windows say. I will ensure Leo remains in your care, do not worry." She lifted the cup again. "Besides, if Rudyard manages to take over, he'll turn us out of this house, and the estate, and I am too old to move to new quarters."

Caro astonished the woman by leaving her seat, coming around the table, and enfolding the dowager in an embrace.

"Thank you, *Maman*." Caro pressed a kiss to her mother-in-law's powdered cheek, while the dowager stared, her cup frozen in her fingers. "You have a tender heart as well, as much as you pretend you do not."

The dowager continued her cold gaze for a moment, before she softened. As Caro released her, she winked. "Tell no one, my dear. I have a reputation to uphold."

Caro laughed and kissed her again, then returned to her seat, daring to let herself hope a little.

———

"Are you certain you want to do this?" Sam asked Eamon.

Eamon was again in the tavern in Maiden Lane, having made himself leave Caro's house at sunset and not think of an excuse to ascend to her bedchamber.

"Very certain."

Sam Noble, who occupied the inglenook once more,

regarded Eamon severely over the glass of strong whisky Eamon had stood him.

"I like you, Stone. But ye know what happens if I never see my money again, don't ye? I can't make an exception for ye, lad."

"I repay my debts," Eamon said without worry. "It is why I haven't fled to the Continent a half-step ahead of my creditors like so many dandies who spend far beyond their means."

"The best way to stay out of debt is not to have any in the first place," Sam said sternly.

"Such wise words. If only you could have talked that sort of sense into my father. Not to mention the dukes of Aylesmore."

"Your father was beyond listening to sense, though he could finagle his way out of anything, that man. You have his gift of gab, and well you know it." Sam's eyes went flinty. "How do I know you're not using it on me now?"

"I am a little bit," Eamon admitted. "To persuade you that my cause is just. I am trying to save a lady, as I told you."

"Better throw the money into the gutter and have done, then. Ladies are insatiable. She'll bleed you dry, son."

"You haven't met my lady." Eamon warmed as he thought of how Caro's eyes would light up when he returned the painting. She might thank him with a few kisses as well. "Besides, it's not only for her, but for her son, a little lad I'm taken with. I think you befriended a similar lad some years ago."

"More fool me." Sam scowled, but Eamon knew he'd already won him over. "The money will be delivered to ye."

Eamon moved his not-too-clean glass on the table. "Delivered?"

"Ye wouldn't make it a step down the road if I gave it to ye here. I don't want to trip over your sliced-up body on my walk home."

"I'm fairly tough, Sam. Not the spindly little boy you knew."

"Yes, yes, and you've been through the wars." Sam nodded wearily. "But fighting on a battlefield's a different thing from besting cutthroats on the streets. You go back to your cozy boardinghouse and wait. My man will have it there in the morning."

Eamon raised his brows. "You trust him to bring it to me without running off with it?"

"I trust him to want to keep his balls attached to his body." Sam shrugged and slurped his whisky. "You'll get it."

"All right then." Eamon saluted Sam with his glass. "Thank you. You're a good man."

"No, I ain't." Sam took another slurp. "Remember that when ye try to explain to me why you're late on a payment or short of cash."

"That will not happen." Eamon knew it wouldn't, because he'd planned carefully. "And I'll invite you to the wedding."

"You're jumping way ahead of yourself, lad," Sam said darkly.

Eamon knew he was, but he couldn't help it.

He realized that the odds of him ending up with Caro as his wife were much longer than his chances of paying back Sam every penny, even with the man's exorbitant fees.

But Eamon had to try.

———

IN THE MORNING, AS PROMISED, AN UNSAVORY-LOOKING gentleman turned up in Oxford Street, ordering Mrs. Temple to rouse Eamon. As Eamon was already up and breakfasting, he hurried outside before Mrs. Temple could shout for a watchman.

The man handed Eamon a paper-wrapped bulk then stamped away in a huff when Eamon offered him a shilling for his trouble.

As Mrs. Temple watched in great curiosity, Eamon carried the package upstairs to his chamber. He shut his door before Mrs. Temple could bustle in after him on pretense of changing his bed linens, and carefully peeled back the parcel's paper. What he saw inside satisfied him very much.

Eamon counted out what he needed, hid the rest in the cavity behind a fireplace brick, and returned to breakfast. Mrs. Temple gazed at him in hope he'd satisfy her curiosity, but Eamon had to disappoint her.

Once he finished his repast, he donned his coat, took up gloves and hat, and called for a hackney to take him to Cheapside and the shop of Hieronymus Clive.

CHAPTER 23

At breakfast the next morning, Caro waded through her correspondence, which had increased since she and Louise had discussed what to do about Rudyard.

Jo was proving particularly helpful, as she and her family were acquainted with so many residents of London. Those acquaintances had servants who knew more about the goings-on of the *haut ton* than anyone, as well as men of business and solicitors with gossipy clerks, chatty footmen, or concierges in St. James's clubs.

The letters Caro had collected over the past few days allowed her to piece together a picture of Rudyard and his true motivations.

Even so, she strove to keep her hopes in check. Though Rudyard might be revealed as a brutal thug who'd lock Leo in a dungeon, courts tended to favor male petitions over those of ladies. Caro needed a clever man of law on her side as well as a sympathetic judge.

On the other hand, the actions of those in polite society weren't always dependent on the courts. Opinions of the Upper Ten Thousand held much sway, and if Rudyard's misdeeds came to light, he might be convinced to withdraw his petition for guardianship. Already he'd garnered much disapproval, if the letters Caro read were any indication.

Singleton entered and made a deferential cough. The dowager, on the opposite side of the table, glanced up from her own correspondence.

"Yes, what is it, Singleton?" the dowager demanded. "Or are you coming down with a cold?"

"Mr. Stone has arrived, Your Grace." Singleton addressed the dowager then turned to Caro. "He is asking to ascend to this floor. He says he has something to show you."

"What does he have?" the dowager asked irritably. She hated when people were cryptic.

"I do not know, Your Grace. He has brought a rather large parcel."

"Send him up, please," Caro said before the dowager could argue. Caro could see that her mother-in-law was curious, but the woman believed it never did to betray eagerness.

Singleton bowed and glided out.

Caro's hands went to her hair, self-consciously smoothing it before she gathered her scattered letters and stacked them neatly. The dowager bathed Caro in a stare before returning to her cup of chocolate and the letter in her hand.

Eamon must have already been climbing the stairs, because less than a minute elapsed before Singleton showed him in. Eamon entered in sidesteps, the large square wrapped in brown paper he toted not letting him move any other way.

"Good morning, Your Graces," Eamon said breezily. "Forgive me if I set this down." He rested the parcel's end on the carpet with a thump and a gasp of breath. "It grows heavy after four flights."

"I did offer to carry it, sir," Singleton told him disapprovingly.

"You did, but I did not want to let it out of my hands until it was safely in this room." Eamon grinned at Caro, who'd risen from her chair, trying not to let her heart flutter.

Did he always have to be so handsome? Climbing stairs with a heavy package hadn't dampened Eamon's energy one whit. His dark hair was a trifle mussed, but Caro didn't mind that. She could straighten it later, which might lead to more mussing and hot kisses that melted her.

Eamon's blue eyes sparkled, as though he read her thoughts.

"Tell us what it is," she cajoled him, flustered. "Don't tease."

Eamon's smile widened. "Very well. Singleton, will you assist?"

Eamon removed a knife from his pocket, cut the twine that bound the package, and then carefully began tearing at the paper. Singleton joined him, and the two men peeled off the wrappings from top to bottom.

A canvas slowly came into view, one in a thin wooden frame that Caro could tell had been hastily nailed together. The front of the canvas faced Eamon, hiding whatever was on it from the Caro and the dowager.

Caro waited with some impatience as Eamon and Singleton finished unwrapping, then had to wait longer while Singleton gathered up the papers and carried them out.

Eamon lifted the painting and turned it around.

The dusky background at the painting's top edge surrounded a darker gray and brown beret that was perched over a man's pale and slightly wrinkled forehead. Large tufts of graying, curly hair poked out on either side of the hat. The man had a bulbous nose, which went with his craggy face and intense dark eyes. A collar cradled the lower part of the man's face then blended into his brown coat, with a hint of russet at the coat's opening.

Caro regarded it in stunned surprise. She understood now why Eamon had instantly known that the painting in their gallery had been false. This one glowed with truth, as though the artist had only now laid down his brush.

Before Caro could utter a word, she heard a strangled noise behind her. She turned swiftly to see the dowager half-risen from her chair, her hand at her throat.

"*Maman?*" Caro hurried to the dowager's side. "Are you unwell?"

The dowager drew herself to her full height, recovering her dignity. "What is *that?*" she inquired in an imperious voice.

"*That* is a self-portrait of Rembrandt van Rijn, painted in about 1659," Eamon answered. "The genuine one. I cleaned it up a bit, because it had become very grimy, but do not worry. I am something of an expert at painting restoration. My landlady complained of the smell of my potions, but it was worth it."

Caro agreed. The paint had the clarity it must have possessed a century and a half ago.

"Wherever did you find it?" Caro asked, her excitement building. If Eamon had located one painting, he might have found others as well.

"Mr. Clive's secondhand shop in Cheapside." Eamon's voice went hard. "If his warehouse is searched, I'm certain it will reveal others. You might want to bring suit against him, Your Graces, because the entire time he worked in this house, he was slowly robbing you."

Caro drew a breath to express indignation but broke off as the dowager moved with astonishing vigor to stand before the painting and Eamon.

"How dare you meddle in our affairs?" she demanded. "You stupid, stupid boy."

"*Maman,*" Caro said, aghast.

Singleton, who had returned to the room, placed himself behind Eamon's shoulder, as though ready to escort him out.

Eamon fixed a sharp gaze on the dowager. "Of course," he

said as though a puzzle had been solved. "It wasn't your husband or your son selling the paintings, was it?"

The dowager looked neither surprised nor ashamed. "Why not? They were mine to sell. My father brought the Rembrandts and the Canalettos with him when he fled France before the *ancien régime* was overthrown. Papa saw the way the wind was blowing and asked for refuge with us. He sold the paintings to my husband for a nominal fee, as compensation for taking him in. Upon both their deaths, the paintings were willed to me."

She stated this with regal defiance.

"Why, *Maman*?" Caro asked in amazement. "And why did you never tell me?"

The dowager turned to Caro, her face stiff. "I sold them before Leopold married you. He could never have afforded a wedding otherwise. And when Leo came along, I knew more would have to go. My husband was a spendthrift, and my son had no head for money at all, had no idea what the things in his collection were worth. Clive told me he knew copyists who'd replace them without Leopold knowing the difference."

Caro's bewilderment turned to anger and remorse. Anger that the dowager had kept this to herself, not trusting Caro with the secret. Remorse that the woman had forced herself to part with her beloved father's artworks so that Caro's husband and son could live in some comfort.

It took courage to do what the dowager had done, Caro realized, and sacrifice. All the while the woman had been sipping chocolate and disparaging her acquaintances, she'd given up something dear to her heart so the family could keep fires burning in their chambers.

"Then why on earth did you let me hire Mr. Stone?" Caro asked her. "It was my idea to being in Cheswell's, and you did nothing to stop me. You encouraged me, in fact."

"Because I thought there might be paintings Clive had

missed," the dowager said heatedly. "Clive wasn't the brightest of men. I thought I would continue my scheme with Stone here, but he turned out to be too damned clever for his own good."

Caro swung to Eamon, who'd watched the exchange with a neutral expression.

"You said you thought the paintings had been copied years ago," Caro reminded him. "That some of the pigments were no longer obtainable."

"True." Eamon nodded. "I will guess that Clive already had some of the forgeries in stock—he has a warehouse full of them—and leapt at the chance to make use of them. He might have had difficulty selling the fakes, especially if it was known the originals were in the duke's collection."

"My husband did like to show them off," the dowager said with exasperation. "My son, however, never spotted the forgeries. Few visitors came to the house to look at them after the Fifth Duke died, in any case. Leopold preferred burying his nose in a book to speaking to people."

"So Her Grace has mentioned." Eamon shared a glance with Caro. "Out of interest, Your Grace, how much did Clive give you for this painting?"

"I scarcely remember," the dowager said. "I'd say about three hundred guineas. Sometimes he'd go as high as five."

Eamon's face turned a faint shade of green, and Singleton winced.

"Clive can turn around and flog them for thousands," Eamon informed her. "Since you sold the paintings to him legitimately, he actually does have the provenance he claimed. He swindled you, madame."

The dowager shrugged. "I knew they were worth more, but Clive promised to be discreet. He said nothing to my son or Caro, so he did hold up his end of the bargain."

"Even so, whenever he found a buyer for the originals, he

should have given you the lion's share of the profit." Eamon's gaze was firm. "He cheated your son and grandson out of a fortune. I will return to his warehouse and search it, though I will guess he's already sold most of the others for a hefty sum to buyers who didn't question him."

"I've told you, this is none of your business," the dowager said, her haughty self once more. "I agreed to let Caro hire you, because I never thought you'd find the damned paintings I sold and bring one home. Did you steal this from Clive? Or threaten him to make him hand it over?"

"I purchased it," Eamon said calmly. "For more than Clive paid you for it, though I talked him down from the price he originally stated."

"You bought it?" Caro blurted. "Why? How?"

The corners of Eamon's eyes crinkled. "I have my resources. As for why." He tipped the canvas toward Caro. "To give it to you."

Caro gaped at Rembrandt, who gazed staunchly back at her. "You cannot *give* it to me. *Maman* sold it, and you purchased it. That means it is yours."

"Yes," Eamon agreed. "And, as it belongs to me, I can do with it what I wish. I wish to make it a gift to you. Or, if you refuse to accept it for yourself, I will give it to Leo."

"Do not quibble, Caro," the dowager broke in. "I am not happy with Mr. Stone, but the damage has been done. Now, he is bestowing a valuable painting on you so that you might sell it again for some much-needed cash."

Her mother-in-law's frank speeches about money always left Caro breathless, but that did not mean she was wrong.

"I'm not certain I will sell it," Caro began. Leopold had been fond of the painting, even if the one he'd proudly showed Caro had been a fake.

"Nonsense," was the dowager's assessment. "Of course you should sell it."

"I do have an interested buyer," Eamon said. "One you would approve of. He is willing to pay twenty-five hundred guineas for it."

Caro grasped the back of a chair for support. "Twenty-five hundred ..."

"That would pay some of the more egregious bills," the dowager said without a flinch. "And allow you to hold your head up again when you go back into society, Caro. With enough left over for a decent frock. You truly need a few."

The dowager wore gowns from the late 1790s, simple affairs that had come into fashion after the high hair and wide panniers had fallen from favor. They were comfortable, she claimed, and she saw no reason to trade the style for any other. She'd always been rather critical of Caro's clothes, however, believing her daughter-in-law ought to dress in the first stare of fashion.

"I will think on it," Caro managed.

Twenty-five hundred guineas would stave off the nastiest of the dunners, the ones who cared nothing for a duke's rank.

Once the deepest debts were paid, and some of the accounts who'd been more patient brought up to date, then Leo's family would be considered creditworthy again. Whispers that Caro had been the cause of the duke's being a bankrupt might cease.

There would be more whispers about where the money had come from, but Caro would know—as would anyone who bothered to find out—that the source was legitimate, a painting inherited by her mother-in-law and bestowed upon Caro and Leo.

"I suppose you'll take your commission," the dowager said to Eamon with her usual cynicism.

Eamon shook his head. "Not at all. I will broker it as a favor to you and your daughter-in-law, and my liege, Leo."

The dowager's brows rose. "Then I will revise my opinion of you, Stone. You are nothing like your father."

Something flickered in Eamon's eyes. "I believe that is the best compliment I've ever received, Your Grace. Thank you."

"Now, then, none of your beguiling. Caro, will you sell it?"

Caro pondered a moment longer, then drew a deep breath, and nodded. "I think so."

"Good girl." The dowager gave her a cool nod and made her slow way back to her chair. "Singleton, bring me a fresh pot of chocolate, if you please. This one's gone cold."

"Very good, Your Grace." Singleton bowed, his smooth self. "Shall I take the picture down to the gallery?" he asked Caro.

"Please, Singleton. Thank you."

"Take good care of it," Eamon said as he relinquished the painting to Singleton's slim, gloved hands. "I worked very hard for that."

"Of course, sir." Singleton looked down his nose, affronted, and slid out of the room, making certain the painting didn't brush the doorframe.

The dowager picked up the letter she'd been perusing, proceeding to ignore Caro and Eamon, though Caro saw the paper tremble.

Caro seized Eamon's arm and half dragged him into the hall, closing the door behind them.

"You can't mean not to take a commission," she said in a near whisper when she faced him. "It cost you much to obtain that, did it not? *Maman* believes everyone ought to cater to us out of respect, but that is not the way of the world."

Eamon quirked a smile. "Never worry. The buyer has offered to clear my expenses, but the twenty-five hundred for the painting is all yours. Also, this is a private sale, so Cheswell will not swoop in for his cut, either."

"You will not tell me who this buyer is?"

"Not yet." Eamon brushed a lock of hair from Caro's face, his smile deepening.

Caro shivered under his touch. "You do like to tease."

"Only when it makes your eyes sparkle."

Caro's heart was full. Though she stood in a hallway where her mother-in-law, son, or Singleton could spring upon her at any moment, she wound her arms around Eamon and pulled him to her for a long and heartfelt kiss.

CHAPTER 24

*E*amon returned Sam's money the next evening, once more in Maiden Lane.

Sam scowled at him across his table. "Ye should have sent word and waited for my courier."

"I wanted no chance it wouldn't reach you." Eamon plunked himself down on the bench and pushed a brown-paper parcel to Sam.

"If a footpad had followed ye, I'd even now be watching your body be pulled out of the Thames."

"I'm a little more careful than that." Eamon accepted the strong brandy brought to him but didn't drink.

In truth, he'd noted plenty of shadows slipping after him when he'd departed Colonel Harper's, leaving the painting there, and sought a hackney. And again, when he'd left the hackney in the Strand and walked up narrow streets to Maiden Lane.

Had thieves of the underworld known about his transaction and the funds he'd been carrying? Or was he being followed for different reasons?

Once he'd ducked into the tavern and walked straight to Sam, his trackers had lost interest.

"Don't be cocksure, lad," Sam warned. "Some will roll you for a penny. This is all of it?" He rested his hand on the packet.

"Every pound, shilling, and pence, plus your ruinous fee."

Colonel Harper had been surprised Eamon wanted a cash transaction, instead of letting his man of business and Leo's handle the sale, but he hadn't questioned him. Eamon had left Colonel Harper gushing gratitude to Caro, the dowager, and the young duke, and turned to paying his debts.

Sam slid the package out of sight under the table, complimenting Eamon by not opening it and counting the money.

"What would ye have done if ye couldn't have repaid me?" Sam asked with curiosity.

Eamon grinned. "First of all, I had no doubt. Second, I'd direct you to take the cash out of Clive. I gave him a thousand guineas—that was your loan plus generous donations from other friends and what I could raise myself. If you went after Clive, you could have your cut back, and more, for your trouble."

"Pah." Sam made a face. "He's a pustule on the world's backside. Why the devil did you give *him* a thousand pounds?"

"To purchase something worth far more than that. I've made my investment back, never worry." Caro's face this evening when she realized Eamon would return to her house with twenty-five hundred guineas was payment enough.

"Ye should have told me," Sam growled. "I'd have done Clive over and given you whatever it was for nothing."

"Generous of you, but I needed a legitimate sale between legitimate buyers, with paperwork and the like. A legal trail. It's important."

"I see." Sam's eyes twinkled as he raised his tankard to his lips. "I hope the lady you've been going on about is worth it."

"She is, indeed," Eamon said warmly. "I told you, I plan to save her life."

Sam's skepticism returned. "And she'll reward you by marrying you? Only happens in stories, lad. Either that, or you're stuck with a shrew and regret being such a gentleman."

Eamon sat back, enjoying himself. "I write my own tales. They turn out how I like."

"That arrogance will take you down in the end," Sam said darkly. "Mark my words."

"As I say, I'll invite you to the wedding."

"Kind of you, lad, but such a lady will never let me in the door."

"She will." Eamon was certain of it. "She has the kindest heart and loveliest face of anybody you will ever meet."

"Has she now?" Sam gave him a frank stare. "Then why hasn't another gent already snapped her up?"

"Many complications," Eamon said, his enthusiasm dimming slightly. "A few more obstacles to navigate. But worth it in the end."

"It had better be." Sam took a noisy slurp of brandy. "Good luck to ye, is all I can say, since you won't take my advice and run far away."

"I won't," Eamon assured him. He never wanted to be further from Caro again than he was at this moment.

"In that case, I *will* go to your wedding," Sam said. "See this miracle for myself."

"You won't regret it, Sam."

"I already do." Sam set down his glass and wiped his mouth. "But you're a good lad, Stone. If anyone deserves a little happiness, it's you. God go with you, my boy."

————

EAMON LEFT THE TAVERN FOR THE DARK STREET, CLAPPING ON HIS hat and settling his coat. He walked toward Covent Garden, whistling cheerily.

He knew they'd waylay him in the darkness between Covent Garden and where he hoped to pick up a hackney in Long Acre. It stood to reason they'd wait until after he'd visited Sam and be off his guard, and would gamble that he had more money in his pockets than what he'd given Sam.

They'd be incorrect, though even the clothes on Eamon's back would fetch a good price.

Eamon had his knife out, his back to the wall before they rushed him. There were three men, all with foul-smelling breath and evil in their eyes.

They didn't bother taunting him or demanding he hand over his coin. They simply attacked.

Eamon fought hard. He wasn't so much bothered about any coins he carried as he was surviving to live another day. Sam was right that his arrogance might mean he was one more body in the Thames for the River Police to find.

One of the men cried out, and then he was mysteriously gone. A second grunted, and Eamon found himself one-on-one with the remaining attacker. The man glanced behind him worriedly, allowing Eamon to land a good punch on his jaw.

The assailant snarled and redoubled his assault. Eamon jabbed and struck, his knife held in a steady hand. The knife forced the man to duck and dodge, though he continued to rain blows down on Eamon.

Swearing in a strong Shetland accent came to him, along with annoyed mutters that signaled the presence of another former soldier. Wolfe's physician often admonished him about overusing his bad leg, but Wolfe just as often ignored him.

Between the three of them, they wore the ruffians down. Eamon's man stayed the longest, but when Eamon's knife came close to his eyes, he backed off and lumbered into the dark lane from whence he and his friends had come. Booted footsteps retreated into the night.

"Didn't bring any slow matches, did you?" McCormick asked, his grin flashing.

"Unfortunately, no." Eamon caught his breath as he slid the knife back into his pocket. "Or powder either."

"If you two are finished congratulating yourselves," Wolfe growled. "It's best we get indoors. You can thank us with an ale later, Stone."

McCormick had already raced off, whistling for the nearest hackney. One turned from the end of the street, McCormick climbing aboard as it passed.

"Thank you for springing to my aid," Eamon said as the hackney neared. "Very timely."

"We weren't risking you losing all our cash."

The hackney halted. McCormick opened the door for them, and Wolfe more or less heaved Eamon inside before climbing in behind him.

"No fear," Eamon said as the hackney pulled away. "Your money is tucked safely away, as is Caro's share."

"Tucked away where?" Wolfe asked with his usual suspicion. He dropped to the seat beside McCormick and opposite Eamon. "In a box under your bed?"

"I left it with Colonel Harper," Eamon informed them. "I'll fetch it tomorrow. I never planned to swan about London with Caro's funds in my pocket. I'm an idiot, but not that much of one."

"Notice he doesn't mention *our* hard-earned funds," McCormick said as the hackney bumped along St. Martin's Lane.

"I had noticed." Wolfe nodded.

"You'll have your money tomorrow, gentlemen," Eamon assured them. "Shall I call on you, or do you want to meet at the office of your man of business, Wolfe?"

"Leave it with Kennedy," Wolfe said. "McCormick and I will fetch it for ourselves."

"A sensible arrangement," Eamon said. "Then *you* can worry about thieves trying to relieve it from you, and I will retire to the nearest pub for refreshment."

"Were they common robbers, do you think?" McCormick asked, cutting through Eamon's banter. "Following you about, thinking you had a few coins to rub together?"

"No." Eamon recognized hired thugs when he saw them. Less desperate, more determined. "I believe they came courtesy of His Grace's cousin."

McCormick scowled. "I thought that might be the case. We have to do something about that bastard."

"Not a bastard," Wolfe broke in. "He's a legitimate heir. Berridge will be duke, no matter what his actions, if anything happens to Leo."

"Then we must make certain Leo grows up to be happily married and produce seven sons of his own," Eamon said firmly. "I'll never let Rudyard stand in the way of Leo having the life he deserves."

"A cause I can strive for," Wolfe said with a nod. "Berridge is an idiot who should be revealed as such."

"I am pleased I can count on your assistance." The fact that Eamon had such friends warmed him, though he'd never embarrass them with these sentiments. He'd been very much alone when he'd been deposited at Hallbridge, but adversity had found him two fellow castaways who'd become like brothers to him.

"You will always have my help," McCormick promised. "You didn't make much out of this deal, though, with the painting, did you? Once you've paid us back and taken the lion's share to young Leo, there isn't much left over for you, is there?"

"It's enough." Eamon's share was minuscule compared to what he'd borrowed from McCormick, Wolfe, and Sam to obtain the painting, but it was plenty for what he would purchase with it.

McCormick studied him quizzically, but Eamon kept his silence.

———

"Are you certain of this?" Caro regarded Lady Carmichael with a mixture of hope and revulsion. If what Lady Carmichael said was true, Rudyard was the most heinous of men.

"Of course I'm certain," Lady Carmichael returned in indignation. "I wouldn't have said so, otherwise."

The two sat in Lady Carmichael's large and luxurious drawing room in South Audley Street, where Caro had been summoned to take tea. Caro had expected a formal gathering, but Lady Carmichael's maid, who'd helped restore Caro's coiffure at the ball, had ushered her into an elegant room on an upper floor where Lady Carmichael waited alone.

Another maid carried in a tray with tea things and an array of small cakes and left them to it.

Lady Carmichael took a sip of tea and continued. "That young man is swindling half the *haut ton*. Not me, of course. My money is well secured, and I'd never invest it in anything for any reason. Fools, the lot of them, but they thought they'd be safe with a duke's heir. Why, I couldn't say. The Berridges were never clever with money."

"But you said some people benefitted nicely," Caro said, trying to understand. Lady Carmichael's story tallied with some of the things she'd learned through Jo and Louise and their connections, but it was still puzzling. "Which means some shares went up and others down. I believe that happens with stocks, does it not?"

"Yes, but not with the exact same ones at the exact same time," Lady Carmichael scoffed. "If Lady Featherbrain invests in canals and loses her money but Lady Feeblewit invests in the same canals and rakes in a forty-percent profit, that raises many questions about these shares. Such as, are they real at all? What does Berridge actually do with the investments?"

Caro had never needed to be shrewd about stocks and shares, but she did know that high returns were unusual. Either people were far over-investing, as had happened with the notorious South Sea Bubble of the last century, or there was something shady going on.

"Who could tell me?" Caro asked, though she was more or less musing out loud. She wasn't certain Lady Carmichael would have an answer.

"Rudyard's man of business," Lady Carmichael said at once. "Or your son's. Make them both dig into what Rudyard is doing. I will also dig. I never invest myself, as I say, but I keep an eye on the markets. I'll send my own man to find out exactly what are stocks these people believe they're buying and how Rudyard is covering them. Do not worry, Caro, dear. We will discover all."

Caro had no doubt Lady Carmichael would. When the woman was determined, not even all of Emperor Bonaparte's army could have stopped her.

Unfortunately, Lady Carmichael turned that determination on Caro in the next moment.

"Now then, what about you and this picture man? The one who has been ferreting through the duke's things since your former curator deserted you? I hear he watches you like a lost sheep. Do you reciprocate his sentiments?"

CHAPTER 25

Caro couldn't very well exclaim, *I don't know what you mean,* to Lady Carmichael, when she'd already been so intimate with Eamon.

Intimacy Caro had relived in her heart every day and night since. Each kiss they stole tasted of it, each smile and touch brought the rush of desire flaring to the surface. It was agony to know Eamon was so close but at the same time had to remain remote.

Eamon always made certain to leave the house at six in the evening, Singleton locking up after he'd gone. Caro knew she was wanton enough to beg him to stay, hang the scandal, but Eamon was being very careful with her reputation. Caro ought to be grateful, but the hunger he'd stirred could not be sated.

Caro only hoped her heated discomfort at Lady Carmichael's questions did not show too much on her face.

"I am a grown woman," Caro said stiffly. "And a widow, not a foolish ingenue."

"I know that, my dear, but your mother-in-law tells me that you and the picture man are rather inseparable."

The dowager always discerned more than she let on, which

burned Caro hotter still. She strove for dignity. "I do not believe it is anyone's business."

"If you marry him, it will become many people's business," Lady Carmichael said with her stern practicality. "This Mr. Stone will have influence over Leo and all those who want to be close to him. Including Cousin Rudyard, which is why he is being so troublesome. Rudyard wants guardianship of Leo, does he not? Hence you fishing for any dirt on him you can find."

"I can't give Leo to Rudyard," Caro said, her desperation returning.

"I agree with you. Rudyard will do everything it takes to gain the title, especially if he owes people money. If nothing else, once he is duke, Rudyard could make laws in the House of Lords that keep him from having to pay back what he's taken." Lady Carmichael waved a black-gloved hand. "Possibly. I have no idea what they get up to in the Lords. A great deal of empty posturing, I'm certain."

"Please help me stop him," Caro begged.

"You poor darling. Of course we will stop him." Lady Carmichael's voice gentled. "You do realize that, in order to keep Leo safe, you might have to send your picture man away. Are you prepared to do so?"

Was she? Caro had long understood she might have to tell Eamon to leave, and she would, if she had no other choice.

Once Leo was grown and Caro was old and decrepit, and no one cared what she did, perhaps she and Eamon could meet again and have their affair—if Eamon remembered her at all by then.

Caro felt herself break down. She'd resolved to remain businesslike while she spoke with Lady Carmichael, to gather her arsenal to face Rudyard.

But the thought of sending Eamon away, of weathering a bleak, lonely future without him, washed her in despair. Caro had never meant to lose herself like this, but it was too late now.

Caro's tears blurred the creams and blues of the drawing room and the black-clad form of Lady Carmichael. "Why does it have to be so difficult?" she asked shakily.

"Because life is always difficult, dear, in great ways and small ones." Lady Carmichael patted Caro's hand then handed her a large linen handkerchief. "Love is difficult as well. But worth fighting for, in my experience. Leave it with me. I will find out specifically what Rudyard is up to, and we'll have him. Few people can abide him anyway, so they'll be happy to shut him out."

Caro wiped away tears, grateful for the pragmatic handkerchief. "Will that be enough to keep Leo safe?"

"Possibly. We can't change the line of inheritance or Rudyard's blood ties to Leo, but we can make England too hot to hold Rudyard and allow Leo to grow up in peace. Once Leo comes of age, he'll be able to deal with Rudyard himself. And who knows? Leo might produce many heirs of his own, and keep Rudyard far from the dukedom."

Caro smiled tremulously at Lady Carmichael, crumpling the damp handkerchief. "Then let us do our worst."

"That's the spirit," Lady Carmichael said. "Now, drink your tea, dear. It will fortify you for what's to come."

———

WHEN EAMON REACHED THE GROSVENOR STREET HOUSE THE next afternoon, after a morning spent running all over London, he found the Countess of Heyford and Princess Josephine descending the staircase.

Caro glided after them, she in her simple everyday frock while her friends wore the latest in light summer coats and plumed bonnets, though the countess's shades were subdued. Caro was animated, her color high, eyes sparkling like jewels in the dim light.

"Your Ladyship, Your Highness, Your Grace." Eamon swept off his hat and greeted them in turn.

"Mr. Stone." Lady Heyford gave him an elegant nod.

Jo shot him an impish grin. "Mr. Stone, how lovely to see you. And how clever you were to find Leo's Rembrandt. How fortunate, also, that Colonel Harper wished to buy it. Yes, I have my resources and know he was the purchaser."

Eamon couldn't stop himself from grinning back at her. "Indeed. Her Grace has been most fortunate all the way around."

"As have you, but I do not think it was all luck." Jo's eyes twinkled with good humor. "By the bye, while you're searching London for more genuine paintings, you wouldn't look out for a nice miniature—say a Holbein or some such—would you? I'd like to give one to Merry for her birthday."

Eamon nodded. "I know the sort you mean, and yes, I will keep an eye out."

"Splendid." Jo latched her arm through that of Louise, who'd been listening with cool detachment. "We are off to do battle. Good afternoon, Mr. Stone."

"Good afternoon, ladies." Eamon handed his hat to Singleton, who'd emerged the moment the two women reached the ground floor, and bowed once more.

A carriage pulled up before the house, footmen swarming from it to help the ladies inside. Caro waved her farewells until the carriage rolled away and Singleton shut the door.

Singleton took Eamon's coat as he shed it and hung it on the hall tree, then vanished to wherever he vanished to every day. The man always reappeared like magic when Eamon finished for the evening and was ready to depart.

"I have much to tell you," Caro said to Eamon once they were alone in the foyer.

"I have things to tell you as well," Eamon said. "Shall we?"

He gestured up the stairs, as formal as though they hadn't

shared a passionate kiss the evening before or lounged together in her bed the previous week.

"I think mine is more important," Caro declared as they started for the gallery.

"Of course it is," Eamon said. "A lady's news should always come first."

Caro eyed in him exasperation. "Do not try to be witty. But it *is* important. About Rudyard."

Eamon had no interest in discussing the lump, but he drew Caro to the far end of the gallery and turned her to face him.

"Rudyard has been running an investment scheme." Caro bounced on her toes as she announced this. "Taking money from his friends and acquaintances, telling them they were investing in anything from shipping ventures to new canals that will trundle goods across England."

"Has he, now?" Eamon's interest reengaged.

Since canal building was an ongoing activity, and ships from all over the world came and went from London, such a proposal on Rudyard's part would sound plausible. Rudyard could then take the money he claimed would go straight to an investment house and pocket it for himself.

"Everyone believed him at first," Caro went on, "because he'd pay them back handsomely in a few months, sometimes doubling what they'd invested."

"Ah," Eamon said. "I begin to see."

His father hadn't been as daring, because any money Sir Benedict had come into slipped through his fingers immediately, but several of Sir Benedict's cronies had tried such schemes. They would pay the first investor with money from the second, pay the second from the third, and so on, after skimming off a large portion for themselves, of course.

"But then, some people began to grow restless," Caro was saying. "When they'd inquire about how their investment was doing, Rudyard would evade the question or send them a placating letter. I believe Rudyard keeps all the money and has never invested at all."

"I believe you are right," Eamon said, catching her animation. "Have you found proof?"

Caro nodded, tendrils of hair dancing, as they did in every sketch Eamon had made of her. "Lady Carmichael has suspected him of it for a time. She's asked among her friends, and I had Jo and Louise do the same. It turns out that plenty of people have entrusted Rudyard with their money. Even if they don't like him personally, he is the nephew of my late husband, whom they *did* like. Leopold was always painfully honest, and I suppose those who don't know Rudyard well assume he must be the same."

"Which explains why he's so keen to be duke," Eamon mused. "Though there's no money in the title, he'd have lands and some protection if his schemes come to light. Sooner or later, though, he will have to answer ..."

"He will," Caro said in satisfaction. "We are rounding up our army to expose him." She finished with a smile of triumph.

If she would only cease being beautiful for a few moments, Eamon might remember how to breathe.

"This is excellent news," he managed to say. "My friends and I will do everything in our power to help you." Eamon dipped a hand into the pocket of his frock coat. "But as much as I'd like to rush out and drag Rudyard before a magistrate on the moment, I do have something for you."

"Oh, yes, for the Rembrandt." Caro clasped her hands, her smile broadening. "You do not have to give *me* the money, you know. Take it to Leo's man of business. I'm certain he'll be excited to hand it out to the creditors, which will be such a help. Thank you, Eamon."

She would slay him with her praise. Eamon tamped down his impatient desires and forced himself back to the task at hand.

"This has nothing to do with the money. The funds are with

Leo's man of business even now." One of Eamon's errands had been to that gentleman.

Caro regarded him with eager anticipation. "Have you located another painting?"

"Not yet, but please let me finish."

"I beg your pardon." Caro's attempt to be contrite made her more enticing than ever. "I simply haven't been hopeful for a while. What is this something?"

"A small token." Eamon pulled a velvet bag from his pocket. Under the watchful eye of the faux Diana on the table next to them, he opened it.

Caro caught the flash of light within. "What on earth?"

Eamon lifted a thin gold strand studded with diamonds from the pouch. "I've been wanting to see this on you," he said softly.

Caro's lips parted as she stared at the diamonds in wonderment. "No, I could not possibly …"

"You could. Most definitely."

Eamon stepped behind her, as he'd pictured himself doing so many times, and laid the necklace around her throat. He fastened the catch, pleased that his fingers didn't shake.

The necklace was not something he'd simply found at a jeweler's stall. Eamon had run down an old friend of his father's in Hatton Garden and told the man exactly what sort of adornment he'd wanted for Caro.

The man was a genius, setting ten diamonds perfectly along the gold strand. The necklace had taken every last pence of the money Eamon had recovered from Colonel Harper for the painting, but viewing the diamonds resting on Caro's bosom was worth it.

"Really, Eamon, I cannot take this." Caro's voice was almost a whisper.

"I am happy you like it."

"I do." Caro gazed up at him with soft eyes, fingers resting lightly on the chain. "I adore it. You are far too kind."

"It has nothing to do with kindness." Eamon brushed the necklace, her flesh warm through her gauzy fichu. "I want you to be my duchess in diamonds. Nothing less will do for you."

"Because we are lovers now," she said shyly.

"Nothing to do with being lovers, either." Another caress, catching her fingers with it. "I want you to have it. Now you do not have to borrow your friends' jewels when you attend their balls."

"Ah." Caro's look turned teasing. "It is out of pity, then."

"Why does there have to be a reason?" Eamon drew her to him. "My reason is I want you to be happy. Seeing your eyes light like they are now is reason enough."

"Then I will cease being a prig." Caro rose on her tiptoes. "Thank you."

She kissed him.

Eamon forgot everything—Rudyard, paintings, debts, even the necklace—and sank into Caro, parting her lips, letting her sear him.

Caro made that delightful noise in her throat which meant she wanted him. Eamon's longing soared, and he scooped her into him, tasting her joy and need, letting it sustain him.

A draft flowing along the gallery reminded Eamon that they stood in too exposed an area to act on their yearnings. He reluctantly broke the kiss but could not resist leaning down and catching the diamonds in his teeth.

Caro gasped, then her quiet laughter surrounded him. She stepped away, but before the cold of that could slap him, she caught Eamon's hand and towed him to the staircase.

They ascended to the next floor, which embraced them with its silence. Caro guided Eamon a short way down the hall to the small drawing room where he'd first encountered her, when she struggled with a stubborn window.

Caro led him inside, closed the door, and turned the key in the lock.

CHAPTER 26

*E*amon never wanted this afternoon to end. He braced himself against the back of the armless chair they'd ended up on, buried inside Caro, who was twined around him.

There was no sound in the room but their mingled breath and groaned words.

Caro was bare except for the necklace shimmering on her throat. Eamon held her securely as he rocked against her, unable to thrust much in this position, but it didn't matter. Caro's warmth enveloped him, and her soft moans as she squeezed him made this chamber a fine place.

Eamon had imagined this scenario since the first day he'd encountered her here—a quick taste of pleasure on a chair, her skirts around them—but this was so much better. He'd learned that Caro had an even deeper beauty than what he'd first seen, a heart she gave readily, a caring beyond anything he'd ever known.

Caro uttered a cry, descending into the newfound passion she was exploring with him, her face softening in desire and wonder.

"Duchess." Eamon felt his release coming, and he fought it

off to prolong this deep and satisfying pleasure. "You are gloriously beautiful."

Caro's answer was a little sob. "You are good to me," she whispered. "So good." The word died on another intake of breath.

"I'll do anything for you, love."

Eamon heard the words come out of his mouth, including the fateful *love*, but Caro only smiled at him, which made his world right again.

———

"STONE?" AN INCREDULOUS VOICE RANG OUT A FEW NIGHTS LATER.

Eamon paused on the steps that led into a hell called the Nines in St. James's, McCormick and Wolfe on either side of him. Standing before them was a giant of a man with very pale hair and surprised pleasure in his wide blue eyes.

"Hell," Wolfe muttered behind Eamon.

"It *is* you," the blond man went on. "I knew it was. Was telling Monty here it was."

The Viking, whose real name Eamon recalled was Percival Davison, beamed at them from his six-and-a-half-foot height. Wolfe had said the man was bulging with muscle, and his assessment was correct. The middle-aged gentleman next to him, who must be Monty, nodded at Eamon and his companions and made his relieved escape into the street.

There was nothing for it. "Davison." Eamon stepped forward, hand out. "Been too long."

"Call me what you used to—the Viking." The man boomed a laugh and grabbed Eamon's hand in a crushing grip. "I like that. No one else dares give me a moniker so friendly."

Eamon decided not to remind the Viking of the days they'd spent healing from wounds taken in brawls the Viking had started. Eamon realized that the Viking had blurred his memories with nostalgia, until they'd all been friends who'd enjoyed a good tussle.

"Ever see Pebbly?" Eamon asked as the Viking turned to beam at Wolfe and McCormick.

"Eh? Who? Oh, Pollard. No, he absconded to the Continent ahead of his creditors." The Viking bellowed another laugh. "Married a pretty lady and bankrupted himself trying to keep her in jewels. Wolfe—good to see you again. Wolfe and I ran into each other a few weeks ago. We had a fine reunion, didn't we?"

Wolfe answered with something noncommittal, pointedly edging toward the entrance of the Nines, but the Viking wasn't finished.

"And McCormick, still a beacon to ships at sea." The Viking pointed to Hayden's very red hair atop his tall body. "Thought you'd bunged off back to Scotland."

"Not for long," McCormick said, as though unoffended. "Took up with the Army, then London."

"Well, we're all together again," the Viking concluded. "What are you doing *here*? This place has deep play. Very deep. Lost my little all, I'm afraid."

Eamon had brought McCormick and Wolfe here after brandy at the Twenty-Fifth's club and a conversation about Rudyard's wrongdoings. They had enough information now, including what Caro and her friends had supplied, to expose Rudyard for fraud.

McCormick had suggested they adjourn to the Nines to celebrate. As a genius with numbers, he could take his small amount of pocket cash and win whatever he wished.

Eamon longed to return to Caro and tell her their plans—and possibly for other activities as well—but the hour was late. He agreed to accompany McCormick, along with Wolfe, who declared McCormick couldn't be trusted to stay out of trouble.

"We're only here for a small flutter," Eamon assured the Viking. "Wonderful to have seen you again."

"Hang about," the Viking said as Eamon and friends finally glided in past him. "I'll stay too. Maybe you can give me some pointers, McCormick. Always at the top of the class in maths, weren't you?"

McCormick sent him a thin smile, but none of them could stop the Viking from marching back into the building with them.

The gaming room was at the rear of the house, filled with card and dice tables. Plenty of brandy and whisky circulated, as well as silk-clad ladies whose task it was to entice gentlemen to wager more coin.

McCormick knew how to choose games with favorable odds —as favorable as they could be in a gaming hell. That meant whist against three other players or piquet against one. Soon he was deep in a game of picquet with another like-minded sharp, focused on the cards in his hand.

Eamon towed the Viking, who wanted to hover at McCormick's shoulder asking questions, to a table where a riotous game of hazard was taking place. Dice clattered, men groaned or cheered, and ladies hung on the arms of the winners, urging them on.

The Viking soon joined in the fray, throwing down his markers without compunction. Though he'd claimed he'd lost heavily, he came from a wealthy family, who'd likely pay any vowels he accumulated tonight.

Eamon had no interest in gaming and neither did Wolfe, who lounged against a pillar and kept an eye on McCormick. McCormick would probably win a nice sum and need his battle-hardened friends to help him take it home safely.

Tomorrow, Eamon would eliminate Cousin Rudyard as a threat to Caro and Leo. Caro's friends had been instrumental in the last few days in finding people willing to confess that

Rudyard had cheated them. Lady Carmichael had sent Eamon a long list, mostly of women who did not want their husbands to discover they'd trusted Rudyard with their pin money. A few of them, Lady Carmichael declared, were angry enough to denounce him.

Wolfe and McCormick had volunteered to take the evidence they'd collected to a magistrate Wolfe knew was honest. An investigation would ensue to prove actual fraud, of course. But even if the case never came before a court, Rudyard's name would be blackened, his suitability as a guardian to a young duke questioned.

Eamon had even more permanent ideas about what to do with Rudyard, and things were already in motion.

For now, Eamon waited for McCormick to enjoy a rare evening of entertainment and daydreamed of Caro.

Eamon had never fallen in love before, beyond the brief but heated infatuations of youth. He'd never experienced the absolute joy he did whenever Caro entered a room, had never woken in the early morning eager to trudge London's foggy and smoke-choked streets to begin his daily tasks.

His spirits always rose as soon as the Grosvenor Square house came into view, lifted still further as he greeted Singleton and handed over his wraps. Finally, his happy anticipation was fulfilled when he heard Caro's steps descending toward him, when he beheld her curved figure and beautiful smile as she bade him good morning.

Eamon would make certain he could wake up with her every morning of his life and kiss her good night in the dark.

"Stone?" a haughty and much-loathed voice spoke behind Eamon, shattering these pleasant visions.

He turned, hoping his hard countenance would make the man and the toadies who surrounded him go away, but Rudyard Berridge didn't possess the sense to know when he wasn't welcome. Either that or he simply enjoyed being an irritant.

"Berridge," Eamon said coldly.

"Why are you not in Grosvenor Square, sniffing around Aunt Caro's skirts?" Rudyard sneered at him, and the toadies imitated his expression.

Eamon faced Rudyard fully. "Have a care. I am not in the mood to listen to you disparage a lady."

"Hardly a lady," Rudyard drawled. "A countrified miss who got above herself. Landed herself a duke by spreading her dimpled knees."

"I say, Berridge, steady on," one of the toadies said, sounding shocked.

Eamon said nothing. He pictured himself seizing Rudyard by the collar and dashing his face into the nearest wall, pounding him until his nose was a bloody pulp. Had they not stood in a roomful of gentlemen growing more and more interested in the argument, Rudyard would have already been a groaning heap on the floor.

But a dim voice beyond Eamon's rage, the one that had ensured his survival all these years, told him that Rudyard was hoping to provoke Eamon to violence. Was counting on it. Rudyard supposed his toadies would keep him safe while Eamon would either be hauled to Bow Street or subdued by the toughs who kept order in this hell.

If Eamon was arrested for assault, Rudyard would no doubt prosecute, and Caro would lose Leo. Rudyard could claim that Caro's lover was a dangerous and savage man, and that Leo would be far safer with his own cousin, away from London and his unprincipled mother.

There was one solution to his dilemma, which Eamon was certain Rudyard would not like.

"You need to be taught manners, Berridge," Eamon said calmly. "My seconds will call on yours in the morning."

Rudyard's mouth popped open and some of his bravado evaporated. "Are you challenging me to a *duel?*" he managed. "As though you are a gentleman?"

Eamon lifted his brows. "Are you refusing?"

"I do not duel with those beneath me." Rudyard tried to stick his nose in the air and stroll away, but he was hemmed in by the interested crowd that had formed, and he couldn't move a step.

"I will second," Wolfe announced beside Eamon.

"And me," McCormick, who'd obviously deserted his game, said on Eamon's other side.

"You are a pack of nobodies," Rudyard scoffed.

The man who'd expressed shocked disapproval at Rudyard's nasty comments about Caro moved to Rudyard's shoulder. "Have a care. That's Lord Dominick Wolfe. Hardly a nobody. And Stone's a dead shot."

"Name *your* seconds, Berridge," Wolfe said. "And we'll arrange the meeting. But know that if Stone decides not to waste powder on you, I'll shoot you myself."

Eamon warmed at Wolfe's offer, but he continued to regard Rudyard with a firm stare.

"Of course you need your friends to fight for you," Rudyard said nervously. "How convenient for you, Stone. I heard you were honored for your bravery at Waterloo, but that was all balderdash, wasn't it?"

This was as close as Rudyard could come to calling Eamon a coward without actually saying the word. He must enjoy teetering on the edge.

"I suppose you will find out when we meet," Eamon said in a mild tone. "It is bad form to continue to speak about it. I issued the challenge, and you will answer it. Our seconds will discuss it from now on."

Eamon deliberately turned his back on Rudyard and without haste strolled away, leaving Wolfe and McCormick to close in front of Rudyard.

The Viking's voice rose above the sudden swell of conversation. "Swine," he bellowed at Rudyard. "How dare you call my friend a coward?"

The sound of fist meeting flesh echoed, and Rudyard grunted. Eamon reached the fray in time to see the Viking pull back his massive fist and plant another blow on Rudyard's face. Blood streaked Rudyard's skin, and the man cried out in pain.

The Viking took a step back, still furious, but he made no other exertion. Rudyard wiped his face, blood staining his glove.

Just as the surrounding men relaxed, deciding the brawl was finished, Rudyard launched himself at the Viking. Both Eamon and Wolfe blocked him.

"Enough," Eamon said in a commanding tone.

Rudyard surged forward, mindless rage propelling him. He kicked Wolfe in his bad leg, and Wolfe cursed, stumbling. He managed to pound Rudyard once in the jaw before half-collapsing.

McCormick took Wolfe's place. McCormick grinned at Rudyard, a bad sign. McCormick was at his most deadly when he smiled at his enemy.

Rudyard swung at Eamon. McCormick got in front of him, deftly intercepting the blow and returning one of his own. Rudyard snarled, spitting blood, but continued to flail.

Eamon wound an arm under Rudyard's and around the back of his neck, locking him in a hard grip.

"Time you were gone." Eamon half dragged, half carried Rudyard through the parting crowd and out of the game room. Rudyard's coterie seemed to have deserted him, none coming to his aid.

The Viking and a dozen others followed, McCormick assisting Wolfe. When they reached the front hall, Rudyard struggled anew, but Eamon propelled him to the front door, with Viking and the others surging with them.

The beefy man who guarded the entrance sprang forward and opened the door.

"Not only is Berridge craven, but he owes me a packet," the Viking boomed. "I gave him scads of cash to invest in this canal scheme of his months and months ago. He assured me it would pay out handsomely in only weeks, and others have had plenty back from him. But not me. So where is my blunt, eh?"

Rudyard, in Eamon's headlock, could only splutter.

"*I* invested with him too," another tightly angry voice came. "What have I to show for it? Not a sausage."

"He's cheating us," the Viking declared.

"He is indeed," another man said coldly. "I've been after him for months to show me his returns, and he puts me off. I'll see you in court, Berridge."

"Or we could beat it out of him now," the Viking suggested eagerly. Eamon reflected that the man had not changed one whit from their Hallbridge days.

Others joined in the call for Rudyard's blood.

Rudyard yelped and turned pleading eyes to Eamon. "For God's sake, Stone. They'll kill me."

They might, indeed. These gentlemen were angry, and the Viking was a strong man who could deal out a great amount of pain without realizing it. That likely hadn't changed from his school days either.

"McCormick," Eamon commanded. "Hackney."

McCormick released Wolfe—who was arguing that he could stand by himself, *blast you*—to whistle and wave at a black carriage in the square.

Eamon dragged Rudyard to the hackney that lumbered toward them, and McCormick yanked open its door.

"I'd leave the country," Eamon advised as he bundled Rudyard inside. "Even if these gentlemen don't kill you, they'll blacken your name and bring suit against you. You've ruined yourself, Berridge. Time to go."

Rudyard landed on the seat, blood, mucus, and tears on his face. "This is *your* doing, Stone."

"Actually, no, you did this on your own." Eamon wrenched a small bag from his pocket, which clinked as he pressed it into Rudyard's hand. "I mean leave the country *now*. Tonight. There's enough there to pay an unscrupulous ship's mate for a crossing."

As Rudyard stared at the bag with incomprehension, Eamon climbed into the coach himself. The coachman, thinking Eamon was another fare, started off, the open door banging.

McCormick slammed the door for them, waving them off. Eamon plunked to the opposite seat from Rudyard and shouted a direction at the driver through the hatch in the roof. Wheels skidded on cobblestones as the coachman steered them into Pall Mall and headed east.

"You're coming with me?" Rudyard asked in a tremulous voice.

"Only as far as the London docks. To make certain you get *on* a ship."

"I can't leave England," Rudyard bleated. "I'm a duke's grandson. My cousin's heir. You'll steal him from me, beguiling him and his mother."

Eamon shook his head. "Leo's an amiable chap. I imagine he'll set up some sort of allowance for you, even if the rest of the world advises him to cut you entirely." He leaned to Rudyard, forcing the man to meet his gaze. "And if anything happens to Leo—an assassin in the dark, a hunting accident, if he even so much as skins his knee—I will come after you, and I will end you. Make no mistake about it."

Fear flared anew in Rudyard's eyes. "You can't. You wouldn't dare."

"I would. As that fellow in the Nines told you, I'm a dead shot. I'm also very good with knives."

"You'd hang." Rudyard's voice was barely above a whisper.

"As long as I have my revenge, I won't mind. And who knows? A magistrate might think me justified. But know that I will protect Leo and Caro from you with everything I have. *You* will be out of their lives. For good."

Rudyard listened with his jaw slack. "Why are you doing this to me?"

Eamon sat back. "You did it to yourself, Berridge. Cheated people, juggled their money to make the influential believe you honest while you skimmed off the rest. Did the money run out? Is that why you want the dukedom—you thought it would protect you from the men you swindled? Trust me, you can't outrun your confidence tricks forever. You'll have to flee sooner or later. You might as well flee tonight."

Rudyard stared. "How do you know all this?"

"I know a great deal about you," Eamon said with finality. "I make it my business to learn all I can about people, always have. Now, I am tired of talking to you. Let us enjoy the remainder of the journey in companionable silence."

Rudyard continued to gape, so Eamon gazed out of the window, pretending he could discern things among the smudgy fog, made opaque by the coach lights.

He half expected Rudyard to leap out of the carriage or maybe attack Eamon, and Eamon readied himself to forestall him, but Rudyard only sat like a lump. Fear had at last penetrated his arrogance.

For now, anyway. Rudyard would likely try to wriggle out of his fraud when he was safely in France or Italy and attempt to return to England with vengeance on his mind. However, Eamon knew plenty of people throughout the Continent, thanks to his father's travels. While Sir Benedict had left distrustful acquaintances behind, Eamon had made many friends.

One of them was the captain's mate on a ship loading at the London docks. Eamon had alerted the man through Sam Noble, and had met up with him the other morning, asking him to be ready. Eamon had planned this departure for tomorrow but tonight would serve as well.

When the hackney halted, Eamon stepped down and whistled a signal. Several burly men appeared out of the fog to haul Rudyard from the hackney and toward the gangway of the small ship, which sailed for Amsterdam in the morning.

"All right, Stone?" the mate joined Eamon on the dock amid the swirling activity, while Rudyard limped up the wooden gangplank between men not about to let him go.

"I am now." Eamon couldn't stop a grin. "When you're next in port, I'll thank you properly. You won't pay for a drink for your entire shore leave."

The mate chortled. "You've done me plenty of favors over the years, including my post on this ship. Captain is a reasonable man."

"You deserved it," Eamon said warmly. "You kept ruffians from beating a frightened lad senseless in this very dockyard. I'd have been dead or maimed for life if you hadn't happened along."

"You'd have talked your way free if I hadn't," the mate said with an answering grin. "You have the gift, Stone."

"When your jaw is half broken, speech does no good." Eamon touched his face, recalling how blood had filled his mouth when the older, tougher boys had wanted to teach him who ruled the docks. "Your rescue was timely."

"That may be." The mate held out his hand. "Well met, once again."

"And you, sir." Eamon accepted the firm handshake. "Make certain Berridge doesn't fall overboard. He's an idiot, but I think his best punishment will be having to live with himself."

The mate's eyes twinkled as he released Eamon from his grip. "He might be a bit sick on the crossing, though."

"That, I don't mind." Eamon turned up the collar of his coat against the damp. He'd come away without his greatcoat or hat, and the night had turned wet and smelly, especially along the river. "Until next time, my friend."

"Get yourself indoors," the mate advised. "It will be a foul night."

"I think it's beautiful." Eamon scanned the thick fog, into which the masts of the merchant ships disappeared. "A splendid evening, one of the most splendid I've seen in my life." He laughed at the mate's incredulous look. "I'm in love, sir. With a beautiful woman who just might love me in return. Life is sweet, and all the world walks in beauty."

The mate shook his head. "Well, you're lost, ain't you? Good night, Stone. God keep you."

"And you." Eamon sketched a salute, then turned and strode, whistling, into the fog, toward the waiting hackney.

———

CARO LEANED BACK IN THE DESK CHAIR, SURROUNDED BY Leopold's books and papers in his old study on the third floor. She rarely came into this room, finding reminders of her brief but contented time with Leopold too painful.

She'd been fond of Leopold for his kindness and quiet affection, for his love of books, and the art he liked to gaze at. For the amusing way he'd shield her from the nude statuettes they happened to pass. For his pride in Leo the few years he'd been able to know his son.

What Caro felt for Eamon was different but did not diminish her tenderness for Leopold. He'd had a special place in her life, one she'd never regret. How could she, when Leopold had unashamedly loved Caro and given her Leo, her greatest joy?

Now Eamon, out of the deep kindness he tried to hide from the world, had provided Caro with some means of helping Leo resolve his father's debts and start him on a path to do great things. Hence, Caro's morning spent looking through Leopold's desk.

Most of the estate's bills were with Leo's man of business, who was now busily paying them with proceeds from the sold Rembrandt. But Leopold had kept other vowels here, personal debts to friends or bills for indulgences such as little gifts for Caro or Leo.

Caro was determined to have their man of business repay these debts as well. Leopold's friends had mostly been understanding about them—they'd lent the money to Leopold out of affection for him in the first place, as they knew how feckless he could be.

Caro did not wish Leo to be obliged to these friends in any way, so he could begin life free of worry. Many aristocrats lived awash in debt, but Caro's simpler upbringing had taught her that being beholden to no one was a more comfortable way to exist.

She sighed and continued to leaf through the ledger before her, noting that Leopold had marked a page of unpaid debts with a loose piece of paper. An old piece, Caro realized as she touched it.

No, not paper, her fingers told her, as her heart beat faster. Vellum.

Caro turned the sheet over, and wonder met her eyes.

CHAPTER 27

*H*er Grace wishes to see you in the study, sir," Singleton announced as he took Eamon's wraps the morning after Eamon had escorted Rudyard to the docks.

Eamon had overslept, after sinking into his bed late the night before, full of whisky and relief. He'd won a battle for Caro, and it felt splendid.

There would be more battles to come, Eamon reminded himself. Other gentlemen might try to control Leo and his upbringing, hoping for influence over a future duke. Eamon would be there to help Caro defend Leo against them, whether she wished what they'd begun between them to blossom or not.

"The study," Eamon repeated. He had no idea where that particular room was.

"Third floor, sir." Singleton carefully folded Eamon's coat over his arm. "In the back of the house."

"I will attend at once."

Eamon's anticipation rose as he hastened up the stairs, wondering whether Caro was inviting him into another unused chamber for more of what they'd done the other day. She could be wickedly delightful, all the while beguiling him with her innocent smile.

The memory of holding her on that chair for some of the best lovemaking of his life quickened Eamon's pace. They could celebrate the vanquishing of Rudyard with great enjoyment.

As soon as he opened the door, he realized that Caro, though she wore the diamond and gold necklace he'd given her, had nothing of the sort in mind.

The study was small and cluttered. Bookcases filled with old and worn tomes lined the walls, and smaller shelves held similar items. None of them worth much, Eamon decided with a calculating gaze, though he'd have to examine each to be certain.

The desk Caro reposed behind was piled with ledgers and old papers that begged an efficient secretary to put in order.

Caro had four ledgers spread open before her. When she glanced up at Eamon's entrance, did she smile in welcome? Open her arms and beg him to come to her? Even thank him for sending Rudyard packing?

No, she regarded him with impatience, excitement in her eyes.

"I've been waiting ages for you," she exclaimed. "Come and look at these. I believe they are the answer to everything, but I might be wrong. I don't know antiquities as well as you do."

Mystified, Eamon crossed to the desk and gazed down at what lay on the ledger Caro turned around to show him.

He ceased breathing.

Glowing up at him with heart-stopping colors and the gleam of gold, was a manuscript page. Not just any manuscript page, but an illuminated gospel with a massive, decorated capital letter entwined with flowering vines and stylized serpents. Gold-leafed interlace patterns lined the margins, hailing from the centuries before William of Normandy sailed over from France to try his luck at being king.

A few Latin letters flowed after the initial capital, reawakening the language in Eamon's brain that had been drilled into him by relentless Hallbridge tutors.

In the beginning was the Word ...

It was the only line on the page, fit in among the riot of decoration. Once upon a time, a monk in a cold monastery on an Ionian island had traced these letters and drawn these glorious pictures, the colors as vivid now as they had been the day the ink had first dried.

"Gah ..." Eamon's words lodged in his throat and wouldn't come out.

"There are more." Caro turned back the leaves of another ledger, and another, and another, revealing pages as pristine and beautiful as the first. Some papers held more writing—one bore only a glorious initial capital—each page a tumult of color and design.

Eamon found a chair beside the desk and collapsed into it, his eyes never leaving the beauty Caro had uncovered.

"The lost gospels of St. Columba," he whispered.

"They are real, then?" Caro asked anxiously.

"Oh, they are real." Eamon sat up, allowing himself to touch the beautiful, ancient, and smooth vellum. "You can feel them, *here.*" He tapped his fist to his chest, right over his heart. "This manuscript was created on Iona in a monastery set up by St. Columba. The monastery is a ruin now and many of the pages have been lost for centuries. And your husband had them stashed here in his study?"

Caro nodded. "He used them to bookmark pages in his ledgers."

Eamon regarded her limply. "Used them to bookmark pages ..."

"They were very important pages," Caro said, her eyes wide.

Eamon fell back into his chair again. And laughed.

He let his hands dangle over the arms of the chair as he abandoned himself to joyousness he hadn't felt in many years.

Caro's golden laughter joined his, the sound filling the room. It felt so good to simply laugh after so long a time of emptiness, resignation, and uncertainty.

"Are they as valuable as they look?" Caro asked when they both had regained their breaths.

Eamon pried himself from the chair, wiping his eyes. "Oh, yes. These pages are legendary. I'm no book expert, but even I know about them. Collectors will pay a fortune for these, and you will become a hero in the art world's eyes."

"Only if collectors believe they are real," Caro said, her enthusiasm dimming.

"They'll believe it." Eamon regarded the gold leafing that glittered from the pages. "Records of where your husband obtained them would be helpful, but I suppose that's too much to expect—"

He broke off as Caro produced a leather-bound tome from under more scattered papers and held it out to him. "All the transactions are in here. My husband's grandfather, the Fourth Duke, purchased the pages from a cardinal in Rome in 1742."

Eamon leafed through the book in wonder. Caro had marked the page with the transaction but there were others as important. Records of purchases of more paintings, including one by Claude, one for an enamel and gold medallion by Cellini, and receipts for statuettes, including the Diana that had been replaced by a recent copy.

"Where did you find this?" Eamon asked as he turned the pages. "Behind a brick in the fireplace?"

"Under the cushions of that chair." Caro gestured to the seat where Eamon had fallen in mirth.

Eamon stared at the piece of furniture in shock. "You will have to chastise Singleton for not tidying up."

"Leopold never allowed anyone into this room but the family. We left it as it was when he died, and in any case, the maids and footmen soon departed. All the records were supposed to be in the gallery, with Mr. Clive's notebooks and the artworks."

And many had been, but they'd not been complete. Perhaps Caro's husband had been cannier than he'd been given credit for, or perhaps simply absent-minded. They'd likely never know.

"What made you come into this sanctuary today?" Eamon asked.

"To look for more debts to be paid. I want the slate to be clean for Leo."

Eamon's gestured to the manuscript pages, which sang at him from the desk. "With these, they will be. You can make the creditors happy and have plenty left over to hire staff to help Singleton, as well as purchase suits for Leo and new frocks for yourself."

Caro remained uneasy. "Will anyone buy these? If they've been missing for so long, should they not go back to the Vatican or a monastery somewhere?"

Eamon shook his head. "The place they originated is long gone, and while they might have been stored in the Vatican for a time, I imagine they got there by means of war, looting, or some such in the turmoil of medieval days. The sale to the Duke of Aylesmore *was* legal, according to this notebook, probably by accountants trying to keep a pope solvent. They belong to Leo, my dear, without doubt. His to do with what he wishes, including making them into pretty bookmarks." Eamon felt his laughter rise again.

"My husband didn't always know what he had," Caro said with some fondness.

No, the man had been a fool about value ... except for Caro. The duke had recognized *her* worth. And because he didn't care what things cost or their pedigree, he'd loved her for herself, hang what anyone thought.

Caro was like these manuscript pages, hidden away, cared for, and immensely beautiful.

"Luckily, tucking them away here kept the pages from light, air, and dirt that would deteriorate them," Eamon said. "As to who will buy them, I know certain collectors who'll fall all over themselves to obtain them, including those who purchase for museums. I can make certain the right person takes them—someone who will treasure them and let others enjoy their beauty as well."

"Yes, please arrange it," Caro said eagerly.

The fact that Caro placed perfect trust in him did strange things to Eamon's heart.

"Only ..." Caro trailed off, her gaze going wistfully to the first page with its medley of gold leaf and bright colors. "Could we keep one? To honor Leopold. And also, it is so very beautiful."

Eamon grinned at her. "Keep whatever you like. Sell it, hang it in your gallery, sleep with it under your pillow." He flinched. "No, not the last, please. It would crease."

Caro let forth her wonderful laughter again. "Very well then, do find a collector for them all, except this one." She gently drew the first page toward her.

"It shall be done," Eamon said. "I'll fix up a cabinet for the page so it can be displayed in the gallery, as it should be."

"Thank you, Eamon." Caro's voice was quiet, her eyes holding gentleness.

Eamon longed to enclose her in his arms, but not here, not in the study of the man she'd liked so well. Eamon didn't believe in ghosts, but he certainly felt the spirit of the Sixth Duke of Aylesmore hovering here.

He cleared his throat. "I came this morning for an entirely different matter—to tell you that Rudyard is gone, his reputation ruined. He is unlikely to be back to bother you again."

Caro drew a quick breath of surprise. "Are you certain?"

"Very certain."

Eamon had received messages that the ship, departing early this morning, had already reached Amsterdam. He'd sent messages of his own the previous night to those who would ensure Rudyard stayed far away from Caro and Leo and caused them no more trouble.

"Thank you," Caro said again.

"You achieved it yourself, you know. You and your friends are more resourceful at gathering information than Wellington's scouts ever were. A pity ladies aren't allowed into the army. Wars would be much shorter and more decisive."

"I had to do *something* to expose him." Caro quieted. "It was either that or send you away."

The simple words told Eamon she had seriously considered dismissing him, and that though it would have hurt her, she'd have done it to keep Leo safe.

His heart ached.

"I am glad," Eamon said softly. "I don't want to be sent away."

Caro studied him as though on the verge of telling him what he meant to her, but she only nodded. "Good."

Eamon rested his fists on the desk, carefully not touching the manuscript. "I also have something to ask you," he said.

"Yes?" Caro's trepidation returned.

"May I speak to Leo a moment?"

She regarded him in bewilderment. "I suppose you can. He is with his grandmother."

"All the better." Eamon drew Caro around to his side of the desk and kissed her fingers before twining her arm through his. "Then let us ascend."

———

Leo leapt up eagerly from the writing table when Caro led Eamon into the fourth-floor sitting room. Leo had been restless all morning, as though he knew his fortunes had changed, though none of them had realized how.

Eamon released Caro and made his formal bow to Leo, addressing him as *My Liege*. Leo grinned, enjoying the game, while the dowager languidly looked up from her embroidery.

"May we sort through more of the books now?" Leo asked Eamon in excitement. "I've studied enough, haven't I, Mama? My head is stuffed."

"If you like," Caro answered. She'd not deny her boy anything today.

Eamon held up a hand. "First, I must ask you a question, Leo. It is a very important one, the most important I will ever put to you."

Leo's zealousness faded at the seriousness of Eamon's tone. "What is it?"

"Shall we sit?" Eamon directed Leo to the writing table and pulled another chair alongside the lad's.

Leo hopped onto his seat and waited in consternation for Eamon to settle himself.

"Please ask," Leo said. "Or I'll burst."

Caro sympathized. Her heart was hammering, and she clasped her hands to keep them from shaking. The dowager fixed her eagle-like stare on the three of them and waited as impatiently.

"It is nothing terrible," Eamon said, quickly reassuring. "What I want to ask you, My Liege, is—would you mind if I married your mother?"

The dowager gasped. Caro froze in place, her breath dying on her parted lips.

Leo leapt to his feet in delight. "You mean you'd live with us for always?"

"I would." Eamon put a hand over his heart. "If you'll have me."

"Of course," Leo all but shouted. "That would be splendid."

He swung to Caro. "You'll marry him, won't you, Mama? Then you can kiss him all you want, and we can move to the country together and go riding and have all sorts of larks."

Caro couldn't move. Leo's exuberance, the dowager's interest, and Eamon's wicked smile seemed remote, as though she viewed them through a fog.

Eamon rose, his smile softening as he moved to her. He took Caro's hands, his so warm, and gently squeezed them.

"Will you marry me, Duchess?" Eamon asked softly. His gaze fell to the necklace Caro had determined to wear every day of her life. "My duchess in diamonds?"

Caro swallowed the lump in her throat that threatened to choke her.

Eamon was offering her everything she wanted—love, happiness, joy for her son, a life free of the petty worries that had dogged her since Leopold's death.

Could it be real? This handsome, devilish, but generous and loving man offering to be in her life forever?

Caro pressed Eamon's hands, trying to reassure herself that he was here in truth. That he'd asked her a question she hadn't let herself yearn to hear.

"Yes," she whispered.

Leo whooped. Caro had meant to extend her speech but knew she'd never be heard over Leo's yells.

Eamon jerked once as though he wanted to leap in the air and shout as well, but instead he pulled Caro into a hard embrace, his body solid against hers. Despite their audience, Eamon kissed her.

Caro met his kiss with a hungry one of her own. Dimly she heard the dowager rustle past, leading a still-whooping Leo out of the room. Leo's footsteps pounded in the outer hall, and his voice rose again.

"*Singleton.* Guess what's happened?"

The door shut, leaving Eamon and Caro alone.

Caro clung to Eamon, her pillar of strength. The kiss turned deep, his mouth tender but arousing, sending fire through her blood.

She found herself being lifted to the table where she spent most of her mornings, Eamon skimming up her skirt and stepping between her thighs. He drew kisses down her throat, lingering at the diamonds on her bosom.

"Caro." His breath burned her skin through her thin frock, then he raised his head. His eyes swam with desire, hope, and also fear. "My duchess. I love you. I love you so much I might perish of it."

"Please don't." Caro touched his cheek. "I want you here, with me."

"I am going nowhere. Never again."

"Good." Caro laced her arms around his neck and rubbed one slippered foot along his strong calf. "I love *you*, Eamon. My charming, handsome, picture man."

Eamon drew back the slightest bit. "Is that what you call me?"

Caro's heart thumped. "I will address you as anything you like. My beloved. My darling. My dearest one."

"I'd like it if you just called me Eamon." He ran his thumb across her lower lip. "You are the only one who does."

"Eamon." Caro loved the taste of his name. "I love you. Please kiss me now."

"Now and always." Eamon's rakish smile returned as he came down to her. "Caro. My duchess."

His kiss erased any other words Caro might have said, but she didn't mind at all.

She laughed in pleasure as Eamon gathered her to him and began loving her with a passion that guaranteed they'd not be downstairs to celebrate with Leo, the dowager, and Singleton for many hours to come.

EPILOGUE

June 1816

The drawing in Eamon's notebook blossomed as he sat in the garden at Mayfield Hall in Kent, the estate of the Dukes of Aylesmore. The weather was cool, summer slow in coming, but the air was fresh, the breeze gentle.

Eamon had carried his sketchbooks with him on this country sojourn on the off chance he'd have a few minutes for them, but upon arrival, he'd started drawing and couldn't cease. Not copies, but more originals, springing forth from his pencil without hindrance.

He sketched the overgrown garden, a bit wild with only one gardener trying to keep it tame, Leo romping with the Countess of Heyford's sons, or the spread of landscape that opened out below the manor.

Mostly, though, he drew Caro herself. His duchess in the garden laughing with her friends, smiling at him across the sunny drawing room, glowing and mussed after chasing Leo about the grounds. They were the best pictures he'd ever done.

The large house hadn't been ready for so many guests, to Singleton's dismay, though Eamon and his friends offered to pitch in with the labor when necessary. The sale of the manuscript pages to one of the Prince of Osagard's extraordinarily wealthy and well-vetted friends, vouched for by Colonel Harper, had brought in a welcome influx of funds, but clearing all the debts and then purchasing necessities would take some time.

Eamon didn't mind the house a bit untamed, the garden an unrestrained riot of spring and early summer flowers. Naturalistic landscapes were all the rage now, he'd assured Singleton, who wanted the entire estate to be perfect.

Watching Caro wander the house with purpose and vigor, planning what was to be repaired or renewed in each room, stimulated more than Eamon's muse.

They'd agreed to marry in July, which would give them time to put the house and garden into some kind of order as well as have the banns read. The ceremony would be held in the village church, and if the weather was kind, they'd have the wedding breakfast in the garden afterward.

Eamon, like Singleton, barely contained his impatience, though for different reasons.

Eamon wanted Caro in his bed every night, from now until the wedding day and then forever after. But they could only steal moments here and there, because the house had filled with people the day after he'd made the journey down.

The Countess of Heyford—Louise—who traditionally invited Caro, the dowager, and Leo to her older son's seat in Berkshire for the month of June, had decided they'd have the summer visit at Mayfield Hall instead.

July usually saw Caro spending time with Princess Jo and her family, but that had also been changed to Jo and her niece Merry traveling with Louise to stay until the wedding. Prince Rupert and Princess Maude would attend the wedding and then linger at Mayfield through July before the royals in exile progressed elsewhere, taking Merry with them.

The impending visit of Jo's parents was giving Singleton palpitations. He was certain the prince and princess would have apoplexy at the state of the Aylesmore house, no matter how many times Jo assured him that they wouldn't care one whit, so long as they could have their coffee every morning.

Eamon's friends had also turned up not long after his arrival at Leo's ostensible invitation. McCormick and Wolfe had been ill at ease with the other guests at first, though McCormick's natural cordialness had broken the ice for him quickly. The dowager found him charming, and McCormick obliged her by escorting her through the garden or attending her in the drawing room whenever she wished.

Wolfe, when he wasn't helping McCormick and Eamon assist Singleton, spent much time riding. Good exercise for his leg, he said. *Good excuse for being misanthropic,* Eamon amended silently. The three boys were fascinated by Wolfe, and he unbent enough to give them a few riding lessons.

All these people in the house meant that Eamon had to satisfy his yearnings with art alone. The wedding night was long in coming.

He shaded the lines he'd made of the frock Caro wore as she walked and chatted with Louise, Jo, and Merry. A breeze had sprung up as he'd sketched, and he'd drawn Caro's hair and skirts fluttering, along with the loose ribbons of her bonnet. The gown caught on her curving legs, outlining them in a most enticing way.

Though Caro stood with her friends, Eamon's drawing held only her.

A little way down the path, the dowager strolled in a stately fashion on McCormick's arm, her old-fashioned, broad-brimmed hat with large feathers defying the wind. No gust would dare disarray her.

Leo, Harry, and Jack yelled as they dashed through the meadow beyond the garden, while Wolfe, on horseback nearby, kept an eye on them. From the house, Singleton's voice rose as he directed the newly hired men-of-all-work like a general harrying his troops to meet Bonaparte.

Caro broke off from her friends and came around the fountain to where Eamon sat on his folding stool. Singleton had cranked to life the rusting mechanism that worked the garden's fountains, and water pattered quietly, though Eamon had moved his seat far away enough so that the spray wouldn't ruin his work.

Caro leaned to Eamon and pressed an uninhibited kiss to his cheek. "Is that what I look like? So untidy."

"So beautiful." Eamon used his finger to blend the charcoal shadow behind her. "Perfect."

"You are very flattering." Caro bestowed another kiss, this one to the top of his head. "You've been drawing quite a lot, haven't you? I'm glad."

Eamon shrugged, but in truth, the outpouring of creativity had brought him jubilation. "I always thought I could only copy others' genius. It turns out, I only needed the right subject." He tilted his head back to send Caro a hot smile.

She flushed, her pulse beating in her throat. Eamon sensed, from her whispers when they met, the kisses they stole on the stair landings, and the way she watched him across the long table at meals, that she longed for him as much as he did her. The weeks before them stretched far too long.

"I came to ask you about the wedding breakfast," Caro said.

Eamon smothered a groan. "When *aren't* you asking me about the wedding breakfast? It started as a few tables for immediate friends, and now I think half of England is coming."

"The dowager believes it's a good way to show Leo's acceptance of our marriage, not to mention that of the Prince and

Princess of Osagard, Jo, Louise, Lady Carmichael, Colonel and Mrs. Harper ..."

"And the rest of London, yes." Eamon flicked another few lines to the folds of Caro's drawn skirt. "Wolfe and McCormick are rounding up their respectable friends as well. I don't have any of those, so I have to bring in my *unrespectable* ones." He'd sent an invitation to Sam Noble, but it remained to be seen if the man would appear.

"*Anyway.*" Caro cut through his meanderings. "What do you think of the summerhouse as a place to set up extra tables?"

She gestured to a building originally erected to resemble a small Greek temple—a folly built by one of the previous dukes, probably more for fashion's sake than any romantic notions about the past.

Eamon glanced at it. "Will they object to being shut away in there?"

"No, indeed. The folly's terrace is wide, and the doors can be folded back. Some might enjoy being out of any wind or damp." Caro held out her hand. "Come and see."

The summerhouse was nicely shielded from the garden by a hedge that Singleton had vowed to one day lower or have removed. When the folly's doors were closed, anyone inside would be quite private.

"Very well, if you insist," Eamon said in pretended resignation. He shut his notebook, returned his pencils to their case, folded his stool, and put all of this under his arm. "Lead on, my lady."

Caro tucked her hand into the crook of his elbow, and together they strolled unhurriedly toward the summerhouse, Eamon's heartbeat far outracing their slow pace. No one noticed them go, which was to his satisfaction.

When they reached the folly, Caro led Eamon up the few steps to its entrance. From there, they had a view across the garden and down the line of fountains to the rear of the house, which stretched its Palladian arms across the green.

On one path, the dowager and McCormick encountered Louise, Jo, and Merry. Louise greeted them with her cool friendliness, Merry with a wide grin. By contrast, while Jo nodded respectfully to the dowager, she turned a frown on McCormick. The tall McCormick sent a bellicose stare down at her.

Jo said a few words to him that Eamon couldn't hear, but from her expression he knew they were biting. McCormick, never one to be cowed, responded in turn. The dowager and Louise looked on in surprise, Merry with great amusement.

"Curious, do you not think?" Caro said softly next to him. "I believe your Mr. McCormick is smitten."

"As is your princess," Eamon returned.

He also had not missed the way Louise's gaze strayed to Wolfe whenever he was near. She might pretend she was looking after her sons who hovered around him, but she'd turn her head to follow Wolfe's progress. Wolfe returned the scrutiny when he believed no one was observing him.

"Nothing can come of anything between Jo and Mr. McCormick," Caro said, her tone turning sad. "No one is allowed to court Jo, the poor girl."

"There's nothing to object to in McCormick," Eamon said with conviction. "He's the most honest man I've ever encountered."

"He's a paragon," Caro agreed. "But it will take more than that to surmount the barriers around Jo."

"McCormick is also resourceful." Eamon took Caro's hand and pulled her into the summerhouse. "I think we should leave them to it for now."

Caro sent a last glance toward her friends then followed Eamon inside.

Eamon had been right that the folly gave them privacy.

Singleton had obviously been in here with his new army, cleaning in anticipation of its possible need for the wedding breakfast. The seats that lined the windows were free of dust, some of the cushions new. Several folding tables waited compactly against one wall.

Eamon set down his sketching things and closed the double doors before he led Caro to the bench with newest cushions.

All restraint of the past days fell away. Eamon divested Caro of her bonnet, catching her tumbling hair in his hands. He pulled her to him for a fierce kiss, which she returned as fiercely.

They fumbled at laces, buttons, and hooks, until items of clothing floated down to rest on the newly swept floor.

The bench was wide enough for Eamon to sit on and have Caro wrap herself around him on his lap. The window behind them gave out into thick, pathless woods, the aristocratic idea of wild country.

The view assured Eamon that no one would observe them as he lowered Caro onto his waiting hardness, that none would hear their groans of pleasure as he began to thrust in the dim silence.

Caro was warm and lush, her cries of passion unrestrained. Eamon answered her with his own, calling her *Love, Caro.*

True to her word, Caro wore the diamond necklace he'd given her. Eamon kissed her breasts beneath it, enjoying the velvet taste of her nipple before he licked the chain and raised his head for more kisses.

"I love you, my duchess."

"Eamon." Caro touched his face, her eyes heavy with desire. "I love *you.* You have given me everything."

"In return, I have you." Eamon rocked against her, speech becoming difficult. "Mine is the best of the bargain, I think."

"Hardly." Caro kissed his mouth. "We did it together. Always. Together ..." Her words faded as need overpowered her.

"Always," Eamon promised, and it was the truest statement he'd ever uttered.

Caro cried out as Eamon's thrusts sped, and his voice joined hers.

The joy of the moment with his duchess in diamonds wound through Eamon, erasing the emptiness of his past and promising a future of love stretching endlessly before them.

The Untamed Mackenzie

The Wicked Deeds of Daniel Mackenzie

Scandal and the Duchess

Rules for a Proper Governess

The Stolen Mackenzie Bride

A Mackenzie Clan Gathering

Alec Mackenzie's Art of Seduction

The Devilish Lord Will

A Rogue Meets a Scandalous Lady

A Mackenzie Yuletide

(**in print** in A Mackenzie Clan Christmas)

Fiona and the Three Wise Highlanders

Mackenzies II

The Sinful Ways of Jamie Mackenzie

ABOUT THE AUTHOR

New York Times bestselling and award-winning author Jennifer Ashley has more than 120 published novels and novellas in mystery, romance, historical fiction, and urban fantasy under the names Jennifer Ashley, Allyson James, and Ashley Gardner. Jennifer's books have been translated into more than a dozen languages and have earned starred reviews in *Publisher's Weekly* and *Booklist*. When she isn't writing, Jennifer enjoys playing music (guitar, piano, flute), reading, knitting, cooking, and building dollhouse miniatures.

More about Jennifer's books can be found at
http://www.jenniferashley.com

To keep up to date on her new releases, join her newsletter here:
http://eepurl.com/47kLL